OTHER
Harlequin Romances
by JULIET ARMSTRONG

THE
FLOWERING VALLEY

by

JULIET ARMSTRONG

HARLEQUIN BOOKS   TORONTO
WINNIPEG

Original hard cover edition published in 1972
by Mills & Boon Limited, 17 - 19 Foley Street,
London W1A 1DR, England

© Juliet Armstrong 1972

Harlequin edition published May, 1972

SBN 373-01585-2

Printed in Canada

For
SMALLIE
with love and gratitude

CHAPTER I

Her face tense with concentration, Penny Foster took the awkward turn into her stepfather's yard, and brought her blue mini-car to a standstill precisely where she intended: by the trade door of his pharmacy-cum-stationer's shop in the hilly, straggling main street. Then quickly relaxing, she jumped out into the bright West Indian sunshine, her long-lashed hazel eyes dancing.

'How's that, Dad? Not one real hitch all that dodgy climb up from the coast! Are you still dubious over giving me such a super present?'

Robert Dale, emerging with rather less spring from the small car, laughed.

'Could be my shrunk bank balance I've been concerned about, Penny, not your skill. But seriously, I'm delighted for you to have it.'

'Well, I'm thrilled to bits. And think of the save it will be, having me to do your errands.' She reached up to give him a quick kiss. 'Thanks a thousand, darling Dad. I shan't forget my nineteenth birthday in a hurry.'

They had started in the first faint flush of dawn, after a quick breakfast prepared by her mother, and driven down in the family Rover to Port Leon, capital of the small, mountainous island of Santa Rita which was their home. There, in the town's chief garage, they had left the big car for servicing and collected the brand-new Mini in which Penny had taken her lessons and passed her test.

Now, with Penny driving, they had completed the hour-long return journey to their village—Val Fleury, Vale of Flowers—lying in a slit of the foothills, and watered by a quick-flowing, silvery stream. Aeons ago, it was said, this stream which made the valley so fertile had been a mighty river, forcing its tumultuous way down to the coast from the high rain forests. Even in later times it had occasionally, through the centuries, swollen alarmingly, forcing people near its banks to take refuge on their roofs, if not to evacuate their dwellings altogether.

But it was long since this had happened—certainly not in living memory. The fame of Val Fleury, which it watered so effectively, rested now on the beauty of its glorious flowering trees, the delicious coolness of its nights.

Legends of old gods haunting the source of the stream for good or evil had well-nigh passed into oblivion. And few penetrated to the ruins of their ancient shrine.

Robert Dale, active despite his bulk, was in the shop and making his way into his little office before Penny had finished backing the car into the shade of the samam tree which spread its great branches over the yard. He hated to be late at work.

Penny herself did not linger long. There would be plenty of time later on to restore her new treasure to its first spotlessness. Meanwhile there would be fruit-juice and cookies waiting, she knew, in the office.

But as she passed through the spacious shop, where daily she presided over the photographic section, a scatter of employees from other counters, and some customers, too, held her up, eager to wish her a happy birthday and to see the new car.

Out they all streamed into the yard, and the compliments and congratulations might have lasted much longer had not Juan Garcia, the grey-headed assistant dispenser, emerged to tell her with unusual solemnity that the Boss wished to see her at once. Would she come immediately, please.

The bunch of well-wishers melted, and Penny hurried to obey the surprisingly peremptory summons. What was the matter? Surely her stepfather couldn't be cross with her for emptying the shop for a few minutes on this special occasion. Not like him at all. Nor was he annoyed now—only agitated, with a mixture of joy and anxiety, it seemed.

'Sit down, my dear, and drink your lime-juice,' he said. 'I've just had a cable with some very unexpected news. After all this time, Gloria is coming over from California to visit us. On a literally flying visit, she says.'

For a moment Penny stared at him in silence—completely taken aback. Then, recovering herself, and try-

8

ing hard to speak with at least a reasonable show of enthusiasm, she said quickly: 'But, Dad, how lovely for you. And about time. After five years away from home. I'm—I'm delighted.'

'My darling, I hardly expect you to share my pleasure.' He gave her a faint, whimsical smile. 'She wasn't a very kind stepsister to you, I'm afraid, and an even less satisfactory stepdaughter.'

'Well, I'm glad for your sake. And Mum—she'll be terribly pleased for you, too.' She hesitated, before continuing diffidently: 'I guess I can understand a lot better now why Gloria resented Mama and me. Losing her mother in that dreadful car accident must have been a devastating experience. Oh, I know Mum tried hard—'

'I'm sure Gloria will appreciate her more, now she's older—and has been married and widowed herself. Did so well, too, before that, as a hair stylist, or whatever you call it. That should help.' Robert's tone was optimistic. 'She'll have mellowed with all that experience of life, I don't doubt.'

Penny forced a smile.

'And I'm no longer a prickly, over-sensitive schoolgirl, which should help too. When does she arrive, Dad?'

'This very night. And as the Rover is out of action, I can't take the short cuts from here and meet her at the airport. She'll have to use the bus and travel by the long route, going right down to Port Leon before coming up here. Unless you're agreeable to my taking your immaculate Mini along those narrow side roads.'

'Of course you must borrow it, Dad. In fact I'd normally suggest fetching her myself—getting Eric to share the driving. But we're supposed to be dancing and dining in Port Leon to-night as a birthday celebration—making a four with Sybil Marsden and Joe Rodriguez. Table booked and everything.'

'Of course you mustn't mess up your evening. So long as you really don't mind my borrowing the precious Mini!'

'You don't have to ask me, Dad.'

'That's all right, then. Now you must get one of the other girls to take over your counter for the rest of the

9

morning, and go home to break the news to your mother. Help her with preparations. But just a minute!' He reached for a packet on his desk. 'This roll of film has just come in for Stephen. If you're not too tired and can find the time to deliver it to him, before you dash home—!'

She smiled. 'I'm never too rushed or tired to go to the Forestry Office.'

'Well, here's the key to their post-box in case no one's around. Don't lose it.'

Pleased at the prospect of putting the little blue car into useful service so soon, and hoping that it would be Stephen Vaughan whom she would find at home—or anyway, not Isaac, his surly old servant—she was soon passing the self-service store, nearly opposite, where her friend Eric Hoskyns worked as assistant manager, then a few more shops and houses, the recently modernised school, and finally the white, Spanish-type church, the oldest building now in Val Fleury. Leaving all these behind she was soon climbing the road which led to the mountains and woods which constituted so much of the island's beauty, and contained so much of its unexploited wealth.

She had not far to go—barely a mile—before she reached the low wooden buildings which served Stephen and his junior, Pete Rodriguez—Joe's brother—for home and office.

At the sound of her horn a young Airedale came bounding to welcome her, followed at a more leisurely pace by Stephen himself, lithe, dark-haired, clean-shaven, his strongly marked features notable chiefly for the cleft in his chin. The sign of an ardent nature, some people said. She'd certainly never seen any signs of it herself—though *she'd* hardly do so, she thought with slight amusement. She was aware he had a temper, yes, though she had never, thank goodness, happened to fall foul of it. From her point of view one could hardly have a kinder, more level-headed person—and fun, too, often.

'Happy birthday, Penny,' was his cheerful greeting. 'So this is the famous car we've been hearing about. Let's have a look.'

She beamed with pride as having conducted a genuinely interested examination he pronounced the little car to be ' just the job for these parts ', and then invited her to come inside for a soft drink.

' I mustn't be long,' she told him regretfully, ' and anyway I've just had a lime-juice. I've come chiefly to deliver you this parcel of film, and then I've got to scoot off home. Dad's just had a cable to say that your glamorous cousin is coming over from California on a flying visit.'

' Gloria?'

' Who else?'

' A second cousin only, I might remind you.' His first, startled look was replaced by one of annoyance. ' Well, it's surely time she came to see her father. Come inside, Penny, anyway. I've a present for you.' And he led her into his barely furnished sitting-room, adding as she sat down : ' I can do without any invitations to meet Gloria. Don't encourage your parents to ask me along, please.'

' She'll invite you herself, I expect,' was Penny's dry response. ' Anyway, I'm trying to be charitable. Now I'm older I can understand better what a shock it must have been losing her mother—'

' When she was ten. Oh, I know all that. But she couldn't have been given a kinder and sweeter step-mother. Too like her own mother, that's Gloria's trouble.'

Penny stared out of the window at a cassia tree on the other side of the road. Tall and heavy with brilliant gold blossom, it reminded her a little, in its opulence, of her stepsister.

She said, after a moment : ' Steve, you and I ought to be able to talk freely. We've been friends long enough. Ever since you were a lanky school-leaver—giving me pick-a-back rides and chocolate bars. Tell me, what's the mystery about Gloria's mother? Dad and Mum are like oysters. But other people are apt to make cryptic remarks about Dad being so happy in his *second* marriage —as though he was miserable in his first. One old woman—she was a bit mad, of course—even said something about her death being retribution.'

Steve tapped with his empty pipe on the wooden table. ' Is that all that's reached you?' he asked.

She nodded.

'I guess I missed a lot of gossip, being away so much at boarding school. I only know that she went on a trip to stay with relatives in America, and died in a car crash soon after she got there.' And then she added reflectively, as he made no comment on this: 'I'm glad no one's mysterious about my father. I can't remember him at all. As you know, he died when I was two. But people often talk about him, and very nicely.'

'So they should. Everyone knew and respected Dr Foster, so I've heard. And there's that tablet to his memory in the town hall.' Now he was filling his pipe, and when he had done so to his satisfaction, he went on: 'Vera, Gloria's mother, if you must have the truth, gave your father a hell of a time with her infidelities. Finally she ran off with a well-known American business chap. When she died in that crash, soon after landing in New York, the fact of her being with him was hushed up—as much as it could be. As for your stepfather, he came up to Val Fleury with this ten-year-old daughter: bought and greatly improved his present business. A year later he met and married your mother, down in Port Leon, and provided Gloria with a loving and lovable stepmother.'

'And me with an adorable stepfather.'

'He's a good chap, too fair and too sensible to blame any of my family for Vera's behaviour. At least I trust so.' He lit up. 'Well, keep what I've told you to yourself, my dear. And let's hope Gloria will be nicer to you these days. And now here's my birthday present. I hope it won't bore you. But you've shown such interest in what some folk call my "silly old trees" that I've got you a book called *Forests of the Caribbean*. Even if you find some of the letterpress tedious, it's got fine illustrations.'

Penny's face lit up.

'I'll devour it. And please, Steve, take me on another little trip before too long.'

He gave her an odd look.

'I'll try some time. But I wonder how long you'll go on enjoying such simple pleasures—what with all your gay times in Port Leon. How are you spending your birthday evening, by the way? With the latest boy-friend?'

'Why do you say it like that? You know very well that Eric's been around for ages! And yes, he's taking me to dine and dance. Pete's brother Joe is coming along, too, bringing Sybil Marsden.'

'Dried-up old bachelor as I am, I'd prefer to take my girl out on her own!' He, too, was standing now, looking down at her with a faint, ironic smile. Bronzed and lean and sinewy—but not, she reflected impatiently, dried-up at all. Remarkably strong and healthy, in fact.

'It's certainly time you acquired a girl,' she told him. 'Someone really nice.'

'That would of course be an advantage—though I always think "nice" rather a soppy adjective. Any more qualifications?'

She grinned then.

'Someone I can get on with, too, who won't absolutely monopolise you in that fearfully possessive way some women have. Whom I can be friends with.'

'So we can go on trips *à trois*?' he suggested mockingly.

'Well, why not—after you've settled down comfortably together, of course!'

'Sounds marvellous, I must say! But come to think of it, we might make a quartet—though your Eric, handsome fellow as he is, has hardly the build of a climber.'

Quick to sense criticism, she said defensively: 'But he's grand at games. Incidentally, you talk as though we were definitely engaged. Well, we're not. We've a kind of understanding, that's all.'

'No ring? No nothing?'

'We've certainly something,' she returned with dignity. 'A very pleasant friendship.'

'Friendship!' he returned slowly. 'Well, that's something, of course! But, Penny-girl—' he used an endearment for her which went back to her childhood—'you're a very young nineteen!'

He opened the door of her car for her.

'Thanks for coming,' he said. 'Have a good time this evening!'

Her chin went up.

'I'm sure I will. And incidentally, it's no sign of

13

immaturity not to go rushing into marriage.'

'I couldn't agree more! It's often a sign of commendable common sense!'

'Then no more gibes about my age, please!'

'Sorry, kid!'

'There you go again,' she exclaimed. But his use of that old nickname had touched her all the same. 'Goodbye, Steve dear,' she added hurriedly, and before he could say another word had driven off, calling over her shoulder: 'And thanks very much for the book.'

Brenda Dale, a plump, silvery-haired edition of Penny, received the news of her stepdaughter's impending arrival with momentary horror—an emotion quickly smothered, and succeeded with praiseworthy speed by a cheerful smile.

'Thank goodness for that,' she observed equably. 'It's high time, to put it mildly, that Gloria came to see her father. But my goodness, to give us so little notice! What a lot we shall have to do in almost no time. Ask Pearl to come along, and we'll plan our jobs.'

At the open doorway, Penny hesitated.

'Mum, do you think Gloria will expect to have her old room back?'

Mrs Dale looked shocked.

'What an idea! Of course not. You've had it for the past five years, and made it your own in lots of ways. She can content herself with the little room you used to have. It's been good enough for visitors—and it will do very well for Gloria.'

In the kitchen, Pearl, the stout daily who had 'done' for Brenda ever since her marriage to Robert Dale, had evidently overheard this conversation. She was kneading a lump of dough with alarming vigour, a scowl on her usually amiable black face.

'So Mis' Gloria comin' to trouble us all again,' she exclaimed, giving the dough a particularly vicious thump. 'S'pose Ah'm to sweat mah soul out, tendin' to her needs. Mis' Penny, strikes is fashionable dese days, an' if dat beauty play me up, dere'll be a one-woman strike here.'

And then she gave a shamefaced grin.

' Don' yo' tak no notice ob cross ole Pearly, mah lamb. Tell your ma, I get dis 'ere dough in de oven, and come rightaway.'

She was there within three minutes, ready for the fray, scrubbing-brush in hand. Her high standard of cleanliness made this implement extremely important, and while she laboured, Penny and her mother turned out some drawers and the little wardrobe which had served Penny for many years, carrying unwanted articles out into the garage.

Then it was lunch-time, and a pleasant surprise.

Eric Hoskyns, the current boy-friend—under-manager at the self-service grocery store—had arranged to drive her stepfather home in his car, his reward being an invitation to a pot-luck meal.

He was a shy, good-looking young man of twenty-two, and he stammered a little as he explained matters—quite unnecessarily, it seemed to his hearers.

' I happened to notice that neither the new Mini nor the Rover were in the pharmacy yard, and it occurred to me that Mr Dale might be glad of a lift home.'

Robert gave Penny a wink.

' None of my staff have cars,' he said gravely. ' I'd have been in sore straits.'

Poor Eric went red.

' All right,' he said stoutly. ' I'll admit to another motive as well. I wanted to see Penny and make sure that her stepsister's arrival wouldn't stop her coming out with me this evening.'

' Very nice of you, Eric.' Penny gave him a demure smile as she passed him the salad. But Robert shook his head in pretended disapproval.

' Sounds as though you hadn't enough work to do, with all you manage to see and hear through the windows of your store.'

' Mr Farrow is always stressing that I must show friendliness to the customers,' Eric explained quickly. ' When they want to chat me up I have to listen. How the news of Mrs Winston's visit began to circulate in the village, I don't know, but—'

' Don't take my husband's teasing seriously,' Mrs Dale said comfortably. ' As a matter of fact, Mr Farrow told me only the other day how well you've been doing since he promoted you. How you're losing that self-consciousness that used to plague you so.'

'I'm still shy underneath,' he told her, flushing again as though to corroborate his words. 'As I've told you, my brothers were much brainier than me—went to the University, both of them. But I don't envy them. I'm glad I got a job here. I'm much happier than I was in Jamaica. Santa Rita may be a much smaller island, but it's a better size for me. And—' studiously avoiding looking at Penny now—'I love Val Fleury.'

After this speech—an unusually long one for Eric—there wasn't much conversation. Lunch was a brief affair, the Dale family being in somewhat of a hurry. But when the two men had gone Mrs Dale found time to make a brief comment on their visitor, remarking that Eric was a most likeable fellow now he was losing that tiresome diffidence and nervous stammer.

'His clever brothers had the same effect on him that Gloria had on me, when I came home for the holidays,' was Penny's comment. 'By understanding what he went through, I may have helped him a little. Though with you and Dad being so sweet to me I didn't endure what he did—with those unsympathetic parents.'

Pearl, when she was helping Penny make up the bed for Gloria, had some dire warnings to get off her chest.

'Now, yo' look out for yo'self, Mis' Penny,' she urged. 'Folks don' change their natures unless by a miracle. An' Mis' Gloria would need a helluva one to make her any different. Mind she don' get her long shiny nails into Mister Eric. She's one to thief any gal's sweet fellow, wit'out de smallest scruple.'

Penny shook up the pillow in its lace-trimmed case.

'Eric, as it happens, can't bear what he remembers of her. He was a pimply junior five years ago, and she treated him like dirt whenever he had to serve her in the store. So he says!'

'Well, he damn good-looking chap now. So yo' look out, Mis' Penny. If she on de man-hunt, 'courage her to make a pass at one of dose forestry officers that live in de woods like monks.' She gave a deep-throated laugh. 'She'd certainly meet her match in dat cousin of hers, Stephen Vaughan. Tried her tricks on him years ago, dey say. Whether she got anywhere, goodness knows.

Plenty talk there was. But he tough fellow, dat one.'

Penny, feeling that the conversation was getting out of hand, and by no means appreciating this linking of Gloria's name with Stephen's, decided to end it.

'Gloria would have to work very quickly to cause any heart-throbs round here,' she said coolly. 'She'll only be here for a week or two. Now let's get on with things.'

Pearl gave a grunt.

'A week or so. Dat what she sayin'? *Huh!*'

And managed to get the last word after all.

After a strenuous afternoon getting everything in readiness for Gloria's descent on Val Fleury, it was a relief to Penny to be out of the bungalow, and driving down through the cool evening air with Eric and their friends towards Port Leon.

Despite her attempts to maintain a sensible and dignified attitude towards Gloria, she dreaded her visit, felt horribly sure of bristling at the first edgy remark, the first hint of faintly malicious banter.

Teasing she could normally take in her stride. Stephen, for instance, had pulled her leg ever since she could remember him, and she had never minded. Schoolfriends, too—they'd never found her touchy. But *Gloria*—!

'You look fabulous, Penny!' Eric's voice was warm with admiration. And from the seat behind came Sybil Marsden's comment: 'Your hair-do's perfect with that flouncy Victorian dress, Pen. I couldn't have done it better if you'd come to the Salon and paid Mrs O'Brien top fees for my services.' A generous remark which caused short stocky Joe Rodriguez, younger brother of Stephen's colleague, and fourth member of the party, to declare that he and Eric were lucky devils to be taking out two such adorable girls.

It gave Penny a cosy feeling to be with these close friends, all near her own age, and held together as a foursome by a tenuous loyalty. Sybil, for instance, would be well aware that the frilly dress was last year's, but she wouldn't feel superior because her own slinky green satin was new. She would appreciate that after giving Penny such a handsome birthday present, Robert Dale and his wife would hardly be able to afford their customary gift

17

of a new party dress.

Eric and Joe, though young and by no means flush, were evidently resolved on giving the girls a good time. Sensibly they had cut out any idea of patronising the Palace, Port Leon's leading hotel, and booked a table at the Ho-Yutang, a newly opened restaurant which boasted excellent Chinese food and a pleasant annexe for dancing. Over the meal the conversation drifted inevitably to Gloria's visit, the news of which had spread with the speed of a cyclone through Val Fleury. It was flying through Port Leon, also, judging by the number of quite distant acquaintances who came up to them, first at their table, and later on to the little dance floor, to ask how long Mrs Winton would be in Santa Rita—if she was as exotically beautiful as ever.

Fortunately these interruptions tailed off as the evening went by. And in spite of them Penny admitted as the evening drew to a close that she had thoroughly enjoyed herself: had been partially successful, with the help of the rest of the foursome, in keeping Gloria at least from the forefront of her mind.

At midnight Eric went for his car, and they set out for home. And now as they climbed the hilly, curving road and came nearer and nearer to Val Fleury, her nervousness returned. However, the dreaded moment could not be postponed indefinitely. Soon she was making her thank-you's and good-byes, and going slowly up the little path to her home, where lights shone in the sitting-room through the graceful, wrought-iron gratings of the windows.

And after all, the meeting with Gloria proved less of an ordeal than she had anticipated.

The tall girl in the beige silk travelling suit looked much the same, apart from her dark hair now being tinged with a rich auburn. But she was clearly far too exhausted for the veiled sarcasms and teasing which Penny had half expected from her.

Without making any move to get up from the comfortable wicker chair in which she had been installed, she accepted Penny's kiss and said resignedly: 'I'm glad you're back at last. Now I can get to bed.' She yawned and stretched herself with something of feline grace. 'That suit you, Dad—and Aunt Brenda? I'm damnably tired.'

' So are we, as a matter of fact,' was her father's quiet reply. And his wife added pleasantly: ' Don't hurry in the morning, my dear. Have a good lie-in.'

' How sweet and old-fashioned that sounds, Aunt Brenda. Makes me feel like a schoolgirl again.' The words were gentle, but the smile that touched her full lips was not very engaging as she added: ' I thought I'd never want another late morning in the days when I was married to Greg. He was an early riser himself. But he made life so dull and boring for me, there never seemed anything much to get up for.'

It was the first time she had said explicitly that her marriage to the wealthy Gregory Winton had been unsatisfactory, though there had been hints of this in her infrequent letters. But her stepmother smoothed over the awkward moment.

' Call out when you wake up and want your coffee,' she told Gloria peaceably. ' Pearl will be around if I'm out at the shops.'

Gloria lifted her eyebrows then.

' You've still got *Pearl*? Good grief! She must be a hundred!'

' Sixty-two,' was Brenda Dale's cool response. ' Goodnight, my dear.' And then she turned to Penny with loving, if sleepy enquiries about her birthday festivities, assuring her that it was not waiting up for her that had made her stepfather so tired, but the drive to and from the airport, across the difficult mountain roads.

' True enough,' Robert Dale concurred, as he kissed Penny good-night. ' I had to pamper your Mini, as you may well believe, but she behaved like an angel. A good buy, that one, and no mistake!'

Over the breakfast table next day, with Gloria slumbering—it was to be supposed—Robert Dale, still sleepy-eyed, was shaking his head over his daughter's extraordinarily sudden descent on her hitherto neglected family. But before he had got further than, ' I simply can't understand it,' in slipped Gloria through the open doorway, her hair ruffled, her face sallow, without any of her usual make-up, a flame-coloured wrap flung round her shoulders.

'I'm literally dying for some coffee,' she exclaimed, flopping down into the nearest chair. And when Brenda Dale had provided her with a cup, she continued, with a flash of her dark, long-lashed eyes: 'I suppose you're wondering why I've turned up like this, almost without warning. Well, I was too worn out to talk last night. But I can give you now my very simple reason. A wave of homesickness for Val Fleury hit me—and some memories— So I upped and came.'

'You mean you've come home permanently?' For the life of her, Penny could not completely conceal her surprise and dismay.

'Permanent? That's a word for the middle-aged. Like that ghastly phrase, "settling down". I'm here until I sort myself out—if that's agreeable to my ever-loving family?'

There was a strained silence. Then Brenda said, in that quiet, serene tone of hers: 'This is still your home, Gloria. But I can't imagine you kicking your heels here for any length of time. You'll soon get bored, with nothing to occupy you, even if you're in no need of money.'

Gloria's down-dropped eyelids flickered.

'I'll be pretty well off when Greg's estate is settled up,' she told them candidly. 'But the lawyers are taking the hell of a time. And meanwhile, I'm by no means rich—not by Greg's standards, anyway.' She passed her cup over for more coffee, but declined toast or rolls. 'It's not the lawyer's fault really, I suppose. At least he and his partners say so. It's Greg's. He was so mad on money he tied everything up in knots, to the last dollar, almost.' She hesitated. 'I don't *need* to take a job, of course. But I might for a time, just to amuse myself.'

'I see. Well, I hope you'll be happy with us for a while, my dear.' And then Robert Dale looked at his watch. 'Time you and I were making a move, Penny. Shall I get your Mini out of the garage, my dear?'

Gloria's eyes opened wide.

'Is that smart little car yours, Penny?' she demanded. Penny nodded.

'Dad and Mama gave it to me yesterday for my birthday. Didn't he tell you?'

'As a matter of fact, he didn't. But I must say I

20

congratulate you all round.' Gloria didn't sound too gracious, as she continued: ' The pharmacy must be doing better. Or perhaps Penny has a way with her. I can't recall aspiring to presents of such magnificence —or even dreaming of them.'

' Penny's using it to do errands for me, as well as for her own pleasure,' Robert said shortly. ' And if you're implying any lack of generosity to you on my part, I may remind you that the costly hairdressing training I paid for you to have in New York, and your living expenses there, amounted to a considerable sum—far more than the price of a small car.'

Gloria looked sulky.

' I was educated here, don't forget, in this potty little island. In Val Fleury, mostly. Penny was sent to a far better school, in Trinidad.'

' Which her mother paid for,' Robert Dale snapped. ' She wanted her to go to her old school. And that wasn't the only reason. She thought Penny would be happier.'

' Sorry, Dad. Put my bad temper down to nerves.' Gloria dabbed at her eyes with a lace-trimmed handkerchief. ' You've been a very good father to me. I may not have appreciated that always, but I do now, otherwise I should hardly be here.'

With this unexpected change of mood, the atmosphere lightened. But it was with a feeling of relief, all the same, that Penny went out to fetch the car.

On the short drive to the pharmacy Robert said half-ashamedly: ' I must try to be more patient with Gloria. Your mother is far more forbearing. She's going to suggest to you that you arrange a little supper-party for Gloria. There must be some of her former acquaintances around, and with a few of your friends to meet her, too—'

' I can't see her fitting in with my contemporaries,' Penny returned quickly. ' Oh, I know she's not all that much older than some of them, anyway, in point of actual age. But she's far too sophisticated to enjoy being with the likes of us.'

' She should have a chance,' was her stepfather's comment. ' Be a sport, Penny, and get out a few names.'

It was difficult, Penny found, to accede cheerfully to this wish of her parents. Gloria, she was certain, would be bored stiff with people like Sybil and Joe and Eric, and they'd be ill at ease with her. As for her 'former acquaintances', as her stepfather put it, he evidently didn't realise that though Gloria had made friends easily, she had never kept them. Anyway, many girls in her age-group had settled down into comfortable domesticity in other parts of the island, or gone farther afield.

She was doodling grimly with her biro when footsteps approached her counter, and she looked up to find Stephen standing in front of her, ironic amusement on his face.

'Plunged in gloom already, Penny? Surely you can stand up to the gorgeous Gloria a little longer than this!' He was speaking very quietly in that deep voice of his. 'After all, you're not without attractions yourself!'

'Stephen, you're the very one!' Used to his teasing, she brushed his flattery aside. 'I don't know why I didn't think of you first!'

'You never do, my dear. And after all, why should you?'

'Do what, Stephen?' There was slight impatience in her tone.

'Think of me first—or even second. I'm a long way down the list.' He spoke in pretended reproach. 'Anyway, what's the reason for my sudden popularity?'

'You're in one of your funny moods this morning,' she told him, a shade irritably. 'But if you want the truth, you're specially important because Dad and Mum suggest I should fix a small party for Gloria this week. Oh, I know you won't wish to come, but Dad may be hurt if you don't.'

His expression hardened.

'I doubt it. However, apart from not intending to be forced into Gloria's company, I shall be away for some little time now, working in the Takhana forests, on that new teak plantation.'

'When are you going up there?' she demanded. 'I— I don't mean to catechise you, Steve, but—'

'Then don't do it, my dear! However, as you're so insistent, I'll tell you that I'll be starting almost at once. And I probably shan't be returning to Val Fleury for quite a while.'

22

She had no wish whatever to see Gloria and Stephen renewing their old friendship. But she knew that they were pretty well bound to meet again in this small, restricted village. Unless, of course, Gloria's visit proved a really-and-truly flying one, and Stephen's stay in the forests inordinately long.

Knew also that Gloria, affronted by her cousin's absence from the party, might very well accuse her of omitting to invite him.

However, he gave her no chance to enlarge farther on the thorny subject. With a brief, ' Be seeing you some time,' he was on his way, whatever purchases he had intended to make forgotten.

As for her mother, she proved far too preoccupied, when Penny and her stepfather reached home in the lunch hour, to discuss supper-parties. Indeed she looked positively worried.

' What's the matter, Mum?' Penny demanded forthrightly.

' Well, I've struck a bit of a problem. Gloria slept very badly, it now seems, and after you and Dad left for work she took some sleeping pills. I told her it was a silly time of day to bother with them; that she'd much better dress and go out in the fresh air. But she wouldn't listen.'

' And she's still fast asleep?' Robert was not greatly concerned. ' Don't worry about her, Brenda. Let's get on with lunch. Later on, when I'm back from the shop, I'll get her to show me what brand she's taking. You'd be surprised if you knew what a lot of people take sleeping pills these days, even in this pleasant, peaceful little island.'

' I'm not fussed about her sleeping late, but about what she said before she took the pills.' Mrs Dale was clearly harassed. She looked from one to the other and went on : ' She declares that she doesn't feel this is home for her any more—sleeping in that tiny room at the back of the house where she hears every noise from the Bennetts' farm. She wants me to ask you, Penny, as a great favour, if you'll let her have her old room—the one you have now.' She pressed her lips together, then added : ' She says you were perfectly happy in the little one for years, so it couldn't make all that difference to you—especially as you're a good sleeper.'

'You mean permanently?' Penny exclaimed in dismay.

'Gloria will never settle down here—I'll be surprised if she stays more than a week or two,' her stepfather observed impatiently. 'All the same, I think she has a colossal nerve to suggest such a thing. She's my own flesh and blood, I know. But Penny's been far more of a real daughter to me, bless her.'

'Oh, she put on the pathetic act, like she so often does,' Mrs Dale told him wearily. 'How lonely she'd be in a hotel—even if there was one in Val Fleury. Doctor's warnings of how important sleep is to her.' She turned to Penny. 'I ended up by promising I'd ask you to give your room up. I didn't commit you.'

'Why should Penny be put upon like this?' Robert Dale fumed. 'I'll have a straight talk with Gloria myself. Ask her what she ever did for her young stepsister when she was living here, except bully and tease her.'

'And can't you imagine the scenes that will follow? All the pills she'll have to take? Why, she might even try to scare us by taking more than a safe dose.'

'Sheer blackmail, that would be,' Robert insisted angrily. But Penny, seeing the trouble in her mother's eyes, and remembering the effect which Gloria's hysteria had always produced on her, said quietly: 'She won't be here long, I feel certain. If she stays in Santa Rita at all, she'll be down in Port Leon, in some glamour job. It's not worth a fuss. And I quite like that little room, and hearing the Bennetts' cockerels. Tell her it's O.K. by me. And now, darling, I'm ravenous!'

In spite of her efforts to be magnanimous, Penny reached home in the evening, in no very genial mood, her annoyance directed even more to Stephen's stubborn refusal of her invitation than to Gloria's egotistical demand.

She found her stepsister looking relaxed and glamorous in a chiffon housecoat—if such a garment could go by so homely a name—and full of sweetly expressed gratitude for Penny's kindness in giving up her room.

'And Auntie Brenda and Pearl have been so good about helping me to move my things!' She took a sip

24

from the long glass of rum and ginger ale which she was holding, and sighed. ' You can't imagine what it means to me to be surrounded by such kindness.'

Pearl, preparing to go home, popped her head in just then.

' Ah'm finished at *last*,' she said, looking reproachfully at Mrs Dale. ' And are mah pore legs achin'? No rest either when Ah gits home. Don' know how Ah carries on—an dat de Gospel truth.'

Penny got quickly from her chair.

' Come on, Pearly,' she exclaimed, ' I'll run you home. You haven't been in the Mini yet.'

Pearl's gloom was replaced by a beaming smile.

' Yo' sure a honey, Mis' Penny. Suit me fine, it will.'

As she and Penny left the room, Penny heard Gloria observing disdainfully: ' It wouldn't have suited me to have had her in any of my cars. I'd have been afraid for my springs. And mine haven't been Minis.'

Evidently Pearl, too, had heard. She stopped short, and asked unhappily: ' Will Ah truly harm anyt'ing? Or is it jest she at her usual trick—makin' folk miserable?'

' Of course you won't break the springs,' Penny told her comfortingly. ' Take no notice of her.'

She was secretly thankful, however, that the drive was a short one. Apart from the question of Pearl's considerable weight, darkness had dropped on the valley, and she needed to concentrate—to shut out, as far as possible, Pearl's deep voice as she expatiated on Gloria's behaviour all through the afternoon. ' Sittin' pretty and havin' me and your ma working like slaves.'

However, she reached the small, wooden house up a narrow lane without too much difficulty, only running into trouble when, unable to turn, she backed down the slight slope out into the main road. Moving faster than she intended, she shot out too far, and a car travelling at fairly high speed away from the village nearly grazed the back of the Mini. Although it was a miss, not a hit, the driver stopped dead, fairly blasting his horn.

She straightened up, and would have called an apology as she drove on, when she saw in the light of the car lamps a broad-shouldered figure come striding, and there was Stephen standing at her window.

' Good grief, Penny, what on earth are you doing out

25

here? Do you realise it takes a skilled driver to negotiate these crazy side-tracks, even in daylight? I might have bashed your car to bits—even killed you.'

Penny, still sore with him, and badly shaken by her narrow escape, eyed him stonily.

'You were going much too fast,' she told him. 'Do you fancy yourself above such things as speed limits?'

'There isn't one here,' he retorted curtly. 'That's why you should have crept out of that concealed turning—if you had to use such a tricky path at all.'

'Well, as there hasn't been an accident, we might as well get going our separate ways.'

'Suits me. But you might remember, Penny, that passing a driving test doesn't make a reliable driver.'

Her hazel eyes glinted.

'And you might remember that flimsy excuses for refusing invitations are paltry. Among people supposed to be friends, that is.'

'Why should I have to spend an evening in Gloria's company when I don't wish to?' he demanded.

'Out of politeness to her father—and consideration for his feelings.' She paused for breath, faintly ashamed of insincerity, then continued with more conviction: 'For my sake, too. Gloria, being the person she is, will think it somehow my fault that you're avoiding her.'

'Take no notice of any of her silly insinuations, Penny,' he told her impatiently. 'She'll not be here long to plague you, I hope. And now, as I've a lot to do before I finish for the day, I must get along. Off with you first!'

She started up and as she began her drive home through the black and silver landscape—for the moon was rising—she heard him give a friendly toot on his horn as he moved towards the hills. It mollified her a little.

She said nothing of this encounter with Stephen when she reached home. Her mother remarked that she had begun to feel a little worried about her, but her stepfather countered by commenting that she had been wise not to drive too fast in the darkness. As for Gloria, she merely yawned, and looking up from the magazine through which she was leafing, enquired whether they would be having a meal soon, as she was starving.

The question of the supper-party came up that evening, and Penny felt a wry amusement at herself for worrying over Stephen's dogged refusal to attend it.

For Gloria did not want to come to it either! She objected, she said, to being exhibited to the neighbourhood as a sorrowing widow. Sympathy would be quite too embarrassing. In any case, the few girl friends she had made during her years at Val Fleury would now be podgy married women with bawling kids. All she wished was to be left in peace.

'Then Penny will just be asking a few of her own crowd along,' Brenda Dale observed equably. 'You needn't appear unless you wish to. Your father and I will probably go to friends for a rubber or two of Bridge.'

Gloria shrugged her shoulders.

'I might rake up someone in Port Leon to take me out to dinner,' was her very casual response. 'I must confess I found more congenial people down there than in this old-world village.' And then after a pause she added: 'Of course there were one or two kindred spirits up here, now I come to think of it. That cousin of mine, for instance, who had some incredibly boring job fiddling around with trees—is he still around? Steve, I mean. Or did he join his parents when they moved to Barbados, and embark on a more ambitious and interesting career— something with a future?'

Penny felt herself flushing with annoyance, but left it to her stepfather to say coldly: 'Stephen has been promoted to the post of Chief Forestry Officer here—something to be proud of for a man of under thirty, even in this little island. He may not be earning an enormous salary, but he's doing a vitally important work, repairing the thoughtlessness and stupidity of the not so distant past by saving valuable trees from destruction—replanting where felling has taken place to guard against any possible repetition of flooding after heavy rain-storms.'

'And he's terribly keen.' Encouraged by her stepfather's eloquence, Penny slid into the conversation. 'Forever trying out new stocks and methods. People in Santa Rita—people who count, I mean—are very proud of him. Even before he went to Trinidad to train, they said—'

But what these important citizens said was not recorded.

Gloria interrupted by declaring that if Stephen wanted to make anything of a career in forestry, he should try for a post in California. At least he would be paid properly, though even then he would be throwing away his talents—in her humble opinion, anyway. And then she continued lightly: ' I've no doubt he'll be turning up some time to see me, once he knows I'm here. We were good friends in the old days. But I'm pretty sure that a party with Penny's contemporaries would hardly be in his line. He was always one for a tête-à-tête, anyway.'

A remark which made her father flash her a look of sharp annoyance.

They came along, Penny's special friends, a few days later. Half a dozen of them, including the three who had made her birthday such a happy one.

Whether Gloria had indeed tried to contact any of her former admirers she did not know. If so, she must have failed to obtain an invitation to dinner, for she retired to her bedroom with a tray of refreshments, a transistor, and a pile of magazines, and announced her desire to be left to her own resources.

On the whole the guests were relieved and settled down cheerfully to play card games and to enjoy the fruit drinks and delicious snacks which Mrs Dale and Pearl had provided for them. True, they had expected to meet Gloria, whom so far they had only caught glimpses of in the main street. But they had been chilled by her bored, slightly disdainful looks as they passed her on the sidewalk, had decided that she would hardly add to their fun.

Eric, indeed, murmured to Penny, when they were out in the kitchen together collecting fresh supplies of lime-juice, that he was delighted that Gloria had taken herself off to her room. She had been a bitch to him when he had first come to the Stores as a young assistant—made his stammer a hundred times worse by her cruel teasing. She wouldn't have the power to put him out of countenance now. All the same, if he had to meet her, he would prefer it to be over the counter. He was on his own ground there, well able to hold his own.

But a couple of hours later Gloria, as always, did the unpredictable thing. At this altitude the nights could be cool, in sharp contrast to the often humid coast, and she came to stand at the open doorway wearing a beautifully cut, long-skirted affair of fairy-fine violet wool, her abundant, shining, auburn-tinted hair piled up on her head, amethysts sparkling at her slender throat.

'Am I dreadfully *de trop*?' she asked with a hint of pathos in her voice. 'I felt so lonesome sitting there in my room, hearing all the talk and laughter. As though I were banished—'

'Of course you're welcome, Gloria!' Penny tried to choke down the resentment which her stepsister so often aroused in her. 'You *were* invited, you know. Come and take a hand at gin-rummy.'

At once room was made for her at the table, but she shook her head.

'No, my dears, I'll watch. It's so many years since I watched these darling, old-fashioned games that I've forgotten every single rule. But first I must renew my acquaintance with some of you, at least. Eric, how good to see you again. But how you've changed. Not the shy boy I used to tease so naughtily. And Sybil—grown-up and sophisticated. Yes, I think I recall every one of you now. And what a lovely feeling it gives me.' She subsided gracefully into a large chair not far from the table. 'All I want now, Penny my sweet, is some of that gorgeous lemon soufflé. Pearl wouldn't give me a morsel when she was preparing my tray. Said it would spoil it to put a spoon into it.'

With her coming the atmosphere had undergone a subtle change. No one seemed completely at ease. It was as though a bird of Paradise had dropped down among a group of house wrens.

'Do you really want to go on playing cards?' Gloria asked, after her wants had been supplied. 'If not, could we have some records? I'm longing to hear calypsos again—on those heavenly steel drums.'

It was Eric who spoke now. He asked, turning to Penny: 'Would you like that, sweetie? Shall I start the record player? Or would you rather keep to rummy?'

Penny did not miss the inflection in his voice. He wished to emphasise that it was she, and no one else, who was the hostess.

'Of course, we'll have some discs. You know where

everything is,' was her serene response. And within moments the room was flooded with softly throbbing music—sweet, sensual, compelling.

Under the spell of the steel drums no one wanted to resume card games, and when Eric had played all the best records, he cheerfully acceded to Penny's suggestion that he and Joe should bring out their guitars and give the party the latest pop songs. The two young men, well accustomed to playing together, settled down contentedly, singing as they twanged the strings a somewhat sugary number which had recently reached the islands from New York.

And suddenly another voice came threading through —a soft contralto taking up the commonplace words and investing them with mockery, passion, sadness.

Nobody spoke when silence fell. Until Penny said evenly: 'We always knew you had a good voice, Gloria, but nothing so wonderful as this.'

'Wonderful my foot! I had a few lessons over in the States. But when Greg—that's my husband—found that I'd never be anything but mediocre, he put a stop to them. My real talent was hairdressing, he said. And I guess he was right.'

There was a short embarrassed silence, broken by Eric who said, stammering a little: 'You've given us a lot of pleasure, anyway. By our standards, you're the tops.' And Joe, leading the clapping which broke out now, exclaimed: 'What fun it would be to form a trio—just playing for charity. Pop, of course.'

But Gloria shook her head.

'And me a widow! Folks would be shocked to the core. Still, it's sweet of you to think of it.'

Sybil, who had been ruminating, came out with quite another idea then.

A very dear aunt in Barbados, who had been taken ill, was begging her to go over and visit her. Normally, she would have asked Mrs O'Brien for leave right away, but the Hibiscus Salon was already short of competent staff, and what with the annual Independence celebrations approaching, she didn't see how she could possibly be spared.

'I suppose you couldn't stand in for me, just for a fortnight?' she asked Gloria diffidently. 'You don't need the money, I know. But maybe it could be a bit boring for you here, just sitting around.'

'I'm out of practice, honey!' Gloria's self-depreciation was not, Penny thought, at all convincing. And she was even less pleased with her stepsister when she went on in that same hesitant tone: 'And if you'll forgive my saying so, hair-styles in the big American cities are rather different from—from what I've noticed here.'

But Sybil was too eager to make the trip to her aunt's bedside to resent Gloria's attitude. All she thought about was winning the older girl's consent to her suggestion.

Mentally Penny shrugged her shoulders. If it suited Gloria to oust Sybil altogether—or even to make Mrs O'Brien to think less of her work—she would have no scruples over doing so. But what could she do about it? Just nothing, she decided.

And then suddenly a new name dropped into the conversation.

Joe, talking to one of the other guests about the forthcoming Independence Ball to be held for the first time in the new luxury hotel in Port Leon, mentioned that his brother Pete was planning to be down from the forests in time for the function and, wonder of wonders, that Stephen might possibly be there, too.

Gloria pricked up her ears at that.

'He wasn't at all a bad dancer in the old days, my cousin Steve,' she remarked casually. 'When he could take his mind off his boring old trees. I wonder, incidentally, if he knows I'm back in Val Fleury.'

'I'll mention it to him, next time I see him,' Joe assured her gallantly. 'He and Pete were both in the bank yesterday, as a matter of fact. I remember now Steve saying he was going up to the new teak plantation at Takhana in a couple of days' time—to-morrow morning, it would be—and would be up there some little while.'

'Well, give him my love, next time you run across him—tell him I'll be seeing him.'

She could hardly have sounded more casual. But when the guests had gone, and Penny was tidying away the remains of the supper, she turned on her young stepsister.

' Rather odd behaviour, to leave Stephen without an invitation to this supper-party of yours. After all, he's my cousin, and——'

' Only a second cousin,' Penny broke in. She knew she was being provocative, but she was too incensed to care. ' If we have to invite all your distant relatives to every little party we give—'

' Put a sock in it,' was Gloria's inelegant retort, an ugly rasp in her voice. ' You know very well—or should, if you weren't completely thick-headed—that he and I were very close friends. So why didn't you ask him?'

' If you want the truth, I did, and he declined. Said he would be up in the forest, working.'

' And he isn't. He's in Val Fleury. What did you say to put him off? You must have said something!'

' No! I haven't your gift for intrigue.' For the first time ever, Penny was standing up firmly to Gloria.

Gloria paled, her eyes snapping with anger, but Penny held her ground, and continued coldly: ' Have you forgotten your own contemptuous refusal to come to my party?'

' Did you tell him I'd not be there?' Gloria spoke a shade more mildly now. ' If so, I can well understand his refusing your invitation.'

' I didn't. As you know, Stephen is a person of few words. He said he couldn't come because he would be away in the Takhana forest.'

' Did he make any apologies to me? Express any regrets? But of course you wouldn't pass them on to me.'

' If you're sure of that why should I waste my breath denying it?' Penny spoke coolly, but heard with relief the sound of her stepfather turning the Mini into the little drive. He and her mother would be in the house in a minute, so Gloria would have no chance of forcing a quarrel on her.

But the older girl managed, as always in the past, to have the last word.

' You're the mean little thing you always were,' she exclaimed furiously. ' I don't believe a word you say. You think Stephen's your property, just because he gives you a madly expensive book for your birthday. But I tell you this—he won't look at you once he's met up with me again!'

Penny stared at her now in utter astonishment.

'What on earth are you getting at?' she exclaimed.

For a second Gloria's chances wavered. Then before she could reply, her father and stepmother had come into the room, and Penny heard her saying in cooing tones, and with the sweetest of smiles: 'Hi, darlings! I just couldn't keep away from Penny's lovely little party. Wonderful food, entrancing music, gay conversation! I haven't enjoyed myself so much in months.'

CHAPTER II

Penny was too tired and sleepy to reflect long, either on
Gloria's acting ability, her lightning changes of manner,
or on that extraordinary reference to Stephen. Her stepsister, she decided, as she dropped off to sleep, had become
more unbalanced than ever to behave as she did. That
being so it was to be hoped she would soon tire of life
in Santa Rita, and leave her long-suffering family in
peace.

But next morning brought her a fresh surprise. She
was coming from the bathroom after her usual morning
shower when Gloria, lying abed, called in an unusually
friendly tone : ' Hi, Pen! Come in for a minute, will
you.' And when Penny reluctantly obeyed the summons,
she patted her bed in an invitation to her to sit down.

' I won't keep you a minute,' she told her, ' but I
really must apologise for the insulting nonsense I talked
last night about you and Stephen. I know there's
nothing in your friendship with him and never could be.
That Eric—such a lovely person as he's turned out—is
the one for you.'

' Why *did* you go on about Steve?' Penny demanded,
trying to subdue the irritation which Gloria always managed to provoke in her. ' Just because he gave me that
book for my birthday!'

Gloria shrugged her shoulders, shapely under her
chiffon wrap ; assumed an air of penitence.

' My proverbially quick temper got the better of me,
I'm afraid. I was feeling furious at his apparent avoid-
ance of me. It was very bad of me, I know, taking it
out on you like that—particularly,'—and now angry
contempt coloured in her voice—' as I don't really care
a damn whether I set eyes on him again or not. It's
evident that the life he leads, stuck up in those dismal
woods for months at a time, has turned him into a boor!'

It was hardly an acceptable apology, Penny felt, but
certainly Stephen hadn't behaved very courteously to
his cousin. And she conjured up a casual assurance that
she would think no more of the matter, and hurried off
to dress.

But she noticed that after that brief conversation Gloria made rather more effort to behave pleasantly, not only in the family circle, but among the people she met in Val Fleury. Within a day or so she had called on Maude O'Brien, the plump, kindly but perennially harassed owner of the rather grandly titled *Hibiscus Hair-styling Salon*, and, to Sybil Marsden's delight, had made an excellent impression there. She had spoken modestly about her undeniably impressive experience in America, and had shown every disposition to co-operate agreeably with the other employees. For what must seem to her a very modest salary she was prepared to work five mornings and two afternoons each week that Sybil was absent.

Full of gratitude, Sybil Marsden was soon packing up and departing for Barbados, seen off by her elderly parents—who were equally edified by Gloria's goodness of heart. After all, Gloria was by all accounts a wealthy woman. She wouldn't need the money. It was sheer kindness on her part.

One person who didn't join in the chorus of praise was Pearl.

' You and Mis' Sybil de most foolish gals in de world,' she declared, chopping up vegetables with unnecessary violence, as Penny came into the kitchen to wash up some tea-cups. ' Mis' Gloria, she gwine thief Mis' Sybil's job for as long as it suits her—throwing it back to her like a bone to a dawg when she tire of it. Spoiling t'ings for her with Mis' O'Brien by hinting Mis' Sybil slow an' ole-fashioned. An' dat not all, Mis' Penny. She get young Eric in her clutches by and by—an' dat Joe, too. Break some hearts and go on her way. Dat's Mis' Gloria. Too like her ma, dat one.'

Nor would any protests or arguments on Penny's part alter her point of view.

Penny's chief doubt was whether Gloria would last out at the Salon for the whole fortnight Sybil was to be away, for she came back from work most days with scathing comments on the poor equipment there, and the old-fashioned ideas that prevailed.

But it soon became clear that Gloria's contemptuous criticisms were strictly for home consumption. Whenever Penny or her mother encountered either Mrs

O'Brien, or friends of theirs who were her clients, they found themselves listening to paeans of praise for Gloria's virtues. She was regarded not only as a first-rate hairdresser, but as a model of tact and charm. She must inevitably find the Salon a trifle old-fashioned, but there was never a grumble from her. She just concentrated on achieving the best results possible with the facilities at her command.

'I think it's horrible, the way she butters people up, then makes unkind fun of them behind their backs,' Penny observed to her mother one evening on her return from work—Gloria having not yet arrived. 'Truly, Mum, I'll be thankful when she takes herself off.'

Brenda Dale hesitated, then said abruptly: 'And so shall I! Though I wouldn't like your stepfather to hear me say that. She makes me thoroughly uneasy.' Again she paused, before adding: 'What's all this about her forming a trio with Eric and Joe? Singing the words of pop songs while they play on their guitars!'

For a second Penny was startled. She had heard no more of the matter since the evening of the party.

Then she asked coolly: 'Oh, is that idea still on? I thought Gloria had turned it down, afraid people would be shocked at a woman who had been bereaved of her husband barely a year ago—'

'If she had such scruples she's lost them now. Joe's parents were talking to me about it only yesterday. They say she's pressing the boys to go on with it—seems to think it a grand notion, as they're only to play for charity.'

Penny flushed.

'Eric's said nothing to me about it. He certainly wasn't keen at first, though he's a far better player than Joe. But if he doesn't wish to tell me, I'm certainly not going to ask him—nor anyone else.'

'I think you're wrong there, dear. Don't let her spoil your friendship with Eric. Treat the thing in a matter-of-fact way. After all, she won't be here indefinitely—not long enough to do much damage, if you behave sensibly.'

'Sorry, Mum, but I haven't Gloria's acting abilities. If I feel annoyed, I show it. I can't coo when I feel spitting mad.'

'Actually you've been very tolerant over Gloria's tiresomeness.' Brenda bent over to kiss her daughter. 'Let's hope she'll take wing soon—that's all. She's an instinctive mischief-maker.'

But it was Robert Dale, sensing that his wife and stepdaughter were not quite so serene as usual, who tackled Gloria bluntly on her future plans.

They were sitting, all four of them, on the back verandah, that night, after dinner, when he asked his daughter mildly: 'And what are you going to do with yourself when your time at the Salon is over?'

There was silence for a moment or two in the scented darkness, but for the whistling of frogs in a distant swamp. Then Gloria returned airily: 'Mrs O'Brien is madly keen for me to stay on—permanently. But she knows really that it's out of the question. It would mean one of the other girls—even Sybil, perhaps—having to go, and that would be most unfair.'

'I should think so,' her father said sharply. 'Anyway, it's impossible you could content yourself living and working in a backwater like this for any length of time.'

'At the moment it's sheer peace being in Val Fleury.' Gloria gave a long sigh. 'Just sitting out here, even, with the lovely scents around one, watching those gorgeous, crazy fireflies, is heaven. Makes me wonder why I ever left the Caribbean.'

'I can answer that in one word, my dear.' Her father's voice was still edgy. 'Ambition.'

'Maybe. Though I can still relax and enjoy myself from time to time, like any other true West Indian.'

'Until you get bored. But anyway—'

'Oh, I've thought things over myself, folks.' She was deliberately including Penny and her mother in the conversation now. 'Sybil may very well ask for a week or two longer, Mrs O'Brien thinks. If she doesn't—perhaps you could put up with me until after Christmas.'

The request startled all three of her hearers. It was now early November, and Christmas seemed a long way off.

But her father, recovering himself quickly, said equably: 'Certainly you must spend Christmas with us, my dear.' And he flashed his wife, sitting next to him in the darkness, an appreciative smile when she backed

37

him up with a quiet: 'Of course she must!'

Only Penny found it impossible to force out a word or two of welcome. Seven weeks more of Gloria's presence in the far from roomy bungalow, occupying the bedroom which Penny had for the past five years made her own. Of her intrigues, her duplicity! How was she to endure it? A trouble-maker, if ever there was one, who would go away precisely when it suited her, leaving factions behind where there had once been peace. An exaggeration? She didn't believe so.

Next day was early closing at the pharmacy. And with Juan Garcia, the elderly dispenser, on call to deal with any urgent prescriptions, Mr and Mrs Dale, with Penny accompanying them, went down to Port Leon in the big Rover, in the early afternoon.

It was a necessary jaunt. Christmas cards and calendars, ordered months ago from the mainland, had only just arrived, and were awaiting collection at a warehouse near the harbour. And there would be supplies of fancy goods of various kinds to be looked over by Brenda and Penny, on whose judgment Robert relied for quick-selling lines.

At the warehouse they ran into several people they knew, including a few from Val Fleury. As they had anticipated, Eric and his boss, George Farrow, were in the section where luxuries for the table were on display—too busy for more than hurried greetings. And shopping around for toiletries they presently encountered Mrs O'Brien, her list of essential goods somewhat lengthened, she confessed, smiling, by Gloria's suggestions.

'She's a most talented girl, your daughter,' she told Robert warmly. 'So sweet-tempered and charming. We think the world of her at the Salon.' She paused, before going on in a confidential tone: 'I expect she has told you, but I'm trying to persuade her to stay on for a while after Sybil's return. I want her to give her and the other girls what I might describe as a few finishing lessons—for an appropriate fee, of course. And I may say, I'd not be ashamed to pick up a few tips myself. We in this little island have much to learn from the outside world—if we're not too proud to do so.'

By the time the Dale family had made their selections

and got them stowed into the boot of the Rover and the vacant back seat, it was growing late—nearing the time when after a brief, glorious sunset, with the sky a kaleidoscope of vivid colours, darkness would fall on the world with the immediacy of a stage curtain.

They were ready to leave before Eric and his boss; and Eric, on the pretence of helping Penny arrange some awkwardly shaped goods on the back seat, tried to get a private word with her.

' I wish we could have fixed things so that I could have driven you home, while Farrow travelled with your parents,' he murmured. ' There's something I want to talk to you about.'

' If it's the trio you're forming with Joe and Gloria, I know about it already,' she said, bending over a large box, so that he shouldn't see her face.

' I'm glad of that,' he returned, clearly relieved. ' The other two wanted to keep it quiet until we'd got a date with the people running the Independence Ball, but I was anxious you should be the first to hear about it.'

' That was thoughtful of you,' she told him coolly.

He looked worried.

' You don't mind, do you, Penny?'

' Why should I?'

He hesitated.

' Well, it means that I can only partner you for odd dances at the Ball. And Joe has the same problem over Sybil. Considering we'd fixed to go in our usual foursome—'

Penny conjured up the blandest of smiles—which even Gloria, she thought, could not have rivalled.

' Don't worry. It's just possible that we shan't find ourselves wallflowers,' she said over-sweetly.

' D—damn it all, of c-course you won't,' Eric stammered under his breath, as Robert Dale, with a friendly nod in his direction, got into the driving seat and started up the engine. ' But, Penny dear, I do *wish*—'

What he wished did not transpire, for Mrs Dale had climbed in quickly now beside her husband, and the big car was moving on its way.

Penny, sitting alone at the back, surrounded by unwieldy packages, was fuming. Not because Eric and Joe were to perform at the Independence Day ball—that would be altogether too petty and unsporting—but because of the way it had been engineered.

It was Gloria's doing, of course. Anyone else would have seen to it that she and Sybil were the first to hear of the project, once it was seriously mooted.

'She has a thoroughly bad influence on people,' she told herself indignantly, and then stopped short, biting her lip.

'I'm affected by it myself,' she thought. 'She brings out the worst in me. Oh, I know now I had cause to feel irritated with those boys, but I needn't have spoken to poor old Eric in that sarcastic way, bringing back his stutter.'

These depressing thoughts were soon submerged in sheer physical tiredness as the car, under Robert Dale's skilful guidance, began the long, steep, zig-zag climb through the foothills. He and her mother, weary too, had lapsed into silence, and she was thankful for this. She was in no mood for conversation.

Darkness had dropped and the strong headlights picked out every tree, every bush, bordering the road, so that they seemed to leap forward menacingly—no longer graceful shapes with gloriously coloured blossoms, but glaring white spectres, stretching out cruel, distorted arms to grab them as they passed. No fragrance, either, nor even the mysterious call of night-birds. Just petrol fumes, and the sound of the car travelling in low gear.

It was a relief to see the welcoming light in the hall, but when they turned into the garage at the side of the house, Robert gave a quick exclamation of surprise.

'Well, I'm damned! Your car's gone, Penny. What on earth—!'

But out waddled Pearl just then, her face thunderous.

'Mis' Gloria take it, an hour or so after you left. A telephone call came an' she got all 'cited. I not tellin' her where you keep de spare keys, Mis' Penny, but she search round an' find dem.'

'The nerve of her!' Robert exploded. 'Borrowing Penny's precious new car without permission!'

'I expect she got bored and went to meet some old friend down in Port Leon,' Brenda Dale observed, trying to pour oil on the troubled waters. 'She's very naughty, of course—'

' And isn't used to driving along our mountain roads,'
Penny chipped in, suddenly anxious. ' I hope she'll be
all right.'

Pearl snorted.

'De debbil look after his own. You'all come inside
now and eat the nice little supper Ah've got for you.
An' den Ah gwine home to mah fam'ly. An' mebbe
Ah'll meet Mis' Gloria. She not goin' to Port Leon. Ah
watch her, an' she gwine de other direction.'

' Towards the mountains?' Penny asked sharply.

' Ah guess so,' was Pearl's brief retort. ' An' now
for goodness' sake come and eat up de supper before it
all spoiled.'

She had hardly gone, stumping up the path when the
lights of a car shone brightly, and an engine purred as
it turned in towards the garage.

It was Gloria returning, they knew, but no one moved.
They had started their meal and were going on with it.
Wasn't it up to her to come in and face them, with her
explanations?

Some minutes later she came into the room—in no
penitent mood, it seemed.

' I suppose I ought to apologise, Penny,' she said
abruptly, as she sat down at the table. ' But I know
beforehand that you'll never understand!'

Penny passed the dish of sauté chicken across to her.

' You got an important telephone message, and there
was no opportunity to get in touch with me about
borrowing the Mini, so you took it. Maybe I'd have
done the same if I'd been in your shoes.'

' Of course you wouldn't, Penny,' Robert began
crossly, but Gloria exclaimed quickly: ' I've no real excuse. That's why I know none of you will understand.
There was no telephone call—'

' But Pearl said—' Brenda protested, her resolve to
keep the peace a trifle shaken by Gloria's assertion.

' A wrong number, that was all. The simple truth is
that I began to get unbearably restless, as though the
walls of the bungalow were pressing on me. I just had
to get out—into the fresh air—by myself.'

Her manner was candid enough. Or was it? None
of her three hearers could be certain. Their doubts ran

41

in different directions.

Joe wanted Gloria to come and rehearse with him, had pressed her to do so, with an urgent telephone call. So Penny and her mother thought.

But Robert had a darker, more troubling thought. Was Stephen, after all that had happened five years ago, about to make a fool of himself once more? It seemed unlikely. He was pretty hard-boiled these days, his eyes wide open to insincerity. But all the same—! Gloria was a beautiful creature—fascinating when she so chose. Like her mother, God rest that poor, false woman's soul!

Well, he wouldn't accuse Gloria of anything sinister. He would content himself with taking her to task to-morrow and insisting with all the force at his command, that if she had another urge to go driving she should telephone to the little garage in the village, and hire out one of the two cars which the owner, Jack Boddy, kept there. They were pretty shabby, he admitted, but he was not going to have *anyone messing* around with Penny's treasured Mini.

With Gloria's meek assurance never to offend again in that way, the matter was dropped. The purchase of goods for the Christmas trade threw so much work on everyone at the pharmacy—Penny being in the forefront of the sorting and pricing—that there was simply no time to think of other things.

Thoroughly tired, she found it even more difficult than usual to tolerate Gloria's all-pervading presence when she went home to lunch. She was still inwardly ashamed of her annoyance over the formation of the pop trio, but couldn't, somehow, recover her poise. Nor did it help when Gloria, sensing her irritation, and finding it unconnected with her ' crime ' of borrowing the Mini, demanded wistfully if she was sore because she was joining up with Eric and Joe to sing and play for charity.

' Because if so, I'll drop the whole thing,' she assured her mournfully. ' I'll be sorry. I should so like to help the poor of the island with my tiny talent. But if you resent my taking up a certain amount of Eric's spare time—well, we're all human! I'd hate myself for causing you to feel the smallest glimmer of jealousy.'

' You haven't the power to do that, I promise you,'

was Penny's cool reply. 'I've a lot of faults, but jealousy isn't one of them.'

Gloria eyed her consideringly.

'Then you aren't human,' she affirmed.

Their tête-à-tête was broken by Robert's entrance with the comment that it was high time he and Penny got back to the shop—and with the offer of a lift for Gloria to the Hibiscus Salon.

'Please, Dad! And don't worry if I'm a little late coming home this evening. I've promised to put in some overtime for Mrs O'Brien. She's always behind schedule, that one.'

In the middle of the afternoon Eric dropped in— ostensibly to hand in a prescription for his boss, George Farrow—but more credibly, since there were less important employees to send, for a word with Penny.

He found her setting out some bargain-price cameras, and asked her quickly if she would come to the cinema with him that evening.

The thought went through Penny's head: 'He's free to-night because Gloria's working late: won't have time to practise.' But she was speaking the truth when she told him evenly that with so much extra to do, she was just about dropping. Come what might, she must have an early night.

'Then I'll ask you again soon, when you feel more like it.' He was bothered, stammering a little. But she could not bring herself to put him at his ease.

Normally he would have tried at once to pin her down to the nearest acceptable date. Now, uncertain of his free time, he was hedging.

More annoyed with herself, oddly enough, than with him, she gave him a tepid, non-committal smile and turned back to her work, and off he went, his shoulders sagging a little.

She bit her lip. If only Gloria had never come back to Santa Rita—upsetting everything and everyone. An exaggeration, of course! But oh dear, to have to put up with her until after Christmas—it didn't bear thinking about.

It wasn't the notion of the trio, as such, that angered her, she told herself. It could have been fun. She could have helped behind the scenes, looking out fresh

43

numbers, copying parts. Sybil—she could have been brought into it, too. But not with Gloria around.

Likeable people, she reflected, had the gift of bringing people together in a happy, harmonious relationship. But Gloria, in some subtle way, spread discord and disquiet, brought out the worst in everyone.

If only Christmas were not so far away.

The whole family, Gloria included, were tired that night, and glad to turn in early.

Penny, painfully sure that she was too exhausted to fall asleep quickly, was actually in dreamland within half an hour, cheerfully waving good-bye to her stepsister as she stepped on the plane which was to take her back to America.

Other more confused dreams followed, and then suddenly she was awake again, starlight silvering her small bedroom, the faint sound of footsteps in her ears. Footsteps in the garden.

She listened and heard, perplexed and a little scared, a man coming quietly up the garden path, saw through the wrought iron grating which filled the window frame a figure pass by, making, evidently, for the back of the house.

She slipped out of bed, but the wrought-iron grating, designed to keep out marauders, prevented her from leaning out. All she could do was to listen, thankful that all the other windows were similarly protected—and almost at once her ears caught the sound of muted voices.

Was it, possibly, someone calling on her father with an urgent prescription? But if so, surely he would have come to the front door.

And then she pinpointed precisely where that muffled conversation was taking place. The intruder was outside Gloria's window, talking to her.

But not for long.

Penny had scarcely time to leap back into bed before the footsteps returned. Just for a moment the man paused outside her window, and in the starlight she recognised by his height and breadth of shoulder who it was who had come calling on Gloria at this unlikely hour.

The last person she would have expected.

Stephen Vaughan.

CHAPTER III

Penny strained her ears for the sound of Stephen's car driving off, but not for a full minute did she hear anything but the quiet sound of his retreating footsteps. Then, and then only, came the soft sound of an engine being started up, and a car, parked a little down the road, sliding away towards the head of the valley, and on, no doubt, to the Forestry Office.

She switched on her bedside light and looked at her watch. To her surprise it was barely eleven o'clock. She and her parents, at least, had dropped off unusually early, after their tiring day.

Odd that those footsteps had not awoken them. But they were notably sound sleepers, rejoicing, normally, in seven or eight hours' solid slumber.

'I simply must get to sleep again,' she told herself fiercely. 'I'll be all in to-morrow if I don't.'

But sleep was long a-coming, and she tossed restlessly about.

That Gloria should so fascinate and bewitch Eric and Joe was understandable, even if, to her mind, regrettable. Unsophisticated, and young by comparison with Gloria, they could never have been in contact with anyone so glamorous. She had bowled the silly boys over.

But Stephen, so confident, so mature. That he should come creeping round late at night—to make an assignation with her, as like as not! It was a shattering thought.

Hadn't he asserted resolutely, angrily, almost, that he wished to have nothing whatever to do with his cousin?

'I was quite shocked at his hard, unyielding attitude,' she thought. 'Annoyed that he wouldn't come to my party to meet her. And all the time, perhaps—'

She remembered Pearl's hints—that years ago, while she herself was still away at boarding-school, Gloria had tried to get him into her clutches. Was she trying again, because he had wounded her pride by his plain omission to contact her? And this time succeeding?

Her mind jumped back a few hours, to Gloria's sudden decision to take a trip in the Mini. Had Pearl's blunt assertion that she had rushed out in response to a telephone call had been well founded? Had Gloria lied when speaking airily of a wrong number?

She switched off her light, as though by so doing she could cut the current of her distasteful thoughts. But she still could not sleep.

Illogically, perhaps, she felt far more sore over Stephen's contemptible conduct, his furtiveness, than by the inconsiderate way Eric and Joe were behaving over their precious pop-group plans.

She could sum them up as 'childish'—in this particular matter, anyway. But *Stephen*!

Ever since her mother had remarried and brought her to live in Val Fleury, and she had first come to know him, a lanky schoolboy, she had warmed to his bluff kindliness, his good-natured teasing. Had puzzled in her childish way that Gloria, who frightened, and even hurt her sometimes when no one was looking, could boast: 'Steve's *my* cousin, not yours at all!'

At first they had only seen him from time to time. Although he and his parents were living in a suburb of Port Leon he was the only member of the Vaughan family who ever came to Val Fleury. But when the Vaughans moved to Barbados things altered.

He underwent part of his training as a forestry officer in Trinidad, his spell there coinciding, for a short time, with her stay as a boarder at a convent school there. And occasionally there had been red letter days, when he had been allowed to take her out to Port-of-Spain's best café, for soft drinks and sweet cakes.

Then, when all his examinations passed, he had been stationed in Val Fleury as a junior, he had been often around. And for the past three years anyway, home from school for good, she had looked upon him as a confidant and friend—someone that much older than herself, that much more experienced in life, whom she could respect and trust.

Now, to think of him as an intriguer—visiting Gloria by stealth, after all he had said about wishing to avoid her. It didn't seem credible. Could one be so deceived about a person's true nature?

46

And yet she had seen him with her own eyes returning from Gloria's window late at night, had heard, she was certain, Gloria's light laugh as he had left her.

What other explanation could there be?

Very little sleep did she get for the rest of that night. There was the inevitable din of cockcrow round midnight, and then again at dawn, with its chorus of protesting dogs. Near silence and then a mocking-bird started up in the garden, pouring fuel by its strange cry on her resentment, her sense of humiliation.

She was looking utterly exhausted and wretched when her mother came in to call her, and when she admitted that she had scarcely slept, she received an immediate injunction to stay in bed.

'Now don't argue, darling,' Brenda Dale told her firmly. 'You've had far too much work piled on you lately. I'm going to tell Robert that he will have to do without you for one day. He'll miss you; of course he will. He's come to rely on you in so many ways. But he'll agree with me, you may be sure.'

Penny produced a whimsical if slightly wan smile.

'You so seldom put your foot down, Mum, that when you do we all submit.'

'Fine. And now, as soon as you've had some coffee and fruit, you're to curl up and go to sleep. I'll keep the house as quiet as I can.'

'But I don't want to stay in bed all day!' Penny exclaimed in dismay.

'Of course not. You can get up as soon as you've had a sound nap. But no work whatsoever until to-morrow.'

She was fast asleep, indeed, the moment Pearl, having clucked over her like a hen over its chick, removed her breakfast tray. And after a solid two hours of deep slumber she woke up, stretching and yawning, no longer weary, but still thoroughly upset by Stephen's paltry behaviour.

She dressed and went into the sitting-room, and pulled out some raffia work she hadn't touched for weeks. It bored her, but so did everything to-day.

'Your ma's gone to the shops,' Pearl called from the kitchen. 'And now you're up and dressed, Ah gwine to de end ob de garden to git up some vegetables for lunch. Jus' take a nice book an' rest yourself.'

'Okay!' But all Penny did was to push the raffia aside and stare wretchedly out of the window.

And then suddenly she was on her feet. For a car had drawn up outside, and there walking up the path was the man on whom her hurt and angry thoughts were centred. Stephen!

He stepped on to the patio.

'Hi, Penny! I've just been to the pharmacy looking for you, and your stepfather told me you were here.'

'Yes,' she said shortly. 'I had a bad night.'

'And so did I.'

'Well, your rendezvous was a bit late, some people might have thought.'

'I'm coming inside.'

'I've nothing to say to you.'

'Oh, yes, you have.' He was in the room with her now, standing and looking down at her, his expression not ashamed at all, but impatient, even irritable. 'You know, you're all kinds of a little fool. Why the heck have you given up that nice bedroom of yours to your stepsister?'

'What do you know about our bedroom arrangements?' she countered sharply.

'Perhaps you've forgotten that I helped your stepfather with the redecoration when Gloria went away to America, and you moved from that tiny room into one of decent size.'

'You mean that you weren't creeping round to see Gloria!' Suddenly a burden was dropping from her shoulders.

'What the hell are you talking about? Of course I wasn't! I wanted urgently to speak to you. I was passing by in my car and at a turn of the road I saw a glow of light coming from what was ordinarily your room "The kid's awake," I thought. "I'll just slip round for a moment." I whistled—'

'Yes, I heard you!'

'And then Gloria was there looking out, smiling like a Cheshire cat.'

'You didn't stay long, I know,' she said uncertainly. 'But I heard her laugh, as though she'd been enjoying a joke with you.'

'Funny for her, perhaps, not for me. I've never felt

48

such a fool. What your parents would have thought if they'd woken up and found me outside Gloria's window at that hour!'

'Perhaps they wouldn't have been very pleased to find you outside mine!'

He was taken aback. 'Good lord! I ought to remember you aren't a kid any longer!'

'And haven't been for some time, if you had the smallest perception!'

He reddened.

'I've realised it quite often lately, as a matter of fact. But now you've chosen to emphasise it, I don't think I'll say what I intended to last night.'

'Oh, come off it, Steve,' she exclaimed impatiently. 'Let's stop sparring. What was the highly important message?'

'You asked me not long ago to take you on a trek into the hills again. Well, I suddenly saw an opportunity, thought you might like to take a day off and come. And now you've got your holiday, but are under orders to rest.'

She was alert at once.

'What time did you intend to start?'

'Around now—or maybe an hour earlier. Why I tried to speak to you last night was to give you a chance of arranging things with your stepfather before going to the pharmacy. Incidentally, I tried to telephone you the other afternoon. I thought I could leave a message with Pearl if you weren't back from Port Leon—having heard at the shop that you were down there with your parents on business.'

'And Gloria answered—and went off in my Mini.'

'Exactly. Well, I can't stop now to tell you just what happened. I must get up to the camp, even if you can't come with me.'

'Of course I'm coming,' she exclaimed. 'I can hear Pearl back in the kitchen. I'll tell her I'm feeling better, and that she must explain to Mum when she comes in that I'm going up into the hills with you.'

'Mind you bring a coat. And put on sensible shoes.'

Pearl's face irradiated delight.

'Do yo' a power o' good, Mis' Penny. An' look here, Ah've got some chicken pasties Ah made for supper

49

to-night, but yo' just take dem along for your lunch. Ah'll pack 'em up nice while yo' do a quick change act.'

Soon they were driving quickly up the straggling village street, past the smaller shops, the bank, the self-service store where Eric worked, with the Dale pharmacy opposite; then the modern school and the white adobe Spanish-type church which stood like the final bastion of civilisation against the primitive world of mountain and forest.

They called in at the Forestry Office to pick up Larry, the young Airedale, who greeted them with barks of joy, and leapt into his usual seat at the back of the car, relapsing quickly into the dignified silence expected of him on a working expedition.

For a little while Stephen and Penny were silent, too. Penny, drinking in the beauty of the blossoming bushes and trees, the glimpses of green glades, with silver streamlets flashing through, was content to have it so. It wasn't for her to open up the question of Gloria's doings. If and when Stephen felt he should do so— well, that would be time enough.

And presently it seemed that Stephen, too, found the subject of Gloria distasteful.

'If you want me to tell you of Gloria's sudden visit to the Forestry Office within minutes of my attempt to contact you on the telephone, I'll do so,' he said evenly. 'But I'd rather not. It's not particularly—shall we say, interesting!'

'But, Stephen, what right has she to pester you?' She couldn't keep the question back. It burst from her.

'Right? None whatever! The fact is, Gloria, like her mother, has always wanted what she can't get, and discarded anything—or anyone—who seemed easy game. And now let's forget her, and enjoy the afternoon.'

It was an immense relief to Penny to find herself back on the old easy terms with Stephen, respecting him not only for his integrity but for his common sense. There was something deeply satisfying, to her at least, in their almost casual companionship, in the feeling that she could so well understand, could even share just a little, in his dedication to the work he so loved.

She could wish, certainly, that he liked Eric better, that he didn't have to be—well, slightly scathing about him at times. But then Eric wasn't exactly enthusiastic over Stephen either. The two were utterly different: that, of course, was the trouble. After all, one began to realise, even when one was at school, that one's closest friends didn't always care for each other, couldn't understand what one saw in someone else.

She knew very well what drew her to Eric, and held her to him: a kind of tenderness, which had something protective in it. From the first, shy, awkward, flushing over nothing, he had seemed to stretch out to her as the one person who could help him. And, touched—perhaps faintly flattered—she had just naturally responded, encouraging him to throw aside his anxious diffidence, born, as she learned, of being the one mediocre member of a brilliant family: to overcome his nervous stammer.

It was irritating to have him so caught up in these everlasting rehearsals with Joe and Gloria. But that was because she so distrusted her stepsister.

If the boys had found a simple, straightforward sort of girl for their singer, she would have been an enthusiastic supporter of the trio, and its efforts for charity. As it was she was already being made to feel an outsider, in a subtle sort of way which the boys might well miss. And she could sense the danger, to Eric, at least, of Gloria thinking it amusing to throw her net over him, and then going on her way, uncaring of what havoc and heartbreak she left in her train.

'A penny for your thoughts, young Penny!' Stephen's eyes were on the road ahead.

'You'll think me absurd, but I'm still uneasy over Gloria. Eric is not a man of the world like you—'

'Hi!' He turned to look at her in sudden amusement. 'Man of the woods, that's what I'm supposed to be, isn't it?'

'Oh, you know what I mean. Sophisticated, and all that!'

'What's "all that"?' he persisted, still laughing. 'Come on now, I'm interested. I can think of more than one interpretation!'

His tone, not his words, made her colour.

'What I'm trying to say,' she said loftily, 'and you'll doubtless think me very stupid, is that I don't want Eric to be hurt.'

His manner changed completely.

'I thought he was supposed to be in love with you, Penny.'

'So he is. But that's what would make it all the more fun for Gloria.'

'My dear, you've got this stepsister of yours on the brain,' he returned sharply. 'Start being tough with her. Demand to have your bedroom back at once. Tell her off good and hard for daring to go out in your Mini without your permission—which you don't intend to give because her driving is so rotten. If you make her uncomfortable enough, she'll soon find a good reason for skipping back to America.' He paused. 'I've done my best to speed her on her way. Drove her into a rage when she put on a sweetly candid act, by indulging in unseemly mirth. Mockery is a favourite weapon with her, but she doesn't like it much when it's used against her.'

His tone was so bitterly contemptuous that it startled her.

'Steve, I didn't know you could speak like that!'

'My good girl, there's quite a lot you don't know about me. "*And all that*", for instance. Maybe it's as well. And now, perhaps you'll do this little expedition of mine the honour of a moment's attention and interest.'

She glanced at him. 'Sorry, Steve!'

'Apology accepted! Well, I'm planning to take you to the Takhana plantation to see the heartening way the young teak trees are coming along. Pete is there already. We'll picnic with him—and maybe some of our worker-comedians will put on a song-and-dance act for you.' And then his voice became slightly ironic, as he added: 'No guitars, or lady vocalists, I can assure you.'

She smiled back at him.

'For which I'm supremely grateful. Calypsos are the tops with me!'

'Some of those we hear up here would need a bit of editing—for feminine ears. But they're damned good chaps, on the whole, our workers. We couldn't have better.'

Quickly she shook off her dark mood, turning her back on Val Fleury not only physically—and indeed it lay

52

far below them now—but mentally. The spell of the high woods was on her, exercising its magic, as it had always done. The flowering trees, so beautiful in the valley, were even more stately and magnificent up here, and their colours brighter. And the air, cool and fresh, delicious to breathe.

For a while they saw, here and there on the hillsides, clearings where peasants were growing vegetables in the fertile soil, and pasturing goats on the surrounding herbage. And occasionally a woman, her head swathed in a brightly-coloured bandana handkerchief, waved a greeting from the doorway of her small white hut. Then the landscape became empty of human beings, and trees and shrubs held unchallenged sway. Only brilliant birds on their flashing flight could be glimpsed, and heard, calling—calling—

Somehow it seemed right that in this world of quiet she and Steve should not be talking. It was a comfortable silence only possible between old and close friends.

Evidently Stephen was feeling the same, for when he did speak it was to comment on having a passenger who didn't keep on asking questions.

'It's ungracious of me, I know. I should appreciate their interest, but when the Tourist Department wants me to bring the city slicker type of V.I.P. up here to admire what we're doing, I could wish that they'd read some books about the Caribbean before coming. Quite elementary ones. I grudge my precious time. But there, I'm a surly devil.'

'You're nothing of the sort,' she exclaimed vigorously, then added slyly: 'You know what? There are men, they say—you're not one of them, of course—who think it makes them more interesting if they acquire a reputation for being tough and taciturn, with an ever-ready scowl!'

'You saucy little wretch!' There was surprise as well as amusement in his eyes as he turned to glance at her. 'You've never spoken to me like that before. Where's your respect?'

'Age gaps narrow as one approaches the twenties,' she affirmed, continuing without a pause: 'You should hear me cheek my stepfather nowadays.'

'*What* a girl!' he exploded. 'Before I can preen

53

myself on being, at thirty, the contemporary of a teen-ager, you shove me on the shelf with a chap of fifty.'

She laughed.

'I've never dared tease you before. It's rather fun. And incidentally, you won't be thirty till next July. But I'll be serious now. I can just imagine the ever-repeated questions you get. "Why do the peasants come up all this way to grow crops?" "Because the soil, once cleared, is so fertile." "Then why isn't there far more felling done?" "Because in a season of really bad rain-storms, we should have landslides that would sweep us all into the sea." '

'Fine! I shall suggest to the Tourist Board that they offer you a job as guide. It would save no end of my precious time.'

Now they could hear distant sounds of men working, and soon were reaching the section of the Takhana forest where teak was taking over from a large area of scrub—the result of indiscriminate felling, years ago, of valuable timber, and failure to replant.

Soon they had reached the new plantation, with acres and acres of young trees in sturdy growth. And men, engaged chiefly, it seemed, in tidying-up routines: chopping up piles of twigs and dead branches which they had collected during recent operations; singing and laughing as their *machetes* flashed, and hurling good-natured mockeries around.

As they got out of the car Pete, Joe's brother, came to greet them.

'So Steve's brought you up to see the results of our efforts.' He was beaming at her. 'He's been hoping to do so some time when young Eric could spare you. Which isn't often, I know!'

'Oh, he's all taken up with his guitar playing now.' She managed to speak with a convincing ease of manner. 'Practising for their first public appearance, on Independence night.'

'Well, let's hope they get enough applause to make them happy, but not enough to swell their heads. They'd have done better without your stepsister, I think. They say she's marvellous, but—'

'Pete, we're ravenous!' Steve jumped in with both feet. 'We've brought a picnic lunch.'

'Enough for you, too,' Penny put in quickly, grateful to Steve for turning Pete's mind away from Gloria. 'Pearl believes in good food and plenty of it.'

'It'll be a sight more interesting than the sandwiches I've brought along.' Pete was visibly pleased. 'Come into the restaurant.' And he led the way to the openfronted wooden hut which served as office and diningroom during daylight hours spent up here in the wild.

'I won't apologise for any discomfort,' he told Penny cheerfully, as he pulled out a couple of folding wooden chairs for herself and Steve, and dragged forward a deal box for himself. 'I regard you as an old campaigner. But we can at least supply some music with your meal. That is, if you'd like a few of these chaps to entertain you. They'll be stopping for their midday break, anyway.'

'Are you sure they won't mind?'

'My dear! They're as eager as my young brother and your boy-friend for a spot of limelight.'

'Then I'd love it. Just for a few minutes.'

'Which is all we can spare.' It was Stephen who spoke now, as Pete went off towards a little group of men. 'That is, if you'd like me to conduct you up to the edge of the true rain-forest—which you've never seen yet.'

'Oh, Steve, I'd adore it!' Her face was radiant. 'But how on earth do we get there? I'm ready to go on my two feet, but there'd never be time to go there and back, with all that climbing.'

'There certainly wouldn't. But we've a new sort of vehicle—a sort of tank-like affair—which can get us up a good part of the way. You see, we shall be working at a higher level before very long, planting palm brakes on slopes too steep to hold anything else.'

'It sounds a thrill!'

He laughed. 'I hope it won't prove too exciting, and that we shan't start running backwards.'

She grinned. 'Don't expect me to get worked up for your amusement. I always feel safe with you.'

He gave her an odd look. 'Always is a long time,' he said.

A pair of entertainers appeared now, and with no apparent rehearsal, and certainly no musical instruments, indulged in a series of calypsos which sent their audience into gales of laughter. All were highly irreverent comments on important island figures.

There had been rumours, ignored by the discreet, of a quarrel between two highly placed ladies in the cloak-room of the Palace Hotel during a recent dance, a quarrel which had resulted in an out-and-out bout of face-slapping.

There had been, so far as was known, not one witness of the brief incident—but the rumour had never been scotched. And here, far away from Port Leon, a couple of sweaty, raggity workmen were joyously indulging in a hilarious imitation of the scene, acting and singing their impudent, home-made calypso, with its barely veiled allusions to the identity of their victims.

From mockery they moved to romance of a sort. Two men loved a girl, and off she went with a third, leaving them to fight over—nothing!

And lastly came the ' hot topical '! Crisp and sweet, in the true calypso rhythm.

> ' Dis Penny in de Boss's pocket
> Worth a t'ousand dollar an' more,
> 'Cos her heart is a golden locket,
> An' she pure as a lily flower.'

The doggerel went on, relating her beauties and her virtues, and the difficulty of finding the key to her heart, the last line of the last verse coming right down to earth, with a burst in which, from near and far, other workers, well primed, joined:

> ' In the woods she play on her holiday,
> But she work in de pharma-cee!'

Out-and-out islander as she was, it took her aback to be recognised so quickly. However, though she didn't altogether relish their idea of her being ' in de Boss's pocket,' she was lucky, she knew, to get off so lightly, showered indeed with compliments.

She thanked the principal performers, duly introduced to her by Stephen, and gave them their modest reward. And well satisfied, it seemed, to judge by their wide smiles, they strolled off, concocting yet another laudatory verse as they went.

'You made a good impression on them,' Stephen told her, with evident pleasure. 'But then I knew you would!'

'That's more than I did,' she confessed. 'Though I certainly hoped they'd be kind.'

'You're young and pretty, and above all, you don't give yourself airs. That's what brings out their mockery. Incidentally, they may find food for good-natured mirth —and matter for another calypso—in our forthcoming trek up into the rain forest on our rather ludicrous-looking vehicle.'

'So long as they don't sing it when they get home— or carry it down to Port Leon.'

'Would you mind much?' He eyed her dubiously. 'After all, it would be very soon scrapped as they found more pungent objects for ridicule.'

She hesitated. After all, it was hardly the thing for a girl of good family to figure with a man friend, however innocuous, in a calypso which was sung in public.

And then suddenly she relaxed and laughed.

'If I did mind, it wouldn't help matters,' she said. 'You'd only have to drop them a hint, to arouse their sense of mischief—and make things a thousand times worse. I'm here to enjoy myself. So let's forget it!'

He took her hand for a moment in his firm grip; pressed it hard.

'You're a sport, Penny,' he told her quietly. 'And a lot more than that. There's no one quite like you.'

'I might say the same—though you make me cross sometimes.' Her voice was even softer, and for some reason she did not want to meet his eyes.

'Same here!' His mood had changed abruptly. He sounded rather amused now, and added coolly: 'Let's go.'

The first part of the trip, crawling up the long hillside in the noisy new contraption, was hair-raising. But watching Stephen's skilful and confident movements, and hearing his lighthearted assurance that he had driven 'the monster' several times already on this very track, steadied her nerves.

'And it won't be any worse coming down again,' he promised. 'The brakes are terrific.'

After a while they reached a flat piece of ground, large

enough to turn the car, and now, faced with no visible sign of a track, they got out and began to climb.

It was strenuous, not dangerous, and Penny found it exhilarating, following Stephen as he moved up from foothold to foothold, showing her where it was safe to pull herself up, here by a protruding tree-root, here by a firmly-set woody shrub. She forgot that she was supposed to be resting all day, after waking up exhausted, forgot, indeed, everything but the pleasure of the moment, the thrill of nearing the rain forest, so different, people said, from the woods and forests below.

And soon they had reached the edge of this strange world and were coming into a wild tangle of creepers and undergrowth. But here a narrow path had been hacked out, and recovering her breath as they stood for a moment on nearly level ground, she asked Stephen in surprise how it came to be there, when no track led up to it.

He laughed.

'You couldn't see it, that's all. But any forester could. I didn't find those footholds by chance. Pete and I know every one of them. Even when the soil shifts, with heavy rain, certain landmarks remain. As you know the mountains in many of the islands are just hard-packed earth, brought down aeons ago by that giant South American river, the Orinoco, and forming deltas which eventually broke away.'

She was gazing into that world of green twilight.

'Even your solid facts don't make it less eerie!'

'You'll soon become used to it. But if you want to penetrate at all we must make a good pace. We've very little time, if I'm to get you home before your parents start worrying.'

They moved along in single file, Stephen ahead—'not only to lead the way,' he observed jokingly over his shoulder, 'but just in case we run across a python.'

Penny gave a shudder.

'I saw one in Val Fleury quite recently; came slipping through a neighbour's fence. Eight feet long, at least. Some workmen killed it.'

'Maybe they had to, down there, before it started raiding the chicken runs. They wouldn't know enough to catch it and release it in one of the swamps. But I have a job sometimes stopping my men killing every snake they see. Most reptiles have their uses, and the poor old python does far more good than harm in his natural surroundings. Eats no end of rats and other pests.'

'So long as we don't suddenly get a boa-constrictor dropping down on us from a tree! That would be far worse.'

'It wouldn't relish me for its dinner. I'm far too tough and sinewy. And even you, dainty morsel as you are, would be a thought too large to tempt it. Unless, of course, it was literally starving—which none of them ever seem to be.'

'I suppose its first reaction would be to escape,' she suggested doubtfully.

'Absolutely. We wouldn't get within yards of it. So —on we go!'

Alone she would certainly have been afraid, but not with Stephen. He knew the forests and its denizens far too well for fear—though a healthy respect would always be there.

She could relax and give herself up to the enjoyment of her surroundings. And indeed there was much to see and wonder at. Tall trees familiar to her, laden with blossom of every colour, mingled with others, gigantic, and totally strange, which stretched to incredible heights in a free-for-all struggle for light and air, their trunks and branches wreathed and intertwined with vines and lianas, all joining in the contest. Here and there, where a tree had abandoned the battle and died, its grey and shrunken skeleton provided space for sunlight to filter through, giving living-room to huge, vivid orchids, and great ferns.

It was a world of silence, pierced only by the sudden sharp call of a bird, or a faint rustling in the under-growth. And yet not silent at all, for all around was the murmuring of insects.

She felt, after a while, that she could have wandered on and on, even alone now, unafraid, because somehow she had become conscious of an inner harmony per-meating the place.

She said as much to Stephen, walking beside her now, and he nodded.

'That's the way it should be. Some of my workmen —the older ones particularly—talk with awe of the spirit of the forest. They would tell you it had laid a hand on you. And maybe it has. But, my dear, you must shake it politely from your shoulder, and turn back. It's time we made for home, unless—!'

'Unless what, Steve?'

'Well, how are you feeling? The source of the river, with its weirdly carved rocks, isn't far off now, if you could manage another ten minutes.'

Her face lit up.

'Of course I could. I'm fine!'

He looked at her doubtfully for a moment, then smiled.

'Come on then. It's worth seeing!'

They plodded on, and suddenly came out into full sunlight: into a glade where a spring came bubbling out of the ground. And there, not many yards away, stood three tall weathered stone slabs, leaning drunkenly against each other at first glance, until one saw how solidly and securely they had been placed. They were far larger than she had expected, and carved with primitive figures crude as drawings by a child in an infant school, with rounded faces and blankly staring eyes.

'It's the work of the Arawak Indians who lived in the islands centuries ago,' he told her. 'A gentle people who were wiped out by fierce Caribs from the mainland even before the Spaniards came.'

She nodded, but said nothing.

There was something strange and mysterious about the spot. One could well understand, she thought, why that ancient shrine still had power to awe later generations— even sophisticated people, who laughed at the superstitions which persisted, of the old gods who still lived in their former haunts.

He would not let her linger, and it was as well. The way back, in all its stages, was rather more tricky and difficult than the ascent. But the light was still good when they reached the teak plantation, picked up Pete, and made quickly for Val Fleury. They dropped their passenger at the Forestry Office, and continuing their swift, smooth way, were soon entering the main street.

Darkness had blotted out the brief tropical twilight. But in the first glimmer of starlight, as they stopped outside the Dale bungalow, they noticed, a few yards away, walking away from them, the outline of two figures, a man and a woman.

Penny, at least, was not interested. She was thinking with dread of being in Gloria's company again, of having the memory of her lovely day torn to shreds by that bitter, mocking tongue.

Almost perfunctorily she invited Stephen to come in, and remembering his expressed wish to avoid Gloria, was a little surprised at his ready acceptance.

' Perhaps I should,' he said easily. ' Just for a minute. I ought to apologise to your parents for keeping you out so long, and involving you in such strenuous activities.'

She smiled. ' I shall tell them I feel far better for it. And it's true.'

They did indeed find the Dales, alone in their sitting-room, a shade ruffled, though the cause was unexpected.

' Come in, Steve, and have a drink,' was her step-father's inevitable greeting, but his tone was distrait, and he went on at once, turning to Penny : ' If you'd got back only three minutes earlier, you wouldn't have missed them.'

' Missed *whom*, Dad?'

' Eric and Gloria. That young man of yours has been sitting here, biting his nails with impatience, for more than half an hour. Particularly wanted to see you. His fidgeting got on our nerves, and we were thankful when Gloria persuaded him to go along with her to Joe's, for an impromptu rehearsal.'

Penny looked at Stephen, startled, and saw compassion in his eyes.

She knew then that those figures they had glimpsed in the starlight were those of Gloria and Eric. And that they were moving in the opposite direction to the Rodriguez bungalow.

Brenda Dale, aware of tension in the atmosphere, plunged boldly now into the conversation.

' He was very disappointed at missing you, poor boy,' she told Penny cheerfully. ' But he'll be ringing you up to-morrow at lunch-time to make a date with you. And now tell me, darling, has Stephen given you a wonderful time, up there, inspecting his precious teak plantations?'

'It's been a super afternoon,' Penny assured her.
'Absolutely grand.'

To her mother's sharp ears, however—and to Stephen's,
too—the enthusiasm sounded a little less spontaneous
than usual.

Perhaps her stepfather, too, noticed this, for he remarked coolly: 'It's kind of you, Stephen, to give
Penny these treats of yours still. But by the look of
her, this one has been a bit too strenuous. She's an
adult now, of course, not the young schoolgirl you were
so careful not to tire. But even grown girls haven't the
stamina of young men.'

Stephen looked shocked—and contrite. But Penny
sprang at once to his defence.

'I didn't do a scrap too much,' she exclaimed. 'I
enjoyed every minute of it, even that last scramble into
the rain forest and up to the Arawak shrine.'

Robert Dale sat up very straight in his chair.

'You took her right up there!' he exploded, eyeing
Stephen more severely.

'Not all the way on foot,' Stephen hastened to explain.
'That first very long slope up to the rain forest could
be hell—but we've acquired a new vehicle that can
manage a fantastically steep gradient, and I took her up
in that.'

'And that last bit we had to tackle on foot was fun,'
Penny chipped in. 'The gorgeousness of it all when
we actually got into the real jungle! The orchids and
the creepers, and the intoxication of being up in that high
altitude! As for the shrine! Oh, Dad, I shall sleep like
a top to-night; wake up to-morrow as fresh as a daisy.'

Robert Dale looked relieved now.

'That makes a difference, cutting out that long back-
breaking trek. It must have been a job clearing the
ground of all that scrub before your new contraption
could get going. I shouldn't have liked to be the first
passenger on it!'

'Robert went up all the way on foot soon after we
came to Val Fleury,' Brenda put in, with wifely pride.
'Ten years ago, that was.'

'Well, our mini-juggernaut has proved perfectly safe,'
Stephen assured them. 'Maybe you and Robert will
come up and test it out some time!'

'We might, at that,' Brenda returned, her eyes sparkling at the thought. And then she turned to her daughter.

'You look—shall we say healthily tired, darling. As though you could do with another early night. I'll get supper right away for the four of us.'

But Stephen refused the invitation with a quick apology.

He would have very much liked to stay, he said, but he had a pile of paper work to cope with, up at the Forestry Office, and a meal would be awaiting him.

And now, as he made his polite good-byes to the Dales, Penny was suddenly very, very tired again.

Despite his remonstrance, she saw him to the gate, and apologised for her stepfather's brusqueness.

'He fusses over me more than Mama does,' she told him, with a faint smile. 'Always has.'

'I'm not worried about Robert,' he said quickly. 'It's about that boy-friend of yours. Don't upset yourself over him, Penny. No man's worth it!' He hesitated a moment, then went on shortly: 'Doubtless he's devoted to you, really. But as you say yourself, not quite smart enough to cope with Gloria's sophistication. Once she's returned to America, he'll come limping back—if not before.'

'I guess so.'

She sounded almost as exhausted as she felt, and he stood for a moment looking down at her, trouble in his eyes. But whatever further comment he was tempted to make remained unuttered.

Abruptly, he was out of the gate, into his car, and turning towards the Forestry Office and the hills.

She was in bed within minutes, and could hardly stay awake long enough to eat the light meal which her mother brought to her. Then, almost before the empty tray was whisked away, she was fast asleep, in a heavy, dreamless slumber.

The Dales made a more leisurely supper, and Robert, at least, had a good deal to say on the subject of his beloved young stepdaughter.

He wasn't sure he was doing right in having Penny working at the pharmacy. She ought to be out of Val Fleury, spreading her wings, training for a proper profession. If only he hadn't spent so much money on Gloria, he might have saved enough to do something worthwhile for Penny now.

'She'll probably be marrying Eric in a year or so,' Brenda pointed out soothingly. 'As for giving her a profession, why not ask her if she'd be interested in pharmacy? You and Garcia could teach her—helped by a correspondence course. Once she passed the official examinations, she'd be qualified to earn a living anywhere, married or single.'

Robert brightened a little at that.

'I have thought of it,' he admitted. 'But it would mean quite a bit of study in her spare time—apart from working behind the scenes, instead of having fun at the camera counter.'

'She wouldn't be free to spend hours and hours up in the woods with Stephen—and I feel that would be a good thing. I like him, and I was quite happy about these "treats" of his when she was younger. But I don't want my girl talked about.'

'As mine was, Brenda, before she left the island.' His voice held pain. 'But Gloria is the kind, I admit, who positively invites gossip. Penny! Everyone loves her. No one would say an unkind word about her.'

Gloria came in just then, and announcing she'd had a meal already, went off to bed without more ado.

'I was sure Mrs Rodriguez would give her a snack,' Brenda observed comfortably. 'And now we can turn in ourselves, and forget these minor worries of ours. They've no urgency at all.'

For some time now Gloria, intent on slimming, hadn't appeared at the family breakfast-table. She took her grapefruit and black coffee in the seclusion of her room, and was usually engaged in the lengthy ritual of making up her face, what time the Dales were starting for the pharmacy.

Mrs O'Brien had agreed to her beginning work at the Hibiscus Salon an hour later than the permanent staff. And though this entailed her walking there, and she was far from keen on exercise, she resigned herself to the thought that it might help the slimming.

Penny always rejoiced at avoiding a breakfast encounter with her, and this morning more so than ever.

She didn't wish to hear where Gloria and Eric had gone last night. And she didn't want any gibes from Gloria on the subject of Stephen and his tedious job, and her own extraordinary tastes in liking to wander about his boring old woods.

But Pearl, arriving earlier than usual, pounced on her on the pretext of helping her turn her mattress, and came out with one of her dire warnings.

'Mis' Penny,' she exclaimed in a dramatic whisper, 'Ah tellin' you once again, watch out Mis' Gloria don' get her claws in Mister Eric. If she not done so already. Mah younger daughter she gone to de pictures las' night wit' her boy-friend. Dey sittin' in de cheap seats at de back, and see Mis' Gloria an' Mister Eric come in from de caff, an' go into de best seats at de front, bold as brass.'

'I suppose Eric thought that if I was out with Stephen Vaughan—'

'Stuff an' nonsense. Everyone know Mister Stephen like big brother to yo' since yo' no more dan a picca-ninny. No, Mister Eric your sweet fellow, and dat Mis' Gloria no right to try leading him astray. Yo' jus' pull yore socks up, Mis' Penny!'

To her relief she heard her stepfather calling to her just then that he was ready to start, and she was able to escape further adjurations from Pearl. She found her mother, kissed her good-bye and was off—sore with Eric, not because he had gone to the cinema with another girl, which he had a perfect right to do, but because that girl was Gloria.

At the pharmacy she soon had something fresh to think about. Steve looked in to pick up fresh film for his ciné-camera, and to ask her in some embarrassment if he had been as inconsiderate as her stepfather seemed to think, by encouraging her to make efforts beyond her strength.

'I'm afraid I'm what they call "a man's man,"' he explained apologetically. 'I spend so much of my time with strong hefty fellows like myself, I forget that girls tire more easily.'

'You needn't worry,' she assured him, adding with a cheerful grin: 'My legs ache slightly—in fact most of my muscles do—but I don't care a bit. It was well worth it.'

'My dear, you're a sport. But I blame myself, all the same. For keeping you out so long, too. Damned thoughtless of me.'

And with that he took his departure.

Another customer who lingered at her counter—she was on the way to the drugs section—was old Mrs Marsden, Sybil's mother, who announced joyfully that Sybil was flying home almost immediately, the aunt whom she had been nursing having made an excellent recovery.

'Her father and I are delighted,' she declared. 'I only hope—' and she lowered her voice, 'that your stepsister won't be incommoded too badly by her return. After all, Sybil's been away longer than she originally intended.'

'Of course she won't, Mrs Marsden,' Penny assured her quickly. 'And I must tell you, I've missed Sybil a lot, too.'

'So—I hope—has Joe,' was Mrs Marsden's comment on this. 'Young men can be awful fools.' And with this cryptic remark, she too was away.

There was a trickle of customers to her counter for the rest of the morning, and then, just before the lunch break, in came Eric.

'Penny, darling, I expect you've forgotten. But it's my birthday. I want you to come dancing with me to-night, down in Port Leon. That's what I came to see you about yesterday evening.'

She had half intended, when he telephoned, to excuse herself amiably from making a date with him. Unfair to him, no doubt. But she just couldn't help feeling annoyed with him.

Now, however, with Eric there in the flesh, looking down at her with such affection, such eagerness, she felt a rush of the old tenderness. He had taken great trouble to make her own birthday a happy occasion, and must clearly be aware that she had forgotten his altogether. And he gave no least sign of petty resentment—the kind which had been colouring her own thoughts.

'Just we two on our own,' he persisted. 'We've not been alone together for days and days.'

'Of course I'll come,' she told him quickly. 'Don't

take me anywhere grand, though. I've no time to get my hair done, and it's terrible after scrambling about in the woods yesterday.'

'Looks fine to me.' He glanced with pleasure at her fair hair. 'I'll be calling for you at seven this evening, if that suits you. Till then!'

As usual Gloria was home for lunch, and with Robert and Brenda Dale there, she appeared to be in a perfectly amiable mood. She heard with equanimity that Eric and Penny would be spending the evening down at Port Leon, and made not one remark about the doings of the previous day.

She, too, had an engagement for the evening. She had slipped into the bank that morning to cash a cheque, and Joe had told her then that Sybil would be returning on the night flight. He would be driving up to meet her, and had invited her to keep him company on the long journey.

No one commented, and she continued, a little wistfully: 'I'll be glad of a change and a rest from rehearsing. Glad of a cheer-up, too.' She took up a spoonful of curry, and after a moment added: 'I was able to cash my cheque all right, but my account is getting rather low, and there was a letter from my lawyer mentioning that there was still a hitch over Greg's will. Not serious, he said, but it would hold up a final settlement for a while.'

'What's gone wrong?' her father asked her, with some concern.

'A few more unexpected debts have come in. But don't worry, Dad, Greg's estate can stand quite a lot of nibbles. Everything will be all right.'

Preoccupied as Penny was with her preparations for the evening, she found time for annoyance with Gloria for her tactlessness and want of consideration for Sybil's feelings.

Even if Joe had pressed her to come to the airport with him, she should have refused. She wasn't stupid. She would know very well how Sybil, good-natured as she was, would resent her presence, what a shadow it would throw on her first meeting with Joe after weeks of separation. And she just wouldn't care.

And this talk about the dwindling of the money in her

current account! Was it true? If so, would it cause her the least inconvenience, when she could give the manager such strong evidence that she would eventually be in possession of large sums from her husband's estate?

Youth, good health, and a normally happy disposition made it possible, as usual, for Penny to banish disagreeable reflections, and to give herself over to enjoyment of the immediate moment.

Even the searching out of her most attractive dress from the narrow curtain-hung space where she had had to hang her clothes since Gloria's appropriation of her room gave her pleasure. It was fun to explore the forests and hills in old clothes of sensible type. But it gave one a kick, too, to aim at a glamorous appearance.

Eric seemed very much his old self that evening, as he kissed her, and helped her into his little four-seater.

'You're the prettiest thing,' he said. 'There's not a girl to touch you—not in the whole of the Caribbean.'

She hesitated, before saying lightly: 'You're getting quite good at compliments.'

'I reserve them for you, my sweet,' he assured her.

'None for Gloria?' she teased, emboldened by his manner to bring out the name so near the surface of her mind.

He glanced at her sharply.

'Don't you realise that what brings me in such close contact with her is our—well, professional connection? This trio we're forming with Joe!'

She could not bring herself to mention that visit to the cinema, made when they were ostensibly practising at the Rodriguez home. It would be too petty. After all, what could she expect when she herself had been out with another man?

And trying to thrust it from her mind, she began to tell him cheerfully of the birthday present she had waiting for him at the pharmacy, if he would drop in to-morrow to collect it. A casket labelled 'For the Masculine Man', containing a flask of the very latest after-shave lotion, with talc powder and soap to match, and a tiny booklet giving the names of famous athletes and sportsmen who were regular users.

'No famous guitarists?' he queried, laughing.

She shook her head in pretended gloom.

'Alas, no! Perhaps they all have beards.' And she added, smiling: 'Keep shaving, and some day you'll get your name on that list, maybe.'

To her surprise, he took that last remark of hers with a degree of seriousness.

'Advertisers' tricks cut no ice with me. I bet half the people mentioned have never used the lotion in their lives. But what wouldn't I give, Penny, to go right ahead as a guitarist! To have everyone recognise my name.' He paused, before continuing: 'Since I've begun practising in grim earnest I'm beginning to feel, without conceit, I hope, that I might have a pretty bright future as a professional player.'

He looked so boyishly hopeful, yet so modest, that she could not bear to damp his enthusiasm. But comparing him and Joe with guitarists she had heard on popular records, she found it hard to believe that without lessons from some first-rate teacher they could possibly have improved to the extent that Eric seemed to believe.

Eric was clearly more talented than Joe. But surely he was setting his sights too high! Had Gloria's flatteries —insincere as they must be, considering her sophistication—turned his handsome head?

Mentally she shrugged her shoulders.

'I'd like to hear you,' she said pleasantly.

'I wish you could, Penny. I nearly left a message with you yesterday, asking you to follow Gloria and me over to Joe's place. We were going to practise.'

She braced herself for his next words. Would they be true—or lies? And then she hated herself for her distrust, for he went on calmly: 'I was glad I didn't leave that message, though, for Gloria suddenly remembered that Joe wouldn't be there, and we went along to the pictures instead.'

'How sensible. You must have got tired of waiting for me to come in. But, Eric, don't do anything rash! To endanger your job at the Stores, I mean.'

'Don't worry, dear. I should want very substantial encouragement before I cut loose from the post I have now—though goodness knows I find it boring at times. The Stores have branches all over the islands, and I might drop into managerial shoes before very long. And then—my love!'

69

She warmed to his tone. How foolish she had been to feel sore with him. The next time Pearl began her dark forebodings, she would give her a quiet but firm snub.

And then Eric was saying something else.

'I'll tell you now why I've been so particularly anxious to see you, Penny darling. I've some great news. It's not been made public yet, and it's to be kept secret for a while. But Manoel Lopez is coming to Rio to attend the Independence Ball, and stay awhile. He's related to the new manager of the Palace, Tom Perez.'

She gave a little gasp.

'But he's one of the top men in the pop world!'

'Of course he is. Plays every sort of musical instrument—saxophone, guitar, trumpet, piano—and sings in a way all his own, a way that just about pulls the hearts out of his audiences.'

'But, Eric, a chap like that will completely overshadow the efforts of your trio!'!

'My dear, he won't be performing! He'll be enjoying a rest period just then, Mr Perez says, in the mood for a real Caribbean holiday.'

'Well, if you're sure of that. But if people recognise him and start shouting for him—! You know what these pop stars are!'

'And I know what fees they get. According to Mr Perez, the Palace Hotel cost such a heck of a lot to put up, and the running expenses are so high, it's only just about breaking even. There simply isn't the money available to tempt Lopez—not this year, anyway.'

'What is he like, this Mr Perez?' she asked idly.

'You'll be seeing for yourself this evening.'

'Eric, you're not taking me to the Palace!' She wasn't quite sure if she was angry or thrilled. 'Me in this old dress—'

'And me without a bean to spare!' he chuckled. 'I happened to mention you the other day, when we were down there, discussing the programme for our trio on Independence night. I said that we were more or less engaged to be married, and that I'd have to find you a nice partner for the Independence Ball—'

'I can find a partner for myself,' she interrupted, flushing a little.

'Darling, don't take me up like that. The point is that Mr Perez gave me a cordial invitation to bring you down to dine at the Palace any evening but Saturday—which is their busiest night. I thought my birthday would be an appropriate occasion, so I rang him up to fix things, and here we are.'

'I'm sure it will be wonderful. But I can't help regretting this old dress. I'm saving up to buy a new one to wear at the Independence Ball.'

'When I shall have very little chance of dancing with you.'

And then, as they came to a short stretch of level road, he slipped an arm round her.

'All your dresses are pretty. And if they weren't, I wouldn't care a damn. To me, you're the loveliest girl in the world.'

She made up her mind then to think no more of any defects in her appearance, but to give herself up to enjoyment of the evening. And from the moment they arrived at the gaily-lit entrance of the hotel she knew that she had nothing to worry about.

Luxurious it certainly was by her standards. But Mr Perez, noticing them, as he stood in the foyer, welcoming his guests, was so friendly that she was at once at ease. He called the head waiter, told him to put them at a corner table, and expressed his hopes that they would thoroughly enjoy themselves.

'We've a liner moored in the harbour,' he explained. 'A small one by present-day notions, but the giants haven't found us yet. Most of the passengers will be arriving soon, so we should have a cheery evening.'

The food and wine—and the service, too—were excellent, the other women's clothes unremarkable. And Eric was at his best, showing such consideration, and exercising such charm, that Penny wondered how she could ever have felt sore with him.

'He's developed into a very personable and attractive man,' she reflected, remembering how, only a year or two ago, he was still in the throes of conquering his stammer, and his tendency to flush in moments of embarrassment.

A tiny, disturbing thought stole into her mind just then. Had Gloria given him this—this final polish, this air of being an experienced host?

With an impatient, ' What does it matter, anyway?' she dismissed the tiresome little query from her mind. After all, Christmas was not so very far ahead now. And in the New Year, Gloria would be gone, and all would be as before. Quite uncomplicated!

They went outside for their coffee, into the garden at the side of the hotel. Gay with fairy lights, and fragrant with the scent of flowering shrubs, it was divided from the wide, busy pavement, and wider road, by a low white wall of fretted design, overhung with bougainvillea.

From the small round table at which they sat they could look across the sapphire sea, flicked with tinsel gleams from the stars. And then came the miracle, seen so often, but still with power to hold the watcher spellbound. A glow on the horizon, growing brighter every moment, until the stars began to fade, followed by the dramatic appearance of the rim of the rising moon which climbed quickly up the sky to reveal itself in its full splendour and banish darkness from earth and sea.

People were right, she thought, in their proud assertion that Santa Rita was one of the most beautiful islands in the Caribbean. This moonrise miracle was common to all, of course, but where else could such variety of landscape be found? Moonlight shedding its radiance through the green, mysterious rain forest! That would be something to witness, though to be up there at night would never be in her power, she feared.

Mr Perez drifted up to their table just then, and a waiter hurried forward with a third chair, to be followed shortly by another man bringing a tray with a squat bottle of the local liqueur and three tiny glasses.

Before Mr Perez had time to ask politely for permission to sit with them, Eric gave him an enthusiastic welcome. He was clearly delighted to be noticed in this way by the great man, who at once began to talk about the Trio, giving moderate encouragement to Eric but careful not to raise extravagant hopes. Hinting—and this shocked and dismayed Penny—that the weak member of the ensemble was Joe Rodriguez.

She dared not voice her disquiet. Who was she to judge any kind of musical performance? But considering his enthusiasm—!

Tom Perez—the last person to be called by such a homely Christian name, she thought—was talking now about his famous relative, Manoel Lopez.

Yes, he was coming, but strictly for a rest. He had had a terribly tight schedule for the past twelve months, and had been warned by his doctors that a break was imperative.

Whether he would take sufficient interest in this local trio to listen seriously to their performance was doubtful, but there was at least a chance. And he went on to say that ' the luscious Gloria ' would have to exert her feminine influence—seeing that Manoel was reputed to have a keen eye for a pretty woman.

' And she has something more important than beauty of face and figure,' he ended, draining his little glass. ' She has a kind of magnetism which more than a few men would, I am sure, find irresistible—at least for a time. As a vocalist only moderately talented. But in other ways quite a girl, that Gloria.'

With which remark, he got up, wished them an enjoyable time on the dance floor, and left them.

Eric offered Penny another glass of liqueur. She refused pleasantly, and he went on to pour some more for himself.

' Perez is a funny bloke in some ways,' he observed discontentedly. ' Praises people with one side of his mouth, and damns them with the other. I didn't like what he said about Gloria charming men " for a time ". It was almost like saying, " until they find her out ". Considering the fuss he makes over her when she's around—'

' And I was startled by his criticism of Joe,' Penny told him quickly. ' It's unfair, surely. He's good, I should have thought.'

' Of course he is,' Eric exclaimed loyally. ' But he doesn't take things so seriously as I do. Thinks it's going to be glorious fun performing at the Independence Ball, and leaves it at that. Doesn't mind rehearsing, but won't even try to improve his technique.'

' Isn't a natural player sometimes more spontaneous?' she suggested diffidently.

He shook his head firmly.

' Doesn't do when one is playing with other people,'

73

he declared. 'But we've not come here to worry over this and that. We're here to enjoy ourselves. Let's move over to the ballroom, and dance.'

It had been a happy evening. She and Eric had danced together so often in the past year or two that their steps fitted well. And in these glamorous surroundings she felt that they were doing even better than usual. Indeed midnight came too quickly.

She enjoyed, too, the long drive home, glad that Eric did not want to talk much. She didn't want to concentrate to-night on anything, only to snuggle into her seat and maybe sleep a little.

In that relaxed mood she felt no pang when Eric, depositing her at last at her own front door, explained that he would be obliged during the next week or two to spend most of his free time rehearsing.

'That's all right,' she assured him drowsily. 'Sybil will be in the same boat—except that it will be worse for her after having been away in Barbados. But we'll get together and plan our new dresses for the famous Independence Ball. That'll keep us happy and occupied.'

He bent down and kissed her.

'That's my girl,' he said. 'You'll find it's all worth while eventually.'

She rang Sybil up next day at lunch-time to invite her over for the evening, and found her eager to accept.

'I've a lot to tell you, Penny,' she said. 'If you don't know already that is. But I won't keep you now. Until eight o'clock to-night.'

When she came she looked very weary, and at first the Dales, at least, put her fatigue down to her journey from Barbados the evening before: told her with affectionate concern—for they were fond of her—that she should have turned in early to-night instead of coming round for supper, glad as they were to see her.

'I'm more worried than tired,' was her brief reply, as she helped herself to crayfish mayonnaise. 'I don't want to upset Mum and Pop by talking about it so soon. They're not young, as you know. Indeed I ought not really to bother you with my troubles.'

'Much better not to bottle them up,' Brenda Dale

said kindly. 'But try to enjoy your meal first. I can't get those delicious flying fish you have in Barbados. But when Penny told me you were coming, I popped down to the Stores, and found they had some of these small crayfish, fresh from that creek near the mouth of our little river. They were sent up from Port Leon with a whole lot of other fish, packed in ice, of course.'

'Brenda's good at remembering people's favourite dishes.' Robert gave his wife a glance full of affection and pride.

With a palpable effort Sybil conjured up a big smile.

'She's certainly done so this time!' And she let herself be drawn by Brenda and Penny into cheerful talk about Barbados—the fashions, the food, the latest social gossip in this island so much larger and more important than their own, but certainly in their eyes, no more beautiful.

'Of course it's entirely different,' Robert affirmed.

'That's what Stephen always says,' Penny chipped in, bright-eyed. 'Because it's founded on coral, not on piled-up river mud, like ours. No rain forests there, nor mountains. Nothing wild and exciting about it.'

'With no history of the terrible floods Santa Rita has suffered now and then, with our charming little stream turning into a brown torrent,' was Robert's quiet comment.

'Stephen thinks any flooding most unlikely now, with all the afforestation that's going on in the mountains.' Penny spoke confidently, her hazel eyes still shining. 'He says people didn't realise what they were doing in the old days, when they hacked the trees down wholesale, with no thought of replacing them.'

Sybil nodded. 'Pete is forever on that tack. Says Gloria makes him sick when he comes home and finds her talking to his family about his patience in sticking out such a boring job. He's like Stephen: madly keen.'

Skilfully Brenda drew the conversation away from that controversial figure, her stepdaughter, and talk veered to other things.

But when after supper, they were all sitting outside drinking their coffee, and Sybil, gently encouraged to unburden herself of her worries, began speaking, Gloria's name again came up.

'I don't want to criticise Gloria in any way,' she said diffidently. 'Indeed I've no real grounds for doing so. But I wonder if you have any idea how long after Christmas she's likely to be here.'

'I'm afraid we don't know any more about her future movements than you do, my dear.' It was Robert who answered, frowning. 'She's completely vague. But if it's your job you're bothered about, Sybil, I've only one thing to say. Gloria must hand it back to you forthwith.'

'It's not quite so simple as that, Mr Dale,' Sybil told him steadily. 'You see, she points out that she took the post over in the first place simply to oblige me.'

'That's not strictly true,' Penny muttered indignantly.

But Sybil, ignoring this, went on quietly: 'She implies that if she hadn't freed me to go to Aunt Emmie, and had returned instead to America, she would have been able to sort things out with her lawyer right away. She would probably not be in financial difficulty now.'

'In other words, it's largely your fault,' Robert growled. 'I never heard such nonsense!'

'Oh, she doesn't really blame me,' Sybil hastened to tell them. 'She agrees that no one could have foreseen that things would turn out this way.'

'Very kind of her!' Robert was still very angry.

'But it's true that she's a bit short of ready cash,' Brenda reminded him in a pacifying tone. 'She told us, too, Sybil, of some snag that's turned up in connection with her husband's will. Unexpected debts against the estate, we gather. But it's nonsense to say that this temporary predicament of hers is in any way your fault.'

Penny felt like saying bluntly: 'The whole thing may very well be sheer invention on Gloria's part. Why she really wants to stay on in Val Fleury, goodness knows! But at the moment it suits her to live here free of charge, apparently—and to keep on what she must feel is a potty little job.'

Brenda was still talking.

'I can't believe she'll want to remain here much longer. Once this Independence Day Ball is over, and she's had the fun of singing in the trio, she'll be thinking of making tracks for America. I doubt if she'll stay as long as Christmas, even. After all, she knows her father will pay her fare to San Francisco.'

'Of course,' Robert said quickly. 'But it will be tourist fare, not first class. I've told her so candidly.'

'Maybe that's why she wants to stay on and work a little longer,' his wife suggested. 'To be able to travel a little more luxuriously.'

'I doubt if she could save enough from her salary with Mrs O'Brien to pay the difference between the two fares,' Sybil put in drily. 'Of course it eases things to have some spare cash. There are always extras, if one can pay for them.'

Brenda had a bright idea then. It might, she thought, lead to a peaceable solution to the problem.

'Couldn't Mrs O'Brien keep you both on—Gloria on a very temporary basis, of course—and arrange for her two young assistants to take their annual holidays during this period?'

Putting it into words, she wondered whether it was a very convincing suggestion after all. So, apparently did poor Sybil.

'That's just what is in Mrs O'Brien's mind,' was her hesitating reply. 'But she's attaching such odd conditions. I suppose I ought not to feel indignant. Gloria's a better hairdresser than I am. But the idea is that she's to keep all my old clients—the best ones, anyway—while I carry on with what amounts, for the most part, to a junior's work.'

'It's absurd, as well as being most unfair,' Penny burst out hotly. 'Mrs O'Brien was proud of you, before Gloria came on the scene. Anyway, I bet most of the people you always looked after will still want you, once they hear you're back from Barbados.'

'They might, if they knew how I've struggled to improve my technique, and my knowledge, generally, while I've been away.' Sybil sounded a shade more optimistic, then her spirits seemed to sag, as she went on: 'I didn't manage to impress our Maude, though—or not to any extent.'

'What have you been up to?' Penny queried quickly. 'I thought you were going to be tied down to sick-nursing.'

'So I was at first. But for the last fortnight Aunt

Emmie needed me much less. So I plucked up my courage, and with some money she'd given me, I went along to the magnificent new hotel on the sea front, not ten minutes' walk away, and asked the Swiss who's in charge of the hairdressing salon there to give me a crash course in the latest fashions and techniques. He agreed, after striking a pretty hard bargain. But I don't grudge a cent of what I paid. I don't say I'm as skilful as Gloria, even now. But I'm not far from catching her up.'

Mrs Dale shook her head.

'I can't think what's come over Mrs O'Brien, to make her treat you so badly,' she exclaimed indignantly. And her husband added sharply: 'It would serve her right if you shook the dust of her salon off your feet, and found a much better post in Port Leon—as I'm sure you could.'

'I've thought of that,' was Sybil's subdued reply. 'But I can't go to live down there, even though we have relatives in the town. Mum and Pop—they're too old to manage on their own, especially as Pop's health is so dicey. And that drive there and back, in all weathers—I couldn't face it.'

There were expressions of sympathy at once from Penny and her parents, and after a moment Robert said soberly: 'I'd better talk to Gloria about things. We can't have her upsetting applecarts in this egotistical way.'

But Sybil demurred at once.

'If it's only going to be a short time, I'd rather put up with things,' she exclaimed. 'I can't bear the idea of a fuss. After all, even if Gloria insisted on sharing the work fairly, Mrs O'Brien might not agree. And I'm in no position to quarrel with her.'

So things must be left as they were, it was decided —though not to anyone's great satisfaction, and the two girls went indoors now to study the latest American fashion paper, and plan new dresses for the forthcoming ball at Port Leon.

Left to themselves, Robert told Brenda unhappily: 'I ought, I suppose, to send Gloria packing. She's like her mother, makes trouble wherever she goes. But somehow—well, she's still my girl. I remember her endearing ways when she was a tiny child, and how she clung to me at first when she lost her mother.'

' I know, Robert.' His wife's voice was gentle. ' She's flesh of your flesh. You can't throw her out, and risk losing her altogether. We must let things slide for a while, so that when she does leave us, it will be without bitterness, either on her side or on ours.'

' So long as she doesn't upset Penny's friendship with Eric, meanwhile. I couldn't stand for that, Brenda.'

' I've a feeling that Penny, for all her sweetness, can look after herself. Sybil has her hands tied, because of her responsibility for her parents. Penny's hands are free. So long as pride didn't intervene, she could be a bonny fighter.'

Soon they, too, went into the house, and found Sybil preparing to leave.

' Joe said something about fetching me,' she said, ' but I told him not to bother. It would be tiresome breaking off a rehearsal, when I have such a short way to go.'

' Then you'll have to put up with an old fellow for your escort,' Robert insisted heartily.

Brenda beamed her approval, but when the two had gone off, she turned to Penny.

' I wouldn't say it to your stepfather,' she declared, ' but if I only knew when Gloria was going—the actual date. I mean—I'd start crossing off the days. Oh, I know her reasons for wanting to stay on—'

And then Penny came out with an observation which startled not only her mother, but even herself. It seemed to spring out of her subconsciousness.

' Do any of us really know? I sometimes wonder.'

Sybil was a frequent visitor after that, coming in the evenings when her parents were comfortably abed, listening to the radio. She and Penny were both good at dressmaking, and managing a shopping expedition together on a free afternoon, had acquired some very beautiful material in Port Leon's leading draper's.

Penny's choice was rose-coloured chiffon, and Sybil's silver lamé. And soon, despite all efforts at tidying up, shreds of the lovely fabrics were continually turning up all over the sitting-room.

Characteristically, Gloria's admiring remarks had a sting in them. What clever girls they were to go on making their own clothes these days. Brave, too. It was years since she herself had worn a home-made dress—too long ago to remember. But she admired people who had the courage to do so. It must save a heap of money.

'What are you going to wear yourself?' Penny demanded on one of these occasions.

Gloria shrugged her shoulders.

'Something I brought with me, I suppose, an old rag of sorts. But as you know I'm short of money, and Dad doesn't seem inclined to fork out. It will have to do.'

Penny, sceptical, made no comment. Gloria had never exhibited her wardrobe to her family *in toto*. She probably had something special stored away for their astonishment and supposed delight on so important an occasion.

The question of partners for the Ball came up more than once between Sybil and Penny.

'I'm all right,' Sybil pointed out to the younger girl. 'Pete's told Joe he wants to take me, and that suits me fine. What a pity Stephen won't tie himself down to coming. He always insists he's no dancer, but I think he exaggerates. In fact I've heard people say that he used to be very good a few years ago.'

'Well, I shouldn't dream of asking him to take me,' was Penny's quick response. 'I'm not boasting, but I know several boys who like to dance with me. It's not much fun having a partner who doesn't dance.'

'Of course not. Anyway, you'd enjoy yourself far more with someone nearer your own age.'

Penny shrugged her shoulders.

'Not necessarily!'

'Someone who's not quite so dedicated to his work, anyway. He may be an entertaining guide in the forests. But in a ballroom you want someone gay and amusing, who knows all the new steps, and isn't above chat over trivialities. Pete is bad enough, but he's not so *remote* as Stephen.'

Gloria came in just then, her rehearsal having ended, it seemed, earlier than usual. Evidently she had caught Sybil's last words, for throwing herself into a chair she asked lightly: 'What poor chap are you pulling to pieces, my dears?'

'We're not saying unkind things about anyone,' Sybil told her a shade stiffly.

Penny hoped she would stop here, but Sybil, unconscious of any need to do so, continued: 'We were just agreeing that Stephen has become rather too serious, isolated so much in his beloved woods and mountains.'

'Stephen Vaughan! He's become a crashing bore—and boor, too, I'm afraid. Too superior, I gather, to honour the Independence Day Ball with his presence. But who cares? There are plenty of attractive men, married and unmarried, in Santa Rita. He won't be missed.'

The telephone bell rang just then and Penny, answering it, and hearing the voice of the very man they had been discussing, wished fervently that Gloria at least had not been within listening distance.

True, she would not be able to hear what Stephen was saying, but she would not miss a word of Penny's reply. She was a natural eavesdropper. Always had been.

'Listen, Penny,' came Stephen's voice. 'It's about this ball at the Palace Hotel on Independence Day. I've been havering about attending, but I suppose there's no chance of your letting me take *you*? I'm no substitute for Eric, I know. And I expect you've fixed up with one of your many other admirers.'

'No, I haven't,' she said coolly.

'Then what about it? I'm out of practice, but I can guarantee not to tread on your toes. I wouldn't monopolise you, either. You'd be sure to want to have some dances with other chaps—and I'd quite understand.'

'That's fine by me, Steve.' Somehow she didn't care now whether Gloria and Sybil heard or not. 'But you needn't be so self-effacing. Not really your line, if I may say so!'

He ignored that last remark.

'If I could have found the time I'd have suggested taking you down to Port Leon beforehand, so that we could practise together. I'd hate to let you down by a clumsy performance on the great night. But I've just discovered a danger spot up here not far from where the stream rises. The dry season will soon be here, of course, but I don't want to take risks. If we did have some heavy out-of-season rain, as sometimes happens, we might have trouble.'

'That's all right. I quite understand.' And then she asked: 'Where are you speaking from? It's not quite so clear as usual.'

He laughed.

'I'm camping out near the teak plantation. We've had a line fixed up. You can't ring me—with much chance of catching me, that is—but I can keep in touch with Val Fleury.'

'Mind you do. I don't want any last-minute bombshell—a message that you can't come after all.'

'No, I won't let you down. Good-bye, kidlet!'

'Good-bye, Steve. And as a favour please stop calling me by childish names.'

'O.K., Penelope Foster! I'll try to remember!'

When she went back into the sitting-room, neither Gloria or Sybil got so far as to question her about that conversation with Stephen. But unspoken queries hung in the air, and Penny decided to be frank.

'Stephen wants to partner me to the ball,' she said as nonchalantly as she could. 'I told him, as you no doubt heard, that I'd be very pleased to go with him.'

'Rather you than me,' was Gloria's lofty retort. 'Anyway, I can tell you from my own experience of him, years ago, that you may very well find yourself without a partner a few minutes before the band strikes up. He'd throw anyone over to save the life of a tree that seemed in danger—or a sick animal.'

'I really don't think that's true.' It was Sybil who interposed. 'If one of his workmen were seriously injured, he'd probably have to cry off. So would Pete, in such circumstances.'

'Anyway, he's far too old for Penny,' was Gloria's retort. 'Not only in years, but in temperament. There will be a good many snide remarks passed if they're together the whole evening.'

'For which I don't care a damn,' Penny snapped, anger rising in her.

Brenda and Robert came in just then from their bridge four, and no more was said on the subject.

But two evenings later, when Sybil and Penny were alone again, measuring and cutting and basting, Sybil, with no intention of hurting Penny, observed that Pete had been partly instrumental in getting Stephen to ring her up and suggest partnering her.

'Stephen, he says, is so diffident over social things that he felt impelled to bolster him up. It's odd, because Steve is so quick and decided when it comes to matters connected with their work.'

'I don't really see why Pete should intervene.' All Penny's prickles were out. 'If Stephen can't make up his own mind whether he wants to take me to the Ball or not, I'm not interested in going with him.'

'Oh, Penny dear, don't take it like that,' Sybil exclaimed in dismay.

'Well, I do, I'm afraid!'

'In that case, I'll have to tell you something else. Eric was getting restive over your being besieged by other fellows, wanting to take you to the Ball.'

'I've had some tentative invitations, but there's hardly been a queue,' was Penny's curt reply.

'Eric's convinced that some dashing chap will be sweeping you off your feet, once it gets around that he'll have almost no chance of dancing with you himself. So Joe got on to Pete, and Pete got on to Stephen. They knew Eric couldn't possibly be jealous of *him*!'

'And is Stephen in this plot to save Eric's feelings?' Penny's wrath was bubbling up.

'Of course he isn't. And mind you, if he hadn't really wanted to take you, Pete's encouragement wouldn't have moved him an inch.'

'Well, I don't like it,' Penny exclaimed, still indignant. 'All this manœuvring going on behind my back! I've a good mind to give that wretched ball a miss, tell Stephen I've changed my mind, and don't really want to attend it.'

'And miss the Trio's all-important performance? You can't do that, Penny. Eric would be cut to the heart if you weren't there to witness their triumph.'

'I'll sleep on it,' was all Penny would promise. 'But I'm going to be frank, Sybil. I'm more annoyed over all this ridiculous plotting and planning than I've been for a long time. It makes Stephen and me, at least, look a couple of fools.'

'Don't be furious with me,' Sybil pleaded. 'I've

done no scheming. All I've done is to let you know about it. And I realise now I shouldn't have.'

Penny, seeing Sybil's piteous expression, relented. Sybil had more than her fair share of troubles. She mustn't add to them.

'I'm not blaming you at all,' she said. 'It's better to know. I never did enjoy playing Blind Man's Buff. And as far as you and I are concerned, we've never quarrelled yet, and aren't going to do so now. Let's get on with the work.'

An injunction which soothed Sybil's fears considerably, since it implied that Penny, for all her vexation, had no real intention of opting out of the Independence Day festivities.

It wouldn't be like her to do all this elaborate dress-making for nothing, especially with the added burden of homework in connection with her pharmacy lessons.

Besides, she wasn't the kind to bear grudges, or disconcert her friends by adopting a martyr's role.

CHAPTER IV

Perhaps it was a good thing for Penny that she had this homework to do. Both her father and Juan Garcia, took endless trouble over the lessons which they gave her in the office at the back of the pharmacy, and she would have been ashamed to let them down.

Alternating between studying alone in her little bedroom, and snipping and stitching with Sybil in the sitting-room, her evenings were fully occupied. She couldn't really fret at seeing so little of Eric. Her irritation with him had given way to tenderer feelings. Remembering his past shyness, his unsureness, she could even pity him for being jealous—poor, silly darling. In all the circumstances his attitude was most illogical. But at least it demonstrated clearly that Pearl's prognostications had been groundless. He certainly wasn't cooling off, and falling under Gloria's spell.

As for Stephen, it still rankled that he had needed persuasion before offering himself as her partner. But she didn't intend to talk to him about it. Enough to show him a little coolness when the important evening arrived.

He didn't ring her again until the very day before the Ball. He'd been very busy over that barrier they had been building near the source of the little river, and the telephone line which had been put up was out of order as often not, what with blustery winds and the inquisitive habits of monkeys and parakeets.

But he was all set to come down that night to his quarters at the Forestry Office where he could bath and shave and make sure that his evening clothes were in good order. Pete was doing the same, and they were both looking forward to a bit of gaiety after their recent hard slog.

' We've decided to use my car,' he finished cheerfully. ' Then Pete and I can share the driving, while you and Sybil have a good gossip.'

It didn't sound very romantic, Penny reflected with rueful amusement. But then Stephen was a strictly practical person, and Pete hardly less so. Anyway, the driving would be a hundred per cent efficient, even if their performance on the dance floor didn't approach that standard.

Their car arrived at the gate of the bungalow on the dot, the following evening, an hour after Gloria had left for Port Leon with Eric and Joe. And when Stephen came striding up to the front door, Penny had a small shock—but a pleasurable one. He must have taken great trouble with his appearance, for his well-cut evening suit was immaculate, as were his shining pumps, and his normally far from sleek hair was brushed into a thick, shiny black cap.

It wasn't that she liked him better this way. She preferred him, she thought, with his hair a bit ruffled, and wearing his usual casual working clothes. But she appreciated the effort he had made, and felt that he was an escort of whom any woman could be proud.

He was not, however, concerned with his own looks. He gazed at Penny in her rose-coloured chiffon dress, and ejaculated: ' To think that when I first knew you, Penny, you were a flat-chested, skinny little schoolgirl, with gaps between your teeth! And now you're a beautiful young woman.'

She laughed. ' Well, I remember you as a terribly untidy young man, with knobbly wrists shooting out of your sleeves. Now Beau Brummel isn't in it.'

He grinned.

' Oh, Pete and I didn't intend to appear at a swell occasion like this looking like wild men of the woods. Sybil is as pleased with Pete as he is with her. So our evening's off to a good start, don't you think?'

The Dales came to the doorway then to wave them good-bye, but Robert gave a sigh as they came back into the house.

' I wish, all the same, it was Eric who was partnering Penny. I don't want any sentimental nonsense between her and Stephen. Not that I anticipate anything of that sort.'

She knew why he felt that way. It was not only that Stephen was a good ten years older than Penny—often there was a far greater disparity—but because he was a Vaughan—cousin to Vera, who had caused him such bitterness, such anguish of heart.

Reason would tell him it was unfair. He could admit to a genuine liking for Stephen, in spite of that scandal of five years ago. As for Vera, poor wayward creature, she had been in her distant grave a long, long time.

But she remembered the old saying: 'The heart has its reasons!' Remembered, too, talk of race memories; of senseless historical quarrels between one clan and another, between tribes and great families.

It would be useless to argue with Robert, she knew. She would do better to hold her peace. After all, he never spoke in so many words of his dark prejudice. And more important still, she could see no sign whatever of this fear of his deepening from a shadow into something substantial.

Stephen and Penny—it was impossible to believe that their names would ever be seriously linked. Stephen and Gloria—that would be easier to imagine, whatever their present antagonisms. But she shivered a little at that. She liked Stephen, had a deeper knowledge of him, she thought, than either Robert or Penny possessed. For all his toughness and reserve, he would be far from immune to suffering.

But as the four drove down the steep mountain road towards the steamy coast, and Port Leon, they had no such serious thoughts. They were all out to make the occasion a joyous one. The two men were resolved that the girls shouldn't have cause to miss their boy-friends too badly, and the girls were anxious not to let their partners feel they were accounted only second-best.

Well-dressed people were thronging into the gaily lit foyer when they arrived. Tom Perez, busy greeting the notables of the island—the Lord Mayor, the Attorney-General and others with their ladies—still found time to approach Penny with a smile of welcome, and a request to be introduced to the others of her party. Which done, he murmured to them confidentially that he had had a special table reserved for them, which would enable them to hear the Trio perfectly.

'Then I'd better cancel the table I booked by telephone last week,' Stephen told him politely.

'Don't trouble. If you give me the name I'll see to it.'

'Stephen Vaughan.'

Tom Perez' eyes flickered.

'Oh, yes. Gloria's cousin! She said you might be coming—that she was going to invite you, and wanted you to be looked after specially well. But that was some time ago, and I'm afraid the matter slipped my memory.'

For a moment Stephen looked annoyed—or was it, Penny wondered, that he was embarrassed? But the next instant he was saying coolly: 'It's of no consequence, anyway, Mr Perez, as you have been kind enough to make such good provision for us. We shall do fine.'

Although he spoke mildly enough, Penny could see by a little vein throbbing at the side of his temple that he was disturbed. She thought, vexed not only by Mr Perez' reference to Gloria but by Stephen's reaction, that even the mention of her stepsister seemed to bring feelings of stress and strain.

She was glad to escape with Sybil into the cloakroom, to leave their coats and tidy up, and found that Sybil, too, was a little mystified.

'I can't make head or tail of Gloria,' she murmured, as they shared a long mirror. 'She knows very well that the four of us are coming together. What's all this about her inviting Stephen—on her own?'

Penny shrugged her shoulders.

'I suppose she asked him, and he declined.'

'And then she didn't feel like telling Mr Perez. Maybe she was secretly humiliated. People can be absurdly over-sensitive when they're crazy over anybody.'

'Do you really think she's so desperately keen on him?' Penny's hazel eyes were dubious. 'I thought she was damned silly, that's all. Incidentally, she's forever running him down. You must have heard her yourself.'

Other people were coming within earshot now, so they said no more, though Penny herself was thinking hard.

If Gloria was annoying and embarrassing Stephen by her pursuit of him, why were his reactions so strange?

'I know he wouldn't talk to me about it,' she reflected. 'He's far too reserved. But why on earth can't he give her an almighty snub that would stop her nonsense once and for all? I bet if *I* started pestering him,' and she had to smile now at such an absurd idea, 'he'd lose no time in telling me where I got off.'

Meeting their escorts at the entrance to the ballroom, Penny saw with relief that Stephen seemed to have put Gloria right out of his mind.

The dining tables were set all round the edge of the great room, leaving the centre free for dancing, and they themselves had been placed fairly near the tiny stage.

Still closer was a slightly larger table, with flower decorations even more opulent and beautiful than elsewhere. And Penny guessed that whatever grandees would be sitting there, Manoel Lopez would be among them.

There was no sign whatever of Gloria and the two boys, but Pete had the clue to this.

'Because they're being paid, they're being treated as professionals,' he said sagely. 'Feasting behind the scenes.'

'But they're appearing for charity,' Penny exclaimed in amazement.

Pete put his finger to his lips.

'Don't speak quite so loud, my dear,' he told her smiling. 'I happen to know they're getting something on the side. But if they haven't mentioned this to you, I should let it float. It's not much anyway; just enough to cover their expenses, and put a few dollars in their pockets.'

Even Sybil looked surprised. But she said stoutly: 'They deserve it, anyway. All the hard work they've put in, for weeks and weeks, just for this one show.'

'Never mind about them.' Stephen spoke in his usual decisive fashion. 'It's a table d'hôte dinner, girls, so there's not much choice—just room for a few minor preferences.'

They had barely glanced at the highly ornamental menu card, however, when a little party of people, on their way to the place of honour near them, stopped at their table to talk in the friendliest way to Stephen. They consisted of the important personages whom they had seen Mr Perez welcoming, whom so far Penny and Sybil, at least, had only known by sight—the Lord Mayor, and the Attorney-General, with their ladies.

And now for the first time Penny saw with great pleasure the high regard in which Stephen was held by people who counted for so much in the island's affairs. They spoke of his work up in the forests with genuine enthusiasm and, including Pete in their praise, declared that the Forestry Department in Santa Rita, though small, and often short of funds, was becoming noted far and wide for its efficiency.

Penny and Sybil were of course introduced, and it was a very cheerful quartet that sat down again when the great ones passed on to their special table.

Stephen and Pete pretended, of course, to be casual; and Pete muttered a distinctly unfavourable comment about the shortness of funds which had been mentioned. But they couldn't deceive the girls. Their work was often belittled. Teasing remarks floated round about ' wild men of the woods '. Appreciation by those who knew the value of their efforts must warm their hearts.

It was not until the delicious meal, washed down with some admirable light wine, was nearly at an end, that Penny, who had begun to worry a little about the non-appearance of Manoel Lopez, caught sight of him, drinking coffee with Tom Perez at the far side of the room.

It would have been a bitter blow to the Trio if he had failed to arrive. It was partly for his approval that they had worked so hard. But doubtless he, too, had taken his dinner behind the scenes—so escaping unwanted notice. If, indeed, a famous pop artist ever preferred to dodge the limelight.

Soon waiters were clearing the tables with commendable speed and deftness, replacing silver and china with tall glasses and jugs of iced drinks. And then up went the curtain of the little stage, and there were Eric and Joe, looking almost unnaturally neat and composed, and between them Gloria in an exquisite dress of lemon tulle, a magnificent necklace of topaz round her slender throat.

A murmur came from the Attorney-General's table.

' What a gorgeous creature ! '

It was his wife speaking, and clearly her companions were in warm agreement.

' She's certainly a very beautiful woman,' Pete spoke in equally low tones, his eyes fixed on Gloria in open admiration.

And Penny, though remembering ironically her stepsister's declaration that she would be reduced to wearing

' some old rag ' for the great occasion, had to agree.

Sybil came in then with a comment on the glorious dress. It was only Stephen who said nothing. But he stared and stared as though unable to tear his eyes away from the dark, graceful woman in the yellow tulle.

Before the performance began, Tom Perez appeared on the tiny stage, speaking through the mike which Gloria was clearly going to use. Introducing them he spoke pleasantly of his delight in discovering local talent. None of the three had ever sung or played in public before, and they were doing so now for island charities. There would be a box in the foyer, and he hoped that their efforts would be well supported.

He disappeared amid conventional sounds of clapping, and left it to Eric to announce the titles of the songs.

The first number was the latest to reach the top of the pops—*Look Where You're Going*. Gay and brisk, both in words and tune, it soon had the younger members of the audience jigging in their chairs.

But Penny knew then that for once in a way Gloria had been honest when she had said that she would never make the grade as a professional. Helped by the mike, her voice carried reasonably well, but she just hadn't the gift of establishing contact with her listeners. Not, at least, with a snappy number.

So long as Eric and Joe were singing with her, this lack was scarcely noticeable. But as soon as they concentrated on their guitars, and left her to solo lines, it became apparent.

Stephen made no comment, but after two more songs, Pete observed under his breath: ' This is a bit unexpected—Joe and Eric carrying Gloria. I should have thought they would have been the jittery ones.'

' Gloria jittery? Don't you believe it. She's saving herself up for the kind of song that shows off her voice. Something slow and sugary, with a synthetic sob in it.'

The contempt and bitterness in Stephen's tone startled Penny, at least, but almost before he had stopped speaking, the guitars had begun throbbing again, playing the soft accompaniment of a song current a few years ago but seldom if ever heard these days. A song which Penny had loved in her schooldays, until made sick of it by hearing it too often on Gloria's lips, when home for the holidays.

As if in confirmation of Stephen's scornful words, Gloria's voice floated out now bringing to the trite and sentimental phrases nostalgia, tinged with languorous passion.

'Remember the Night,' she sang to the muted music of the guitars, and though there were few signs of enthusiasm, this time, from the younger generation, there was a fair amount of applause from their seniors.

Penny thought, with a spurt of indignation: 'A direct appeal to Stephen, and a pretty crude one. She's reminding him of one particular night, I'm sure.' And she was confirmed in this notion when Sybil commented: 'The boys were all against that number. Outdated and sloppy, they called it. But Gloria insisted, not merely on being allowed to sing something lush, but that particular song.'

'I suppose it went down all right,' Penny conceded, but could not resist stealing a glance at Stephen. But his bronzed face gave nothing away. Indeed, now that the curtain was coming down, there was no sign that he had even been giving the performance much attention. Already he had engaged the attention of a waiter and was ordering a fresh supply of iced fruit cup.

And now Penny looked towards the other side of the hall, curious to see if anything of approval—or disapproval—could be gleaned from Manoel Lopez' expression.

But he was chatting to Tom Perez, his face turned away, and though he was gesturing with his hands they conveyed no particular meaning at this distance.

In any case, a large radiogram began just then to send out dance music. The small amateur concert was forgotten, and the guests streamed out on to the highly polished floor.

Penny, held lightly but firmly in Stephen's arms, found a pleasant surprise awaiting her. It was the first time she had ever danced with him, and he proved a delightful partner. He produced no new steps, it was true, no gimmicks; but he moved smoothly and with decision, and before long she was scolding him for having become so anti-social.

'Absurd of you to boycott all the Port Leon dances,'

she told him. 'Working up in the forests is no excuse for turning yourself into a hermit, and persuading Pete to follow your example. Though he's not as bad as you, I admit.'

'Hi, not so fast!' he protested. 'I haven't the faintest influence on Pete, outside our work. If he found a girl to his liking, he'd soon demonstrate that he was no anchorite.'

'The same thing applies to you, I'm sure.'

'Exactly. Well, try match-making for Pete if you like, but leave me alone. If ever I marry, you may be sure I'll have done my own hunting.'

'It's good to hear that!' She was satirically amused. 'Women are so often accused of being huntresses. But I can prophesy the kind of female you'll fall for.'

'You've already done so. She must be *nice*, and agreeable to your coming on expeditions with us!'

'Ah, but I've thought more about it since then. She must be exactly your age, so you can't complain she's either too young or too old. With splendid muscles and fine nerves—and not a tremor of fear over vipers or pythons!'

Suddenly he was holding her closer—too tightly altogether.

'Stop it, Steve!' she exclaimed breathlessly, half laughing still. 'Talk about pythons! You're more like a blooming boa-constrictor!'

'My dear, I'm merely giving you a warning of what happens to girls who tease poor old hermits too far.'

He, too, was laughing, but there was a note in his voice that she had never heard before. A note that showed even more clearly than his near-violence, that he was very far indeed from being a passionless recluse.

The music stopped then, however, and releasing her he looked down at her in a way that made her flush, saying mockingly: 'You see, I can be provocative, too, when I'm in the mood.'

'Of course, with that cleft in your chin,' she countered swiftly.

'Now, just you listen,' he began, putting on a pretended scowl.

But at that moment Pete came to claim her, and their conversation was cut short abruptly.

The change of partner was, from her point of view, at least, a decided comedown. It made her feel absurdly flat. Like everyone in the islands Pete had an inborn sense of rhythm, and she tried to tell herself that he was really as good a dancer as Stephen. But he wasn't. He was too eager to try out new steps that he wasn't quite sure of. And it was only through hard concentration on her part, and natural facility, that all went well. At least, she consoled herself, he didn't expect her to talk to him. It was the last thing she felt like doing just then.

Turn and turn about it had to be. They had agreed about that, the four of them, on their way down in the car—with Sybil, she couldn't but fail to notice, particularly insistent. And now Stephen had changed. He was once again his usual self. Friendly but casual. It should not have disconcerted her, but it did.

In one of the intervals, when the two girls had a chance of talking on their own, Sybil admitted that she had been anxious to arrange this ' swapping '.

' It's not only that I know by experience Pete isn't too hot at dancing—for all the trouble he takes—but I learnt from Gloria, when we were having a little gossip between appointments at the Salon, that her cousin had once been a highly desirable partner. And she wasn't exaggerating. Indeed, once he relaxes a bit, there's no question but that he's a highly desirable man altogether. Very far, I should say, from the born celibate he might appear.'

' Personally I've always thought he would make an excellent husband for the right woman,' Penny returned, a shade loftily. But her mind wasn't on her cool, sensible words at all.

' I'm sure. But mind you, I'd rather have my dear old Joe—' Sybil's voice went on, without Penny catching a syllable.

A flash of memory had brought back Stephen's intent look as he first caught sight of Gloria, standing on the miniature stage, in the magnificent yellow dress. What had happened between the two of them in the past? They must have been strongly attracted to each other. And Gloria was still drawn to him. But what were his feelings for her? Could they really be summed up in his expressed dislike, his wish to avoid her?

94

When she and Sybil re-entered the ballroom, and made to join Stephen and Pete at their table, they found Eric and Joe waiting there, all set to claim a few dances.

Certainly Eric was an enterprising and accomplished dancer—fun, as a partner, especially when, as now, he was in high spirits and a quickstep was being played. But somehow she couldn't altogether share his annoyance when, pretty soon, the lights went low and a Paul Jones was announced.

'We'll soon be together again,' she promised him comfortingly, ashamed of her secret wish to be for a little while at least in Stephen's arms.

But as luck would have it— ' and it jolly well serves me right ', she thought severely—she fell to Tom Perez, whom she hadn't even realised was on the dance floor.

She smiled charmingly at him nor, such was her self-control, did her smile lessen when she caught sight, all at once, of Stephen and Gloria dancing together, in perfect unison.

It was something of a relief to her when Tom Perez suggested, after a few turns, that she should sit down with him and watch the dancers. She was suddenly aware of weariness.

'I could dance with you for hours,' he said, with a twisted smile. 'You're first-rate. But the truth is I'm dead tired—a remark I could only make to a sweet kid like you.'

She wasn't altogether sure that she liked him—and she was getting a little fed up at being treated as though she was younger than her real age. Just because she happened to be on the slight side!

But she couldn't help feeling sorry for him, and told him seriously that she didn't wonder at his exhaustion. He must have worked terrifically to have made such a success of the evening. She was sure that Port Leon had never experienced anything like it.

He cheered up then.

'It's good to hear that from one of the younger generation,' he said. 'I find it much easier to please the middle-aged. They're not half so choosey. So long as the food and drink are good, they'll be satisfied.'

'What's happened to Mr Lopez?' Penny enquired then, glancing round. 'Was he at all impressed?'

95

' You mean—with the Trio?'

She nodded, on tenterhooks to hear the great man's opinion.

' He turned in some time ago. After all, he's on holiday. But apparently he thought Eric Hoskins had talent that might be developed. I wouldn't be surprised if he sent for him to come up and have a chat, within the next day or two.'

Penny flushed with pleasure.

' Good old Eric! Though I'm sorry for Joe, if he's to be left out.'

' That's life. But don't count on anything—and don't let your Eric get too excited. These stars are notoriously unreliable.'

If he noticed that she had omitted Gloria's name, he gave no sign. But the next moment Penny was forced to think of her. From the corner of her eye she caught the gleam of the full-skirted yellow dress, and along came Gloria and Stephen, still moving like one person over the dance-floor.

Mentally she shrugged her shoulders. What did it matter to her who either of them danced with?

But this philosophical reflection lost its power, when her sharp ears caught a fragment of conversation that floated from a table at a short distance away.

' What a marvellously well matched couple they make,' a man was saying. And the woman with him echoed: ' I'm not sure I like that girl, beautiful as she is. But she's more in his line, I should think, than anyone else he's been dancing with.'

Penny glanced at Tom Perez. But apparently he hadn't heard. He had his own comment, however, to make about Gloria.

' Although my famous cousin didn't think Gloria would ever go far as a vocalist,' he observed, ' he didn't conceal the fact that he found her a damned attractive woman. So she is. But—in confidence, for I know she's your stepsister—she's difficult to work with. Insisted, for instance, on finishing with that old-time favourite, *Remember the Night*. Suited her voice, she declared.'

' So it did,' Penny admitted, a shade unwillingly.

' I know. It was the only number she made much of at all. And it's a lovely thing. But it's had its day.

The younger set showed quite plainly that they didn't like it. Not lively enough for them. Gave it hardly a clap—I was watching them.'

'I suppose it's only fair that the older people should be considered.' Penny was trying to be loyal—if not to Gloria herself, then to the boys who had accompanied her.

'If you want to catch *them*, you must put on some really old stuff. Not things that flared up and died a few years ago. It's like women's fashions. Period dresses are O.K., but not yesterday's styles.'

She was relieved when she found herself dancing with Eric again. He was in high spirits, for he and the other two had received warm congratulations on their performance from a great many of the guests. It was a shade disappointing that Manoel Lopez had said so little, but maybe they'd hear something in a day or so. Tom Perez had hinted as much. Anyway, it had all been great fun. And with visitors from some of the other islands attending the Ball, and lavishing praise on them, it wouldn't be surprising if they collected quite a few engagements before many weeks were over.

'If Gloria leaves Santa Rita directly after Christmas, you'll have to find another vocalist,' she observed, forced somehow to make that remark, though dreading to hear that Gloria would probably decide now to prolong her visit indefinitely.

But she need not, she found, have worried.

'I suppose so,' was Eric's matter-of-fact reply. And then he looked down at her and told her affectionately: 'I wish you could sing, Penny. What fun we'd have doing zingy numbers together, you and I and dear old Joe.'

His manner soothed, just a little, certain sore feelings which that unknown woman's casual remark had engendered. Illogical, but there it was!

'I'd always help you behind the scenes if you needed me,' she said. 'You could count on me for that. But a singer I'll never make.'

Eric smiled at her encouragingly.

'Far more important to make a loving wife,' he said. And seeing something in her expression that puzzled him for a second, added quickly: 'Loving and greatly beloved, of course, my darling.'

She danced several times with Eric after that, and occasionally with Joe and Pete, catching not a sign, however, of Stephen or Gloria. But when, at eleven, supper was announced, and she and Eric began to move from the dance floor, she suddenly found Stephen at her elbow.

'Sorry to claim you, Penny,' he said blandly but with decision. 'But I'm your host for supper, I believe. Pete and Sybil have already gone to our table.' He smiled amiably at Eric. 'So if you'll excuse me I'll take over.'

'Couldn't we all join up now?' Eric suggested awkwardly.

'Oh, I don't think seven is a very satisfactory number,' was Stephen's swift and smooth reply. 'Incidentally, I think Gloria will be looking out for you and Joe, if she's torn herself away from the great Lopez.'

Penny looked at him sharply.

'I thought he'd cleared off long ago.'

'Oh, he went behind the scenes, but not very far away. Anyway, what does it matter? Let's go! I'm starving.'

She tried to give the disgruntled Eric a sympathetic smile, but it wasn't very convincing. Stephen hadn't been with Gloria all this time—he'd probably been in the bar, or outside with some of his friends, smoking. And though it was a matter of no real consequence to her at all, it gave her spirits a lift. She was quite happy to accompany him to the supper-table.

Sybil and Pete were already installed in the seats they had originally occupied, and Pete's face lightened at the sight of them.

'I'm glad you realise, like Sybil, that fair's fair,' he told Penny. 'Those boy-friends have been trying to fix things, not only over the supper arrangements, but to drive you home. Pretended to think we'd like to share Gloria's company, for a little change—if you can believe anything so unlikely.'

'And what did Gloria say to all this?' Penny couldn't keep back the question.

'I wasn't interested enough to enquire. But I gather she's in a funny-peculiar mood, though I may be wrong. I guess I don't understand women too well.'

No one commented on this, certainly not Stephen, apparently absorbed in a study of the supper-menu. And soon a light, delectable meal appeared on the tables, served by waiters who still managed to maintain their brisk and cheerful looks, weary though they must be.

There was to be more dancing after supper, of course, but Penny at least felt she had had enough. She wanted to be home, safe, sound and in bed, and thinking over the events of the evening before slipping into sleep.

It had started to rain when they emerged from the hotel—no very unusual occurrence at this time of year. But with Steve bringing his car right up to the entrance, Penny and Sybil managed to keep their flimsy dresses dry.

' I thought this might happen,' he remarked, as he helped them in. ' I've a nose for rain. If we'd waited until the end, there'd have been a bit of a scrum, with everyone trying to get off at once. You might have been soaked despite my efforts.'

The trickle became a downpour before they were far on the road, and this, combined with the steep climb, made them slow their pace considerably. Soon both girls were dozing comfortably, waking only when, about halfway on their journey, Stephen halted the car and handed the driving over to Pete.

Soon, however, the rain ceased as abruptly as it had started, but with the water gushing down the ditches at the sides of the road, Pete maintained a careful speed. Then the moon slipped out from behind a dark cloud, and a break in the woods gave a glimpse of the little river running almost parallel less than a hundred yards away, tumbling down the hillside like a frayed and crumpled tinsel ribbon.

' It's pretty, but I don't suppose you and Pete like to see it tearing along like that,' Penny murmured sleepily.

' Not to worry.' Pete's tone was confident. ' It's often in spate like that—only more so!'

' All the same, I'll be glad when they push on with the digging out of the river bed, especially near our village,' Stephen put in. ' I've nagged the powers-that-be until I'm sick of it. The dykes and barriers we've been working on so long up in the forests are practically unbreachable. But we want both aspects attended to.'

'Shortage of funds,' was Pete's yawning comment. 'It's always the same cry.'

Penny thought it time now to offer a grain of comfort. 'Shows like to-night's will boost the tourist trade. Then there'll be more money for everything. Tom Perez was talking to me. He's very enthusiastic.'

And that there was something in his hopes and ideas, both men philosophically agreed.

Their serenity was shattered, however, when about five miles from Val Fleury, in a narrow section of the road, a car dashed past them, hooting loudly, and nearly forcing them into the ditch—Eric's car, with three people inside.

'Silly young fools!' Pete exclaimed angrily, adding over his shoulder to the two girls: 'Sorry to criticise your boy-friends, but if they want an accident, that's the way to achieve it. The road's as slippery as glass, with all this mud about.' And he added wrathfully: 'What's Gloria about to allow them to behave that way? She's old enough to have some sense.'

It was a rhetorical question to which he expected no reply. But an answer of sorts did come—from Stephen.

'As you implied yourself not long ago, she's in one of her bad moods,' he said, as though that explained everything. And Penny for one understood, in part at least.

Gloria, in a suppressed fury, was quite capable of egging on two excited and hilarious young men to dangerous folly. Though exactly what she was so upset about she did not know.

She hoped that Gloria would have gone to her bedroom by the time she herself reached the bungalow. An encounter with her was the last thing she wanted.

At first it seemed as though she were going to avoid this, for when the car stopped at last outside the white wooden gate, she saw that the place was in darkness, and she stepped boldly from the car, said good-night to the others—with pretty thanks to Steve and Pete for their hospitality—and walked quietly up the path.

But as she went through the front door, the sitting-room light went on, and out into the little hallway came Gloria.

Penny went white, her mind reaching back, despite herself, to those days when Gloria seemed forever pouncing on her to tease and torment. And the older girl asked her in that same well-remembered, supercilious tone, indeed in the words she had so often used: 'What's the matter with you? Do you think I'm going to eat you?'

But Penny was no longer a nervous and sensitive twelve-year-old. She recovered her poise at once.

'Why haven't you gone to bed?' she demanded sharply. 'Why sit around in the dark?'

Gloria's answer came as an anti-climax.

'Because my zip has caught somewhere. I've been waiting for you to tackle it. Knew you couldn't be long, in spite of the way Stephen's car was crawling.'

Penny began to fiddle with the back of the dress.

'If you'd take your topaz necklace off, I could cope better,' she said. 'I'll unclasp it if you like.'

'No, leave it to me. It's special.'

'It's certainly very beautiful,' Penny admitted.

'And precious!' Gloria hesitated. 'Stephen gave it to me when I told him I was going to wear a yellow dress. He's always liked me in this colour.' She undid the necklace and slid the jewels into her hands. 'Generous of him, isn't it?'

'Very.' Penny's tone was cool, but she didn't feel that way. It was nothing to her what presents Stephen chose to give his glamorous cousin. But there was an air of mystery about his doings—and sayings—which she could not help resenting.

Was he acting a part when he spoke of her so scathingly? If so, why should he do so?

She fetched a tiny phial of almond oil from the bathroom, and putting the merest drop on the obstinate zip quickly had it running free.

Gloria thanked her and shrugged herself out of the lovely dress so that it fell in a flurry of gold to her feet, leaving her standing in exiguous bra and pants.

'He knows my tastes, Steve does,' she remarked, as she stepped out of the dress and picked it up. 'Knows a piece of jewellery is more in my line than a dull old book about trees.' Then, swinging the necklace in her free hand, she went on: 'You'd better not talk about this to anyone—least of all to Steve. He's a funny fellow. Cagey isn't the word for him!'

'My dear Gloria, what Stephen chooses to do is

nothing to me.' Penny spoke frigidly. 'You're free, and we can both get to bed.'

Gloria yawned and stretched herself.

'Free—that's a lovely word,' she said. 'And yet sometimes—'

She did not finish the sentence, trailed quietly off to her room.

Tossing about in the early hours, with the rain pelting down again, Penny could not, try as she might, keep her thoughts away from Stephen and Gloria.

That Gloria had little regard for the truth when a lie suited her best, she well knew. But to utter one which could so easily be disproved wasn't her usual form.

'Except, of course, that she knows as well as I do that Stephen isn't a person to be catechised, even by a person who has a right to question him. As I certainly have not.'

She tried hard now to switch her mind from Stephen to Eric—who belonged to her. To his lovable, boyish qualities, his eager hopes for a career in pop music. But her mind kept recurring, against all reason, to the matter of the topaz necklace.

How and when could Gloria have possibly told Stephen of her intention to wear a yellow dress? She had only, so she said, come to a decision on what to wear at the very last minute—and Stephen had been away then, up in the forest. Even he couldn't pick necklaces off trees and bushes!

And then she began to feel angry, not with Gloria or Stephen, or with anyone else but her foolish self.

'Penny Foster, it's none of your business,' she told herself severely. 'Stop bothering your silly head about things and people that don't concern you. *Stop*, I say!'

Absurdly, as though in obedience to that vehement command, the downpour outside ceased, with the customary abruptness of tropical rain.

She smiled, in spite of herself, curled up, and was soon asleep.

Next day was Sunday, and she awoke in full sunlight to hear the clanging of the bell from the white church up the road. Her clock told her it was ringing for the last morning service, and in vain she tried to shut out the insistent sound.

Indeed she was given no chance to do so. Pearl waddled in with a cup of coffee to warn her that she would be late if she didn't hurry. It was after ten o'clock, and even nowadays when girls went around with almost no clothes on, she could hardly go running down the road and up the aisle in a skimpy see-through nightie.

Penny suppressed the impulse to snap at Pearl. There was an easier way to discompose her for pushing her along what she doubtless considered the 'straight and narrow.'

' Have you been thoughtful enough to call Gloria as well?' she enquired amiably, jumping out of bed and running a comb through her rumpled hair.

And when Pearl merely snorted, she told her airily: ' I'm sorry to have to say it, Pearly, but you've no moral courage. You just haven't the nerve to go into her room and root her out. Unless you think she's so good already— '.

Pearl handed her the pretty wrapper lying on her bed.

' Dat Gloria, she can go to hell for all Ah care,' she declared, her dark eyes rolling until the whites showed. ' An' prob'ly will. But don' tell your ma Ah said so. De truth ain't always polite! Now, git along an' have your shower, mah darlin'.'

There were always young men waiting about outside the church after this last and crowded morning service, and as Penny emerged with her parents, Eric detached himself from the others and joined them, an eager expression on his face.

' You're just the person I wanted to see,' he exclaimed, after a quick greeting to the Dales. ' I had a telephone message from Perez soon after nine this morning asking me to come down to the hotel for lunch. Manoel Lopez wants to see me. I'm off this minute.'

' What about Gloria and Joe?' Penny wanted to know.

' I asked Perez about them, and he said Lopez only mentioned me.' He hesitated. ' I wish I could take you with me, darling, but it would be a terrible bore for you hanging around. But I'll dash round to see you directly I get back.'

Penny smiled.

'O.K. by me. Good luck, dear.'

And off Eric went, to jump into his waiting car and speed on his way.

The Dales, with their usual tact, had moved a few paces away to talk to some friends, and Penny now joined them.

'I'm not coming home right away,' she told them, with a nonchalance she did not altogether feel. 'I'm going to pop into the Marsdens' for a chat with Sybil.'

'Well, give them all our love. We'll expect you when we see you.' And with a cheerful wave, Mrs Dale resumed her innocent gossip with her cronies, then taking her husband's arm set about their stroll back to their bungalow.

How much they had heard of her brief conversation with Eric, Penny did not know. It was, in fact, more than she supposed, but Robert, at least, didn't take it too seriously.

'I don't believe anything will come of it,' was his verdict. 'These popular idols! As if they could go on keeping in mind every talented amateur who's brought to their notice. It's all part of the *brouhaha* which Gloria's responsible for. Once she's gone back to America, we'll all settle down again.'

Brenda pressed his arm.

'I devoutly hope so,' she murmured; but wondered wistfully whether things would ever be quite the same again. Whether, even, she would be content to have them that way.

At the Marsdens' Penny found the old people seated comfortably on the verandah, listening to the radio.

Sybil was in the kitchen, Mrs Marsden told her pleasantly. Just in the mood for a chat over last night's festivities, she was sure.

As always Sybil was, indeed, delighted to see Penny. She was busy putting the finishing touches to a trifle— her mother's favourite sweet, which she always tried to give her on a Sunday. If Penny wanted a job, she could get some grapefruit juice out of the fridge. Joe was coming in for a cool drink round about twelve, and there was just a possibility that Pete and Stephen might drop in, too.

Penny, who wanted to talk to her friend alone, was a shade disconcerted at this. But she decided to take the plunge, and repeated to her just what Eric had told her before rushing down to Port Leon.

Sybil stopped arranging the cherries round the trifle. 'I'm sorry for poor old Joe,' she said quietly. 'But I'm not really surprised about Eric. He's come on a lot since the three of them started practising together.' She hesitated. 'It would be much worse if it had happened the other way round. Eric's far more vulnerable than the Rodriguez boys.'

'I know. He didn't have the same stable background. I can still remember the nervous, stammering person he used to be, when he first landed up in Val Fleury.'

Sybil nodded.

'So can I. And I don't forget all you did to bring him out and give him confidence—long before you were more or less courting.'

For a few moments both girls were silent, busy with their own thoughts. Then Penny said, almost brusquely: 'I hope he rang Joe up this morning, after he got that— that summons to the hotel.'

'Of course he'll have done so. They're real buddies, Eric and Joe. But even if he didn't, and you have to tell Joe yourself, you needn't feel bad about it.' She paused. 'If it didn't prick your conscience too badly, you could even put it in the form of a message from Eric!'

'I suppose so. Anyway, let's hope Eric did the decent thing and told Joe himself.'

The finished trifle was hardly back in the fridge, to keep company there with a chicken salad, when Joe arrived.

'Hi, girls!' he exclaimed genially, and gave Sybil a hearty kiss. 'Still alive after last night's excitements! Seen anything of Eric? I rang his lodgings just now, and that bitchy landlady of his said crossly that he'd gone out.'

Sybil pulled out a chair for him.

'Penny's seen him,' she said lightly. 'You've a message for Joe, haven't you, honey?'

'I only saw him for a minute,' Penny explained. 'He was waiting for me as I came out of church, and in no end of a hurry. Perez asked him to come to lunch and meet Lopez for a chat.'

Joe smiled cheerfully.

'Going to find jobs for our famous Trio?'

'He didn't say. Leapt into his car and drove off.'

Joe took a pull at his beaker of fruit juice.

'To tell you the truth, it doesn't suit me, all this practising. I used to enjoy my guitar. Playing was fun. Now it's getting to be a chore. Of course, I enjoyed last night,' he added hastily, seeing the surprise on his hearers' faces. 'But enough is enough. Apart from feeling stale, I want time to take my girl out,' and he leaned forward and squeezed Sybil's hand.

Sybil returned the pressure.

'I've missed you a lot, Joe. But I'd hate to stand in your way.'

'There you are, it's all got so serious. I tell you, darling, I've no ambitions in the music line, beyond giving myself and my friends a bit of enjoyment.' His round, good-humoured face was serious. 'In fact I'm not ambitious at all. I like my job at the bank, and I'm sure of a regular rise. And if that's enough for you, Sybil, it's enough for me.'

'It's all I've ever wanted,' Sybil told him. 'But what will the others say?'

'I'm afraid I don't care.' He glanced at Penny apologetically. 'If Eric wants to forge ahead, and Lopez, or someone of that sort, gives him solid encouragement, he won't need me—or Gloria, either—to help him on his way.'

'What about Gloria?' Sybil queried.

'She may make a scene, but she won't really care. She knows, really, she'd never make the grade as a professional. Hasn't the temperament—nor even the desire. Anyway,' he added darkly, 'her present ambitions seem to be running in a very different direction.'

If he had intended to elucidate this somewhat mysterious statement, he had no chance of doing so. There was the sound of visitors arriving on the front verandah, of men's voices, and the three of them trooped out of the kitchen to find Pete and Stephen there, apologising for being in their working clothes on a Sunday morning.

'It's Steve's fault,' Pete was declaring cheerfully.

' Insists that we go up to the forest with a few volunteers to make absolutely sure that heavy rain hasn't done any harm to our half-finished work.' He winked. 'Not quite human, Steve isn't.'

'Well, I'm glad you're here, so that I can offer you both an apology for last night's—er—frolic!' Joe wore a half-ashamed grin. 'I hope your car wasn't splashed too badly.'

Stephen gave him an odd look.

'Noble of you to apologise, when it wasn't your fault. I could see you weren't the driver, in spite of the pace you were going.'

Penny felt herself flushing at this sidelong tilt at Eric.

'I expect they were all a bit high,' she observed as airily as she could. 'And one can't really wonder, after their triumph.'

Maybe he didn't hear. At all events he made no comment. And the next minute he was in friendly conversation with Mr Marsden, showing a consideration and respect for the deaf old man which, despite her annoyance with him, she found wholly praiseworthy.

CHAPTER V

It was inevitable that Eric's name should crop up again now.

Mrs Marsden, clearly surprised that he was not of the company, enquired of Penny in the most natural way what she had done with her good-looking boy-friend. And it had to come out, all over again, that he had gone down to Port Leon alone for a special interview with the great Manoel Lopez.

To the old Marsdens this didn't mean very much. They had heard of him through dear Joe, Sybil's fiancé, but their own memories of star performers went back to an earlier day. They couldn't really keep up with the waves of new idols which had come on the scene since those halcyon days.

Stephen alone seemed startled, and then only for a split second. But Penny, noticing this, observed also that his face was unusually thoughtful, and that he did not join in the general conversation for a while.

Penny was the first to make a move to go, and at once Stephen and Pete announced that it was high time they, too, were on their way. They would run her home, if they might, and then collect their picnic lunch from the Forestry Office and drive up to the Takhana Plantation to see how many volunteers had turned up.

'You and Pete are fanatics about your work,' Joe teased them. 'Here we are, nearly at the dry season, and a few showers of rain send you scuttling up the mountainside. You must have been beavers in a pre-existence!'

The two men were not to be drawn. They merely grinned. And a minute or two later they were making their farewells and leading Penny out into the street where their estate car was parked.

'Sorry we can't invite you to come with us this time, Penny,' Pete remarked cheerfully, as he installed her in the one empty space in the back seat. 'Especially as your boy-friend has deserted you on a Sunday afternoon.'

'That's O.K.,' she returned quickly. 'I didn't expect you to suggest it.'

But she wasn't very pleased when Stephen put in, as they neared the Dale bungalow—speaking in a bland tone: 'Our charming Penny won't want to go traipsing about the forests when she gets even on the fringes of the glamorous pop world.'

A remark which Penny decided to greet with silence.

Exactly why she felt so ruffled she didn't quite know. But justly or unjustly, she was annoyed with Eric and Stephen and, needless to say, with Gloria. Indeed she felt slightly irritated with everyone.

It was certainly a relief to hear, when she got home, that Gloria was having a day in bed, to recover from the arduous labours and excitements of the previous night. But even her mother's affectionate concern over her own evident weariness fretted Penny. She was ashamed of betraying ungraciousness without the power to control it.

After lunch she turned down, almost brusquely, the idea of a Sunday afternoon siesta. She wanted fresh air. And no! She wasn't going to bother getting the Mini out. She would take a book and a rug, and cut across the fields to the river-bank. It was cool and shady there, and very restful.

Her parents were too sensible to comment. It was clear that their darling Penny was over-tired. That was why she was in this difficult mood. Wise of her to plump for fresh air after all those hours last night in a crowded ballroom. She would be her old self when she came home again.

The hot sun had done away with all the visible effects of last night's rain, so she noticed vaguely as she crossed the open ground where a few goats were browsing, and made her way towards the line of trees bordering the river.

She loved to hear the sound of the water, all the more so because once the dry weather set in it would gradually diminish until at last, it would dwindle to a sluggish trickle with no beauty at all.

Because of last night's rain she expected to find it brown and muddy, and indeed, though very little deeper, it was not quite so clear as usual.

She had half intended to paddle. The stones were smooth-rounded by time, and it could be a pleasant experience. But today it did not tempt her.

She decided instead to be lazy, and settled herself on her rug, trying to steer her mind away from troubling thoughts. Trying to find peace by steeping herself in the tranquil beauty around her: the reflection of grey-green leaves, shimmering in the broken surface of the stream and, lovelier still, of salmon-pink blossom, hanging in splendour from a nearby water-immortelle: the piercing sweetness of bird calls, the fragrance of flowers from shrub and bush.

She dozed for a while, but the ground was too hard for comfortable sleep, and when she awoke restlessness returned. Impatiently she sat up, pulled out the book she had brought and, frowning, began to pore over lists and descriptions of drugs 'commonly used in medical practice.'

She had closed the book and was scribbling away in a notebook when she heard voices approaching, and looking up saw the spare figure of Juan Garcia approaching. He had several small youngsters with him—his grandchildren—and when he saw her, he waved.

Next moment he was up with her, and the children, with the characteristic friendliness of West Indians, were quickly all round her, with gay greetings, and calls to her to admire this little dress, or that bunch of dried-up flowers, or maybe a toy gun.

Their eager chat and laughter did more to banish her gloom than all the beauties of nature. They brought fun—and that, at the moment, was what she needed.

Presently, with the inconsequence of puppies, they moved off a little way, and Juan Garcia asked permission to sit down beside her.

She made room willingly for the kind old man, wishing she had a cushion to offer him. But he assured her that it wasn't luxury he wanted, just a little rest for his tired legs. He greatly enjoyed his Sunday afternoons with his grandchildren, but the years, he confessed, were beginning to tell.

If his limbs were weary, his eyes were sharp enough. He spotted the brown-covered pharmacy book, and asked her, almost accusingly, why she was bothering about dull old ciphers and figures on this glorious Sunday afternoon.

'Partly because I'm feeling restless, but even more because I know I shall lose ground, if I don't make more of an effort,' she told him.

'But surely, child, it's far easier to study at home, in the peace of your own comfortable and spacious room. It's grand out here, I admit, but in the open air there are so many distractions. Why,' and he laughed wryly, 'I myself am one!'

'A welcome one,' she assured him, smiling.

'Also to concentrate,' he continued, 'you need a comfortable chair and a sizeable table, on which you can spread out your books and papers. It's particularly necessary when you are copying out all these tiresome lists and figures.'

She shrugged her shoulders.

'I could manage better if I had my own bedroom, but I've let my stepsister take it over. It's quieter than the little one I have now, as well as being much larger. And as she doesn't sleep so well—'

He shook his grey head, his lips pursed tightly.

'That is more generous than is reasonable.'

She looked at him helplessly.

'We didn't think she'd be staying with us this long— indefinitely, it sometimes seems.'

He sighed.

'I wish I could think of some way to be of use,' he said. 'If only we had a spare room to lend you for a study until the young lady takes her departure. But we are painfully cramped.' He sighed again. 'Life can be very difficult!'

A sentiment with which she fully agreed.

The children came back now to bear him off. They had surprised a brightly coloured lizard with a crest on its head and wanted to know if it was an iguana. He must come at once and see.

He pulled himself to his feet, smiling, and they all went off with friendly good-byes and much waving, leaving Penny to resume her studies.

'Dear old Juan,' she thought, as she opened her books again. 'Gloria has been mean to him as long as I can remember. Treats him like a fuddy-duddy when he serves her. And he has never a criticism to make of her. Tolerance is his creed. Maybe I'd be better if I copied him a bit.'

She was even less successful now in committing these dry facts and figures to memory. It wasn't so much that the brief encounter with Juan Garcia and his grandchildren had snapped the thread of her thoughts, but the discovery that numerous other people had apparently decided to come out before the sun went down, and stroll along the river bank.

Some of them she recognised with a start of surprise as tourists who had been dancing at last night's ball. Doubtless officials in Port Leon, grasping the chance of promoting tourism, had arranged for a coach to drive them to some of the island's beauty spots. If this was so, Val Fleury would hardly be omitted.

Tempted to go home at once, she hesitated. Gloria would probably have got up by now, and she just didn't want to encounter her a minute sooner than necessary. But while she was pondering a shadow fell across the rug, and down dropped Eric beside her.

' Don't look so surprised, my dear,' he exclaimed, his eyes dancing. ' I dashed along to your home, as soon as I got back from Port Leon—mercifully I was ahead of that blinking coach Perez had organised—and your parents told me where I was likely to find you. I'm glad you didn't disappear into the forest, for once in a way!'

She ignored that last remark. Spoken in fun, Eric could have no idea that it held a tiny barb—because to-day Stephen had made it so clear that he did not want her company.

' How did you get on with the great man?' she demanded. ' You couldn't have been with him very long, surely?'

' Barely ten minutes, as things turned out,' he admitted. ' There were other more important guests at lunch with him. But that was time enough for him to give me not only warm encouragement, but reasonable hope for the future. He wants me to start planning to go to Rio— yes, Rio! Don't look so startled, dear!'

' But what about your job here?' she asked, as coolly as she could.

'Oh, I'm to hold on to it for the present. I need some first-rate lessons—as of course I know very well—and these will cost money. I must save what I can, but he has some wealthy business acquaintances who, he says, will quite certainly give me financial backing, if he convinces them that I have a future.'

She was tempted to say: 'What about me, Eric?' But he hadn't finished his story yet.

'It won't be the first time he's discovered talent, and got solid support for it, he says. And he's emphasising that he won't prophesy stardom. To become leading guitarist in a top-notch combination—that should be my ultimate aim. And it's certainly good enough for me.'

'It sounds sufficiently ambitious,' she observed.

'Exactly. You see, to be a star you have to be a solo singer. The voice doesn't matter too much, because you sing with a mike. But putting it across! That's the crux.'

'Of course. But you could sing with the rest of the band.'

'I'm sure of it. Oh, darling, I'm glad you have faith in me!' And his arm went quickly round her waist.

Gently she freed herself. This was too public a place at the moment for displays of affection. Nor was she in the mood for them.

'I suppose he didn't mention Joe—or Gloria?' she asked him.

'Oh, yes. He said Joe was an out-and-out amateur, and none the worse for that. Gloria? Just that she was a highly desirable creature with strong potentialities for mischief—which it might be amusing to plumb. A funny chap, Lopez, in some ways.'

The little throng of tourists was thinning now, as they began to make their way towards the road where, no doubt, their coach was waiting. And Penny, still wanting no caress from him, gathered up her belongings and stood up.

'Time I went home,' she said. 'By the way, Eric, I take it you'll try to keep all this to yourself. If your boss at the Stores thinks you're contemplating leaving, he may get someone else in quick to train for the job.'

He nodded. 'Of course. But secrecy won't be necessary long, I'm sure. Perez says that when Manoel decides to act, he does so very quickly.'

They walked over now to his car, reaching it just in time to see the coachload of tourists disappearing in the direction of Port Leon.

With every step she wondered when he was going to speak of her own future, which so far he seemed to be ignoring. And at last, as they got into the car, he did so.

'We may have to have rather a long engagement,' he said, 'because it will be some time before I can support a wife. But, darling, it will be gloriously worth-while in the end. My earnings will make my salary at the Stores look like chickenfeed. We'll have a lovely house, two or three cars, a gorgeous swimming-pool—! I've been planning it all on the drive up from the coast.'

'While I stay in Val Fleury helping with the dispensing,' she thought. 'For years and years!'

'It will be hard on you, Penny, I'm afraid,' he went on, starting up the engine. 'But I'd fly back to see you whenever I could. You might even, if you liked the idea, get a job over in Rio, so as to be near me. That training in pharmacy, when you finish it, would be a big help in finding work.'

She managed to smile.

'It's all rather in the clouds at present, Eric. And you know, I haven't a passion for great wealth, for glamorous surroundings.'

He smiled back at her confidently.

'We've never tasted real luxury, you and I. Perhaps when we've tried it, we may enjoy it.' And he added in an altered tone: 'It's not so much riches I'm after, Penny. It's success. I want the family forced to acknowledge that I'm far from being the thick-headed mediocrity they've always thought—the nervous ditherer! I want them admitting that I've beaten them all.'

'They may not think much of pop as a career,' she pointed out lightly.

'Maybe not. But they think a hell of a lot about money,' was his quick response. 'And to think that I'll be able to patronise them. Penny! You can't think what a kick that gives me.'

Soon they had reached her home and now he stopped the car and took her in his arms. 'Oh, Penny darling,' he said, ' it's a little miracle. And whether you like Gloria or not, you must admit, as I do, that we owe it all to her. If she had never come here, we'd be plodding away in the same old groove, with no hope of anything very much better—ever!'

Penny felt like snapping: ' Grateful to Gloria. Speak for yourself.' But she controlled herself. Not for any-thing—certainly not to relieve her taut feelings—would she cast a damper on Eric's happy enthusiasm.

It wasn't altogether praiseworthy that he wanted so badly to confound his unsympathetic relations. But it was understandable.

' I'm glad fate is being kind to you, my dear,' she said simply, and almost mechanically raised her face for his kiss.

She would have liked to tell her parents the results of Eric's interview with Manoel Lopez, but he had spoken in strict confidence. So, though she longed to discuss it with them, to give vent to her very mixed conclusions, she merely told them that Mr Lopez had apparently been kind and encouraging, and left it at that.

Naturally they were not blind to her unrest, but she was making so evident an effort to be serene and cheer-ful that they willingly co-operated, simply by behaving in their normal fashion.

With Gloria still resting in her room, the atmosphere was peaceful and pleasant, and soon Penny, sitting at supper with her parents, was chatting about the tiny events of the afternoon: of the appearance of tourists on the river-bank, of her encounter with Juan Garcia, and his gay little imps of grandchildren.

The Dales, too, had seen the tourists—but only as they passed the house in their coach, on the way, a neighbour had told them, to visit the old Spanish church and the modern school beside it.

From this, conversation centred on the island's hopes of benefiting from tourism—hopes made stronger by the fact that the formation of the bay at Port Leon made the building of a new harbour unnecessary—a heavy expense which several of the islands had been obliged to shoulder.

Altogether a happy, restful evening, just like so many others she had spent in past years. ' We're in a groove here,' Eric would have said, in his newly awakened discontent with his surroundings. And perhaps they were, concentrating too much on the affairs of their little island. But whether she ought to be ashamed of herself or not, she was obliged to concede that insularity had its charms. At least one was not drawn into the rat race of the great world, something she feared and hated.

Monday proved an unusually busy day at the pharmacy. A quantity of long-awaited goods arrived from Port Leon, carried from Canada by the liner that had brought the tourists. And Penny was one of those called upon to help sort them out in the yard at the side of the shop.

Among them were photographic supplies, and when Penny had collected them, and sundry other lightweight items, she packed up her Mini and started off on an extensive delivery round.

Usually the Forestry Office was her first port of call. She had always enjoyed that, sure of a welcome from the exuberant Airedale, at least—hopeful even of a brief, friendly chat with Stephen, if she arrived there when he happened to be engaged on office work.

But to-day he was almost the last person she wanted to see. With Gloria exercising her charm on him, he no longer seemed his old self. He had always been reserved. Now he was evasive. She was no longer truly at ease with him: doubted if she ever would be again.

Her tour this morning took her to out-of-the-way shacks, chiefly delivering baby-foods to isolated families; protein preparations, too, she carried with her for invalids and the very old—all prescribed by the hardworking local doctor, but difficult of speedy collection by people with little or no means of transport.

It was a tiring job, and one which would have defeated any stranger to the island. More often than not she had to abandon the Mini, and climb rough paths in order to reach the widely scattered houses, which bore neither names nor numbers. But the welcome which greeted her was heart-warming. No money passed. Meagre in resources though the island might be, there was enough in the kitty to provide essential medical supplies to the poorest. Instead, it was she who was on the receiving side. Here an orange was pressed into her hand, with a 'God bless you, chile!' Or it might be a coconut, or a little bunch of fresh vegetables.

For they all knew that she was under no necessity to make the journey. Only kindness of heart brought her, to spare them the trek into Val Fleury. Even before she had had the little car, she had done her best to reach them when any kind of hold-up had occurred.

Her final destination was the Forestry Office. Here, not even Larry was there to greet her. But the elderly servant who had been left in charge—a taciturn person devoted to Stephen and Pete, but hostile, it seemed, to the rest of the community—came up to take the roll of films from her, with a grunt which she took as equivalent to a thank-you.

He was seldom in evidence, preferring to let callers cope as best they could. But to-day, to her surprise, he stopped to speak to her. She was even more astonished when she heard the words he muttered.

'You've a witch in your house. A temptress to sin. When the time comes, you just remember what the Bible says. "You shall not suffer a witch to live".'

And with a piercing glance from his black eyes, he turned away, and talking to himself now about fornication and hell-fire—so far as she could gather—went round to the back of the building.

Stephen had told her years ago that Isaac, though utterly trustworthy and an excellent servant, was, on some points, as mad as a hatter. Apparently his muddled brain still held vestiges of strange superstitions reaching back to the days when his forebears, snatched into slavery from the forests of Africa, clung to the only thing that remained to them—their primitive belief, handing these down to mingle with the Christian doctrines which they later acquired.

She was glad to get away from him, to hop into the Mini and make for home. Already she was late, tired and hungry, too.

To her dismay, she found herself walking straight into trouble. The family had finished their meal, but were still sitting round the table. And Gloria and her stepfather were locked in angry argument.

The moment she entered Gloria turned on her. 'If you wanted your bedroom back, why couldn't you have come and asked me about it?' she cried. 'Going behind my back and whining to old Garcia—who's always hated me! Aren't you ashamed?'

'Hold your tongue!' her father thundered. 'We've asked you politely to move your things into the little room, so that Penny has space to study. I'm only ashamed of leaving it to Garcia to point out her difficulties.'

Brenda, on her feet by now, took Penny by the arm.

'Come into the kitchen, my dear,' she said quietly. 'Pearl's keeping your lunch hot for you. Take no notice of what's going on. I knew there'd be an explosion sooner or later. Robert has been getting more and more irritated with Gloria.'

'Maybe she makin' tracks for Californy now,' Pearl observed hopefully, as she cleared a little space on the spotless kitchen table, and set a plate of curried shrimps before Penny. She pricked up her ears. 'Listen. They've stopped fightin'. She off now to her work. We-all can breathe again.'

Penny carried her plate into the sitting-room.

'Dad darling, I never dreamt Juan would say anything to you,' she exclaimed, as she sat down opposite him. 'He always seems so diffident. If I'd guessed for a moment he was going to repeat my silly grumble—'

'He said very little. Just enough to make me realise what an ass I'd been not to see your difficulty before.'

'I thought, myself, that poor old Penny had been kept out of her room long enough. But as it seemed probable that Gloria might decide to leave any time, it didn't seem worth while upsetting her.' Brenda was looking worried. 'I do so hate rows.'

'So do I,' echoed Penny. 'Let's leave things as they are until after Christmas, anyway.'

But Robert would have none of it.

'I've told her she must change rooms with you before the end of the week,' he insisted grimly. 'That would have been the right course even if you hadn't been trying to study. Fair's fair.' And as he went off, leaving Penny to follow in due course, he uttered his parting shot: ' I don't often put my foot down. Not often enough, perhaps. But this time I'm putting it down good and hard.'

When he had gone Brenda told her daughter, with a faint, whimsical smile: ' This is the accumulation, of course, of all your stepfather's irritation with Gloria. She's had him simmering at times, with her general tiresomeness, and now he's boiled over.'

Penny sighed.

' I wish, all the same, that I hadn't moaned to Juan —though it was only a little moan! Now Gloria will be more difficult than ever, and make it even harder for me to study.'

' Don't worry, darling. If Gloria plays up badly, her father will send her packing. He's had enough, he says.'

' But she says she has almost no money—and won't have until her lawyer gets things settled up and sends her some,' Penny pointed out glumly.

' Then Robert and I will have to get together and scrape our respective barrels,' was her mother's quiet rejoinder. ' Eat up your lunch, now. But leave room for some specially good ice-cream. Pearly's surpassed herself to-day.'

Busy as she was, that afternoon, helping assistants at other counters to put away their fresh supplies, she had little opportunity for fretting. But as she went home, ahead of her stepfather, who was working still on some last-minute jobs, she was dreading what might await her.

Would Gloria be there already? If so, what mood would she be in—raging, weeping hysterically, or merely sweetly injured?

Passing her stepsister's open door, she saw that she was in a flurry of packing, and would have passed by quickly, but Gloria called to her—mildly, it seemed—to come in for a minute.

But the mildness was only assumed. She enquired of Penny in frigidly polite tones why, if she had wished to have her bedroom back, she hadn't behaved in a civilised way, and said so. Why did she have to go whining to Juan Garcia—that dimwit?

Of course, it was all part of a plan made by Penny herself and her mother to get rid of her. They had worked on her father until he had acted wholly out of character, and pitched into her without giving her the chance to say a word in her own defence.

Well, she wasn't one to ignore a hint. She was moving out this very evening and going to lodge with Mrs O'Brien—who thought she'd been treated abominably. She'd be much happier and more comfortable there, with a decent-sized room, and permission to make use of her hostess's car.

Penny refrained from observing that Mrs O'Brien's house was not the cleanest in Val Fleury, by all accounts: that she was said to concentrate on a presentable salon, and leave her living quarters to take their chance. Nor that her ancient two-seater needed constant repair.

Indeed she was not even tempted to put these stray thoughts into words.

Gloria was going. There would be peace at home once more.

If Robert Dale was taken aback when he came from work at the way things had shaped, he made no comment. He would, of course, run Gloria down to Mrs O'Brien's when she was ready to leave, he said. And when Gloria retorted that Eric would be taking her, he again put his foot down—though this time quietly enough.

'You can ring him, and tell him not to trouble,' he told her. 'You are my daughter, and you leave my house in a conventional manner. Just tell me when you are ready and we'll go along.'

She shrugged her shoulders.

'Then you'd better ring Eric yourself,' she said. 'Or perhaps dear Penny would like to do so. It's all one to me.'

A remark which sent Robert straight to the telephone for an extremely brief conversation with the somewhat mystified Eric.

Although sure of a rebuff, Penny forced herself to ask Gloria, after a while, if there was anything she could do to help her and immediately regretted her conscientiousness.

'Trying to hustle me off, are you?' was Gloria's reply. 'I'm being as quick as I can. And if I was stuck, I would hardly wish for your assistance. But as you're here, I'll just say this. Now that Eric appears to be on the up-and-up, perhaps you'll stop two-timing him. Even if he doesn't see what you're up to, Stephen does. And he strongly dislikes being pursued, says he wishes you weren't such a scheming little fool.'

Penny flushed hotly.

'You expect me to believe that? When he's made it plain to me that—that he doesn't like you at all?'

Gloria threw back her head in a laugh.

'Nor does he! Anaemic emotions of that sort aren't his line. What Stephen feels for me is something a damned sight more full-blooded. But you wouldn't know anything about that.'

Brenda's voice came then, summoning them both to supper, and Penny, badly shaken, was glad to escape. As for Gloria, when she came along to take her place at the table—Robert having insisted that she had supper before she left—she conducted herself in so sweetly forgiving a manner that Penny could hardly believe she was the same person.

It was a relief to Penny and her mother when father and daughter left, but they could settle to nothing until Robert returned—not even to fixing Penny's old bedroom, so that she could move in right away.

And when he came back, he looked tired and ill, and said something which they both found disturbing.

'She's terribly impetuous, my poor unhappy Gloria,' he observed, sitting down in the nearest chair. 'I asked her how she was going to pay Mrs O'Brien for her board and lodging. Had she received any of the money she was hoping for? No, she declared, she was penniless, but it was of no consequence. She was going to give her services without salary, until her lawyer sent her a draft. I tried to get her to take some money from me, but she wouldn't take a cent. Said it was a matter of pride.' He gave a great sigh. 'She's her own worst enemy—just as Vera was. God knows what will happen to her. But I've done right to let her go. There's nothing else I could do.'

Brenda went and slipped an arm round him, and he turned to her for comfort.

'My darling,' he murmured.

Penny did not hesitate. She left them, and went to the little room she had occupied since Gloria's stay at the bungalow. The bed was still made up, and even if it had been changed, she would have slept there.

For her old room not only held Gloria's exotic perfume—but bitter memories of things she had said, the most cruel being what must count for ever as her parting remark.

Would she ever forget it?

And why, oh, why did it hurt so horribly?

CHAPTER VI

Mrs O'Brien's house, and the salon attached to it, was close enough to the pharmacy to cause Penny and her stepfather a certain amount of embarrassment. Not that they saw very much of Gloria. But when they did, she invariably wore a martyred expression, and they could not but wonder whether some of the Val Fleury people were learning to sympathise with her.

Evidently Mrs O'Brien was taking her part. While reasonably friendly when she dropped into the pharmacy to buy goods at trade prices, she was heard to remark that she loved having a young person living with her, adding in an audible whisper on one occasion, that though Gloria was, perhaps, a trifle erratic, she only needed understanding.

Such observations fell flat, so far as the staff was concerned: one and all were a hundred per cent loyal to Robert. But it wasn't to them she spoke in this way. It was to other customers—people fairly new to the village. And it annoyed Robert so much he began to talk blackly of refusing to serve her—at least at the usual discount. Of telling her to take her custom down to Port Leon.

Penny counselled him to do no such thing, and felt pretty sure that Juan Garcia, the old dispenser, had given him the same advice. At all events he dropped the idea and even refrained from mentioning the matter at home.

By and large, it wasn't a very happy time for Penny. Knowing Gloria's disregard for the truth, she was well aware of her foolishness in letting her words about Stephen rankle. All the same Stephen, whom she had liked and trusted all these years, talking to him with the utmost freedom, had changed towards her: always reserved over his own affairs, he had now become a clam.

Nor could she draw comfort from Eric's affection. Thrilled over the future, his talk became more and more centred on himself, making her feel she was a mere appendage to his plans. What her own feelings were over living in South America, in totally different conditions did not, it seem, strike him as of any particular interest.

Feeling forced to keep any doubts and anxieties to herself, she found as time went by, that she was being too scrupulous.

It was necessary for him to practise his guitar, but even if his landlady had been agreeable to his doing so, he could not get far without someone to accompany him on the piano. At his present level, help of this kind was essential.

Very few people in Val Fleury had pianos, having scrapped them long ago for radiograms. Indeed the only person who possessed one of any merit whatever was Mrs O'Brien, in whose rather tawdry sitting-room an ancient instrument, with a pleated front of green silk, and a pair of gilt candlesticks, held pride of place. She didn't play it herself, but because her late husband had done so, she kept it reasonably well tuned. Gloria could do so, however, and, in her goodness of heart—as Eric enthusiastically phrased it—agreed to give him fairly regular assistance.

The arrangement had barely begun when rumours spread, some of them so near the truth, that he could hardly give them the lie direct. And as so often when he was worried he came hurrying to Penny for advice and sympathy.

'How I hate living in a village!' he burst out when, after supper he was sitting with her on the back verandah. 'One can't make the least move without causing talk. Either I'm having a love affair with Gloria, or else I'm slogging away at my guitar because I'm bent on a professional career somewhere abroad.'

Penny shrugged her shoulders. It was something that Eric still was frank and simple enough to speak impatiently and without embarrassment over a supposed romantic attachment to Gloria: he clearly regarded that notion as ridiculous.

'Why do you let gossip bother you?' she asked quietly. 'The truth is bound to come out soon.'

'Because if I don't walk circumspectly I shall be in danger of losing my job, before I can afford to give it up. Farrow spoke to me this morning, said that if I was likely to leave the Stores at a moment's notice, he must know—not because he disapproved of my taking up work I found more congenial, but because he would need time to train someone in my place. All I could promise, in common honesty, was to give him as long notice as I possibly could. And I'm not sure he was completely satisfied.'

'If you assured him of a clear four weeks, he could hardly complain,' Penny suggested encouragingly. 'I know the work you've been doing since Mr Farrow promoted you is quite complicated, but even so—'

'Darling, you don't understand,' he interrupted. 'If Lopez sends for me to go to him at once, I shall have to fling my things together and catch the first possible plane to the mainland. He's a creature of impulse—that's obvious when one's talked to him for five minutes. If I annoy him by temporising, he may easily wash his hands of me. Perez has warned me of that.'

Penny sighed.

'The world of Manoel Lopez is very different from ours. Are you sure you would be happy in it, Eric?'

He gave a short laugh.

'You think I'd rather stay here? In this cramped little village where everyone knows one's business—or thinks so—before one has even considered it oneself. Not on your life!'

'People here are friendly, even if they do gossip a bit,' she pointed out gently. 'They're always ready to help one out in a difficulty.'

'So they would in a large town—with the resources to do so.' And then suddenly he looked at her, and noticed her troubled expression.

'My dear, you've done so much for me in the past. Surely you're ready to go a step farther, and encourage me to launch out on a splendid career.'

She looked back at him with tears in her eyes.

'Eric, I don't want to be selfish. And I'd be more than happy to see you successful. But I've neither the inclination nor the temperament to join the rat race—especially in a foreign country. I'm not even madly keen on the guitar. You'll think me a nitwit, an ignoramus, but I really enjoy steel band music far more.'

'Chaps with no musical education whatever thumping away on old kerosene tins!' he gibed, suddenly angry.

His contemptuous tone made her fire up, too.

'If I do admire them, I'm in good company,' she exclaimed. 'People flock to the big islands to hear them and dance to their kind of music. If we want to get tourists here, that's what we'll have to give them.'

'Please God, I'll be out of the Caribbean altogether before long,' he snapped. And then he began to look a little ashamed of himself. 'Sorry to be ill-tempered, darling. I suppose I'm on edge. But you seem different somehow from what you used to be.'

'I should have thought you were the one who had changed.'

'I don't know. Sometimes I almost wonder whether —oh, it's silly of me, of course—whether you're going to back out of our engagement.'

'We're not officially engaged, Eric, never have been. I've given you no definite promise. You've given me no ring.'

'Our understanding, then!'

She hesitated.

'Don't you understand, Eric, that I'm bewildered. Even if you and I haven't, as persons, changed in the last few months—and I think we have, both of us—circumstances have certainly altered. The future has a very different look.'

'My dear, you've seen so little of the world, led such a cramped life—you're scared stiff, naturally. When you've had time to consider matters, I'm sure the idea of a different existence in a strange country won't seem so alarming. Anyway don't rush now into decisions you may regret. Let things bide, as my old nurse in Jamaica used to say.'

A strange thought—or was it really so very strange?— flashed into her mind. Surely with the right man—a man truly loved—a woman would go joyously, without fear, to the end of the world.

But she said nothing, and soon after a gentle kiss, he said good-night and left her. A gentle kiss, as always. Sign of a chivalrous nature, she had always thought— influenced more than she knew by the serene, quiet-voiced nuns from whom she had received much of her schooling.

But suddenly thought was swept aside and feelings took its place, which she tried in vain to subdue. Feelings which humiliated her by their very force.

She was, to her shame, imagining Stephen's mouth crushed against hers. Wasn't that how he would kiss the woman he loved—desiring and expecting her happy, warm response?

Then the cold wind of sanity came in a wild gust, bringing chilly rain, like tears, to disperse the madness.

What was all this to her? Nothing! Stephen might pretend to find her attractive, get a kick out of teasing her. But his passion was all for Gloria. He betrayed himself at every turn, whatever he might say to imply his dislike and contempt for her.

Gloria had said as much, and for once, Penny believed, she had been speaking the truth.

'As for me,' she reflected stonily, 'how disloyal can one get? How paltry! Putting a damper on Eric's natural ambition, just because I love—love—'

She choked on the words she was trying to say: 'because I love Val Fleury!' They just wouldn't come.

And almost crying with the sudden pain of self-knowledge—for so, in that moment it seemed to her—she went stumbling into the house.

Tired out, she slept heavily that night, and awoke to the feeling that common sense had returned: that she was once again her level-headed self.

This feverish concern with Stephen's supposed emotions. This even more dangerous straying of her own! It was high time she took a hold on herself and, clear-eyed over Stephen and his surprising propensity for intrigue, put him out of her head.

But even so the problem of Eric remained.

He was a darling, and his gentleness towards her was a virtue, not a weakness. Shameful to think otherwise! But she just couldn't see herself settling happily into the world of show business. And if she wasn't happy, what use would she be to Eric as a wife? With the very best intentions on her part, she might very well become a drag on him.

He would be unhappy, of course, and very sore, if she broke away from him now. But in South America, in a new and wider circle, he would surely find other girls eager to share in his exciting career.

'I shall have to tell him,' she thought, a shade wistfully. 'It will be painful for me as well as for him. For stupid as it is, when he's older and cleverer than me, I've felt sometimes as though he was my child.'

And with the memory of his plea that she should leave things as they were for a while, she was half relieved to carry out his wish. The moment for giving him her decision would come soon enough.

But things did not work out that day precisely as she had anticipated.

In the early afternoon, Stephen came in and walked straight up to her.

'Sorry to bother you, Penny,' he said, in his curtly amiable fashion, 'but that last parcel of film you brought to the Forestry Office was not what I ordered. No good for my cameras at all. Here it is,' and he lifted a package on to her counter. 'You can see by the label it's wrong.'

Penny looked at it in dismay. She prided herself on her accuracy, but this time she had, it was clear, slipped up.

'I'm extremely sorry,' she told him, with a hint of stiffness in her voice—due more to embarrassment at this unexpected encounter than to her mistake.

'Not to worry! But will it take much time to find the right one?'

'A few minutes, I'm afraid. The stockroom's pretty full up just now. Could you call back? Say, in half an hour, to be on the safe side?'

He hesitated.

'Not to-day, I'm afraid. I've just collected the mail, and I find there's some correspondence requiring an immediate answer. But don't look so bothered, Penny! There's not all that much hurry. I could send Isaac down, I suppose, but he's such a funny fellow.'

'You're right there,' she told him. 'He said some very queer things to me, last time I saw him.'

'Nothing to worry you, I hope?' he demanded sharply.

'Heavens, no. Has a thing about Gloria, it seems!' Somehow she could not keep that name back.

For a second his face took on a shut expression. But almost at once he was observing lightly: 'When there's a full moon he always goes off course a bit. Takes a

128

dislike to people he's barely heard of, sometimes. But I'll be off now, and collect the film just when I can.'

'Would you like me to run up with it? It won't take more than five minutes in the Mini.'

He smiled at her. 'Good girl! And I'll see you don't have to encounter poor old Isaac. What time will you come?'

'In the early afternoon,' she promised. And as she went to the storeroom to begin her search, she told herself she was the world's fool. With those nonsensical thoughts about Stephen troubling her peace, as they had done last night, why hadn't she the ordinary sense and strength of mind to keep away from him. There was no earthly need for her to take his parcel up to the Forestry Office this very afternoon. None at all.

She found the correct film more easily than she had expected, and when she carried it up saw that Sybil had come into the shop, evidently on an errand for Mrs O'Brien, since she was ordering a quantity of shampoo powders.

She made her purchase quickly and then came across to Penny.

'Can you come to supper this evening?' she asked. 'Joe's out with the boys to-night, but that's all to the good. I've something important to tell you, something that will surprise you. Once I've got the parents settled comfortably, listening to their radio, we can have a good talk.'

'Nothing too grim, I hope?' Penny tried not to sound too apprehensive.

'Something very odd,' was all Sybil would say, as she took her departure.

She told her father of her mistake over Stephen's order, and of her promise to take the right parcel up to him at the Forestry Office, half-hoping that he would offer to make the run himself, as he sometimes did when not particularly busy.

But he didn't volunteer. He had to go down to Port Leon on a business trip. But though he grumbled a little —for Stephen didn't seem to be in his good books at present—he gave her his blessing, remarking that he supposed as the mistake was hers, it was up to her to put it right. And anyway, she wouldn't be long away from her counter.

Greeted exuberantly by Larry, and less effusively by Stephen, she was prepared to hand over the parcel and leave.

But he asked her casually if she would come in for a moment, as he had something to say to her, and she followed him into his bare, ultra-masculine office and sat on the only really comfortable chair—known to her by long experience as the one to choose.

'I've an invitation for you,' he said. 'In the old days when you sat there in a gym dress and white ankle socks, you would have called it one of my "treats". But you may look on it as a bore now.'

'Give me a chance to judge,' was her cool reply. 'I'm not readily bored.'

'Of that I'm well aware,' he told her drily. 'Otherwise you wouldn't have condescended to come on treks with me. But with these glamorous prospects ahead of you now, one can't expect you to be quite so easily amused.'

'Oh, rot, Stephen,' she told him impatiently. 'What is this blessed treat?'

He relaxed.

'That's more like you, Penny! Pete and I are giving a little film show next week, not only illustrating our work in the woods and forests but giving shots of various places up there which we both regard as beauty spots. We're asking a few friends to come along—people who have shown interest in what we're doing. And we're providing light refreshments. Does it appeal to you at all?'

She nodded.

'Of course it does. Can I bring my parents along?'

'Naturally. And your boy-friend too, if you think he'd find time from his rehearsing.'

She looked at him sharply, but he was giving nothing away. And after a minute she remarked smoothly: 'You and Pete call yourselves hermits, but you don't seem to miss much of what goes on in the village.'

He shrugged his shoulders.

'Bits and pieces of news drift up to the woods,' he admitted. 'And calypsos! The workmen seize on the oddest scraps of gossip and turn them into ribald songs. One can't stop them. And anyway, they can be quite amusing at times—provided they don't come too close to the bone, and puncture one's own self-esteem.'

She stood up then.

' I'll come with pleasure,' she said. ' I'll be off now.'
And then, pausing, she observed: ' If you want help with
the refreshments, Sybil and I would come up a bit earlier
and do what we could.'

He shook his head, laughing.

' Do you think Isaac would permit that? Not for a
minute. He'll get in a couple of relatives and turn out
something pretty good, I'm sure. Anyway, he can't be
faulted for coffee, whatever he lacks in other directions.'

She smiled back at him.

' I thought he'd not want us,' she said.

He escorted her to the car, his manner so pleasantly
prosaic, so impersonal, that she wondered how last night's
crazy thoughts and impulses could ever have stirred her.

But as he took her arm to help her in, she found, dismayed, that she could hardly control a tremor. Terrified
that he might notice—and be secretly amused—she turned
her face away, started up the engine and without even
waving good-bye was off as fast as she could reasonably go.

At work she could hide her unrest. True, there was
not much activity in the photographic section, but with
her father away in Port Leon, Juan Garcia was glad of
her assistance in small routine matters, requiring neatness
and accuracy, rather than knowledge or skill.

Checking the numbers of tablets in various glass jars
was hardly a thrilling occupation, nor were the other
jobs he handed over to her. But at least they called for
concentration. She simply couldn't let her mind go
straying. She must live in the immediate minute.

It was a relief, too, that she was going to supper at the
Marsdens'. An evening alone with her parents would
have been, for the first time in her life, an ordeal. They
would have known that there was something troubling
her deeply; and she could not possibly have given them
her confidence. It was something she would have to
deal with alone as best she could.

With Sybil it would be different. She would be too full
of her exciting news to notice anything unusual about
her friend. She had nothing to worry about on that
score.

And that was just how things turned out.

She helped Sybil prepare supper and sat down to share the simple meal with her and her parents—managing, somehow, to chat to the old people as though she hadn't a care in the world.

Mr Marsden, older by ten years than his wife, and a friendly soul, liked to talk of the past, when there were still a few Caribs living at the far end of the island, with their own primitive way of life, their ancient skills. But Mrs Marsden, able to get about, though not as much as she would have liked, was more interested in modern matters, and full of questions about the fashions prevailing in Port Leon, the latest people to assume importance in the affairs of Santa Rita. Feeling somehow, it seemed, that Penny, though a little younger, would be more up in these matters than Sybil.

Once they were left to their radio programme, Sybil and Penny retired to the kitchen to wash up and—far more important—to talk in freedom.

Until they had cleared up and were sitting down to coffee, Sybil would say nothing of her secret discovery. Then, elbows on table, and a mysterious expression on her attractive face, she told Penny: 'It's about Gloria. You know how she pleads lack of funds as a reason for working at the Hibiscus, and indeed for staying in Val Fleury at all. Well, it's utterly untrue.'

'How on earth do you know?' Penny demanded in astonishment. 'Dad certainly doesn't!'

'Up to now, the only people who must have been aware of the situation are Joe and his manager. And they're under oath to disclose nothing of their clients' affairs—except when the law requires it. But someone, going to the bank at a time when no one is ordinarily there, saw Gloria cashing a very large cheque.'

'But Gloria wouldn't do that in front of any other customer. She's far too fly!'

Penny looked, and felt, incredulous.

'Not if it had been anyone she thought mattered. But it was someone who would never swim into her ken, someone far too obscure. The old mother, in fact, of Rebecca, the girl who comes here to clean occasionally. Apparently some relative in Trinidad had sent her a crossed postal order, and she was told she would have to cash it at the bank.' She sipped her coffee. 'Dim-witted as the old girl appeared to be, she didn't miss the wad of notes which Gloria was pushing into her handbag. And though Gloria doesn't know her from Adam, she recognised Gloria at once.'

'And when did you hear this?'

'Only yesterday, when Rebecca mentioned it to me, quite casually. You see, neither she nor her mother had any idea Gloria was anything *but* wealthy. So the little transaction, which evidently took place some weeks ago, caused them no particular surprise. What puzzled them was why Gloria should want to work at the Salon when, in Rebecca's own words, "she might be living like a lady". Which was rather hard, I thought, on yours truly!'

'What's Gloria's idea in keeping it dark that she's in funds again?' Penny exclaimed. 'We've never expected anything from her—and never had anything. Unless she was planning to diddle Dad into paying her fare to America for her.'

'I'm sure she has a much stronger motive than that,' Sybil told her. 'You see, there's something else I've learnt—only yesterday. I overheard Mrs O'Brien thanking her effusively for something—and promising to keep quiet about it. " I can settle up my overdraft completely now " was what she said. What Gloria's reply was, I've no idea, for I skipped. I didn't want to be accused of eavesdropping, because nothing was further from my intention.'

Penny's amazement had increased.

'But, Sybil, I simply don't understand. Unless it's just an impulsive act of kindness on Gloria's part.'

'Sorry, but I don't think it's anything of the sort. I've noticed in a vague sort of way that since Gloria's been working here, Mrs O'Brien seems to be spending more than usual. And I've come to the conclusion that it's all connected with Gloria's intention of staying on in Val Fleury without causing tiresome comment.'

'But *why*?'

'Because she's crazy over Stephen,' came Sybil's swift reply. 'According to Mother, they were close friends when you and I were away at boarding-school. Caused a bit of gossip, in fact. Then there was a

133

rupture, and Gloria persuaded your stepfather to send her to New York for a hairdressing course. Now, having met up with him again, she's determined to get him back.'

'You mean she wants to marry him?' Penny was suddenly feeling rather sick.

'Not if he stays in his present job, I'm sure. It would be more accurate to say simply that she wants him—and leave it at that. It may be that he jilted her, and that it's a question of pride. But I'm pretty sure that plain, ordinary passion is involved, too. She's a voluptuous creature.'

Penny tried to drink her coffee, but nearly choked over it, and Sybil, leaning across the table, took her hand.

'I'm not blind, Penny; and we've been intimate friends for years,' she said gently. 'Eric's a nice boy. But if you feel he's not for you, break things off with him.' She hesitated before adding: 'As for Stephen, if, as I can't help suspecting, you've come to love him—! Well, you've assets, in yourself, that Gloria has never had—and never will have. So go in and win!'

Penny brushed away the threatening tears, half relieved at Sybil's frankness.

'I'll have a darned good try,' she said. 'Though—' And now she was half laughing, half crying, 'it's a bit like David and Goliath, when I think of vanquishing Gloria!'

CHAPTER VII

Brave words. But that courageous mood didn't last. No longer, indeed, than it took her to reach home again.

Then, lacking Sybil's confident and enthusiastic support, she told herself that the notion of snatching Stephen from Gloria's clutches was not only theatrical nonsense, but utterly childish. Indeed it made her cheeks burn even to think of it.

Stephen was no weakling, like poor—! She stopped short in her reflections, realising that she had been on the point of saying, if only to herself, 'like poor Eric!'

What was coming over her? How could she be so disloyal to Eric? Think of him as weak, when she was such a fatuous fool herself?

And how, for goodness' sake, imagine that she could ever win Stephen to love her?

Even if there were no Gloria to reckon with, there were plenty of other attractive women, sophisticated, and nearer his own age, even in this little island. Women whom he would not think of addressing as 'kid' in that casual, big-brother fashion.

'I must tell Sybil as soon as I can to forget what I said to her to-night,' she decided. 'Explain that I was talking twaddle. And I must put this crazy nonsense right out of my head.'

That last resolution should have been made easier by the fact that Stephen had now gone up to the forests again. She learned this when she dropped in at the Marsdens' home in her lunch hour for a private word with Sybil. Her friend didn't approve of her change of front, but she was not the kind of person to interfere.

'It's your own business, Penny dear,' she said, 'and of course you can count on me to be an oyster,' and then told her, Joe having heard it from Pete, that the two forest officers would be away until the very day of their little film show.

Rather to her relief she saw little of Eric. She had promised to let things slide for the moment, so far as their 'understanding' was concerned. But her mind was really made up. On this matter at least there was no wavering. It was just a question of finding the right time to tell Eric of her firm and unshakable resolve: the time when it would be least likely to distress him.

'And that,' she thought, 'will be when he gets a definite summons to join Manoel Lopez in Rio. He'll be far too thrilled over his dazzling prospects to take my defection to heart too badly. And once he's over there, in that different world, he may even be relieved at my sensible decision.'

It was borne in on her soon, however, that he was far from having reached that stage of placid resignation.

He came down to see her at her home the very day before the film show at the Forestry Office, looking highly elated, and brandishing a piece of pasteboard.

'It's a ticket for two. Tom Perez sent it to me, for that charity dinner to-morrow evening. All the important people in Port Leon are attending, and it's only because of a last-minute cancellation that he's able to get us in. There's to be dancing afterwards—to the steel bands you like so much—and a tombola with marvellous prizes—'

'But I can't possibly go,' she interrupted at last. 'I'm booked to go with my parents to the film show which Pete and Stephen have arranged, up at the Forestry Office.'

He flushed with annoyance and disappointment.

'What's stopping Mr and Mrs Dale going by themselves? You can't tell me seriously that a potty affair like that—a film made by out-and-out amateurs—is going to stand in the way of your having a really super evening down at the Palace Hotel?'

'I'm sorry, Eric, but I've accepted the invitation, and I can't just throw Steve and Pete over because something more exciting happens to turn up.' What a hypocrite she felt saying this!

'You could ask them if they minded. They'd surely understand.'

'They'd say so, of course. But it wouldn't alter their opinion of my manners.'

'Just the kind of petty nonsense one gets in a tiny community like this!' Thoroughly irritated, he began to pace up and down the room. 'Thank heaven I'll soon be out of it. Living among people who'll have something more exciting to think about than silly, shackling conventions. I sometimes wonder how I've breathed this stifling atmosphere so long.'

'You liked Val Fleury when you first came here,' she pointed out, controlling her rising indignation. 'I remember your saying, after a while, that you felt yourself to be an individual—someone who counted—in this tucked-away village. That in your old home, you were swamped—'

'Oh, I know all that,' he broke in hastily. 'But I've developed since then. As one should.'

Those last words held a note of accusation. She was tempted to retort: 'And you think I haven't! That I'm still an ingenuous schoolgirl. Well, you're wrong. I'm a mature and normal woman.'

But even to think along those lines brought bewilderment and unhappiness and she said instead: 'To come down to brass tacks, I couldn't give Stephen even the shortest notice. He and Pete don't come back until tomorrow, just in time to get ready for their party.'

His impatience grew.

'You seem to know a lot about Stephen's movements. What any of you girls can see in that boorish chap, goodness knows. Even Gloria, who ought to have more sense, is nuts about him, though she'd never admit it. My own guess is that they were lovers once, and she still has this *tendresse* for him—if you can use that phrase about such a fiery customer.'

Taken aback, she thought: 'You've certainly changed, Eric, to talk in that man-of-the-world way.' But she didn't believe that his wild conjecture had any truth in it. Not for a moment. Steve was just not that sort of man. He wouldn't have a hole-and-corner love affair—an intrigue—with a girl in Gloria's position, living quietly at home with her father and stepmother.

Eric was still talking.

'All the same,' he was saying, 'if Gloria had to choose between a luxurious evening at the Palace Hotel and sitting on a hard chair watching an amateur film, I think the scales would dip down in my direction. Of course, any entertainment in Port Leon is small beer for her, compared to what she enjoys in America. Still, to dress

137

up and drink champagne has its charms, wherever she finds herself.'

'Then why not ask her to go with you?' Penny suggested. 'She's beautiful, has a wonderful wardrobe. She'd certainly do you credit.'

'I'd rather have you with me, all the same, Penny,' he said then, his old self for a moment. 'There's something about you—oh, I don't know what. A kind of sweetness. It's consideration for the feelings of those two chaps in the Forestry Office, I know, that makes you hate the idea of throwing them over at the last minute. So you must have your way. I'll take Gloria. She'll jump at the invitation.'

She was glad to reach a peaceful conclusion to the argument. Secretly pleased, too, that she would not have to encounter Gloria at the film show.

But things did not work out as she—and Eric—had anticipated.

Gloria rang up at lunch-time the following afternoon, all gaiety and good cheer, to ask if she could go with the family to the party at the Forestry Office.

'Maude O'Brien hasn't been invited,' she told her stepmother, 'and I hate going anywhere on my own. So if you and Dad and Penny could put up with my company—'

Naturally Mrs Dale had no option but to tell Gloria that they would be very glad to have her with them. And Robert, though a little surprised at his daughter's friendly overture, was mildly pleased. Only Penny was disappointed and dismayed, though she tried to put a good face on it.

So Gloria had plumped for a hard chair—and as much of Steve's society as she could obtain. And Eric would be left without a partner. But that, she reflected quickly, need not happen unless he had grown too proud to take one of the girls from the Store, and give them the treat of their lives.

Suppose, however, he got in touch with her now and told her of his disappointment. Could she conceivably throw over those standards of courtesy which she had preached so smugly to him? It wouldn't be all that enjoyable, spending an evening in Gloria's company.

But she shook off the idea immediately. Whether from

praiseworthy motives or selfish ones, she was going to Stephen's show.

In the event, Eric made no move, and there it was.

Gloria, all smiles, and slightly overdressed in a cocktail suit of white and silver, joined them for a light meal. And off they drove soon afterwards, in appearance, at least, a united family, Robert driving, with his wife beside him, Penny and Gloria behind.

Although they arrived in good time, the familiar, somewhat untidy office, miraculously transformed into a miniature cinema, was beginning to fill up. Stephen and Pete, fiddling with the projector, had their backs turned to the door, and it was left to Isaac, neatly sháved and obviously in his Sunday best, to collect the invitation cards from the guests as they came along, and show them, with the solemnity of a churchwarden, to their seats.

Penny, aware that this duty was extra to his work behind the scenes, of preparing refreshments, ventured a friendly word of congratulation to him, and was rewarded, not indeed by a smile, but by a dignified little bow, and a flicker in his dark, hooded eyes which might be appreciation.

But at the sight of Gloria, just behind her, he stiffened. And when she observed casually that she hadn't bothered to bring her ticket, his expression changed. He positively glared.

'No admission without ticket,' he snapped. 'Mister Vaughan, he say so. Otherwise too many people come crowdin' in, an' no room left.'

'Rubbish! I'm his cousin, as you know very well,' Gloria retorted sharply, adding under her breath to her embarrassed young stepsister: 'Goodness knows why Steve and Pete keep on this obstinate, useless old fool. He should have been pensioned off years ago.'

From the piercing glance which Isaac gave Gloria, Penny felt certain that he had heard. But before more trouble could ensue Stephen, having fixed the projector to his satisfaction, turned towards the doorway. Just for a second a look of surprise and displeasure displaced his welcoming smile. But it went as quickly as it came, and he told Isaac evenly that there were some seats left in the third row; he'd show Mr Dale's party there himself.

'I knew everything would be all right,' Gloria observed comfortably, as they all sat down. 'Stupid of me to leave the card on Mrs O'Brien's sideboard. But I've a head like a sieve, I'm afraid.'

Penny, certain in her own mind that Gloria had not received an invitation, that she was simply a gate-crasher, made no comment. But she heard her step-father, seated on the other side of Gloria, remark: 'I'm afraid you've never been one of Isaac's favourites, my dear.'

She laughed. 'Far from it. He's been atrociously rude to me ever since I was a schoolgirl—on the few occasions when I came within his ken. But because, in his own way, he looks after Stephen and Pete pretty well—and discourages intruders as possible sneak-thieves —they won't give him the push. But he's getting on. One day he'll drop dead from sheer ill-temper and jealousy, and then presumably they'll install someone more civilised.'

It was a characteristically ill-natured little speech, Penny thought, and so apparently did her stepfather, for he turned away to occupy himself in conversation with his wife.

But Gloria, it seemed, hadn't finished.

'Oh, he attends chapel and all that,' she went on. 'But as you know yourself, psalm-singing can be a screen for something more sinister! I bet he goes in for voodoo on the quiet. In fact,' and she giggled, a shade nervously, 'I shouldn't be surprised if he'd tried to put a curse on me before now. Made a wax image of me and stuck pins into it. Especially after one unfortunate encounter.'

'Why should he take a dislike to you, of all people?' Penny asked suddenly, her mind flying to that 'guess' of Eric's which she had found so ridiculous.

Something in her tone startled Gloria, but she observed casually enough, the next minute: 'He's insanely jealous, the silly old chap. Stephen and I were, as you know, very good friends when we were younger. And he resented it. Mad, my dear, quite mad.'

The lights went down now, and the show began, Pete manipulating the camera, and Stephen furnishing the explanations.

Relieved at the impossibility of further conversation with Gloria, Penny gave her whole attention to the excellent photography and accompanying talk.

The film, in colour, had many facets, showing aspects of the work of which even she knew little. Large areas were shown, where valuable trees had been ruthlessly cut down without any replanting having been undertaken: or where sheer carelessness had caused disastrous fires—with serious loss of revenue to the island. Then, in more optimistic strain, came scenes where a fresh beginning was made with methodical clearing of such derelict sites: of consultation with the forestry departments of other islands on the choice of the most satisfactory trees to replace the treasure so wantonly destroyed.

'For the trees in our woods and forests are of immense value,' came Stephen's deep voice. 'Tourism is a big help to prosperity, of course, but we shouldn't rely on it, nor need we. With more money and more trained assistance we could increase our exports of *mora* and teak, of mahogany and sandbox, enormously. The world wants timber—and we have it. So let's stop wasting our heritage and learn to appreciate it, not only for its usefulness, but for its sheer beauty.'

'He'll bore everyone stiff, if he goes on like this,' Gloria whispered to Penny.

She did not reply. It was clear that he was holding the attention of his audience. But having made his point with magnificent pictures of the trees he had mentioned, he now turned to the wild life of the forests, which it was part of the work of a forester to protect.

If his audience were interested before—with food for thought—they were now entranced. Birds of every brilliant colour, seldom if ever seen at lower levels, flashed through blossom-laden trees. Manakins were shown in the mating season with males clearing individual patches of ground of litter and leaves, in preparation for their dancing displays, designed to attract admiring females. Humming-birds, too, with plumage bright as jewels, hovering over honey-laden flowers, and bellbirds with anvil-like voices said to carry for half a mile And scores of others.

Mammals came next, some so shy that to photograph them must have taken endless patience, though the capuchin monkeys, eager to entertain, suffered no such inhibitions.

But it was the snakes that caused a sudden quickening of interest, shots of an enormous boa-constrictor lying peacefully in the middle of a woodland path evoking exclamations of dismay here and there.

'Do you have to protect creatures like that?' came Gloria's incredulous voice.

'Certainly,' Stephen returned coolly. 'They're valuable. Rats are a favourite food with them—and other pests. They might go for an unwary human if they were ravenous. But I've never known of a case in all the years I've lived here.' And then he added politely: 'But may we keep questions until the end, please.'

With a shrug Gloria subsided, and Stephen continued his commentary.

To Penny, at least, it seemed no time at all until, the film coming to a stop and the lights going on, he announced an interval for refreshments, to be followed by questions from the audience.

'I expect most of you will be glad to stretch your legs,' he added with an apologetic smile. 'I'm afraid the chairs are not very comfortable, but I'm pressing the powers-that-be to import a skilled cabinet-maker into the island, an artist-craftsman who could teach our carpenters to make far better use of our splendid local wood. Handsome, well-designed furniture could mean valuable exports, and more of the prosperity we all want for our beloved Santa Rita.'

People greeted the little speech with hearty applause, and responding to his invitation, began to stand up and form themselves into little groups. And soon Isaac appeared with two of his young relatives, bringing trays of coffee and tiny savouries. With an adroitness which Penny found remarkable he poured out each cup of coffee individually and handed it to a guest, making a slight inclination of the head as he did so. It was evidently his notion of politeness, and it touched Penny. He wanted to please Stephen, who had probably tried to impress on him the need for courtesy on such an occasion.

Even Gloria noticed his efforts at ceremonious behaviour.

'Stephen probably tore a strip off him for his rudeness to me at the door,' she remarked complacently. 'And it's about time he stopped pampering the old fool. Firmness pays dividends. Why, believe it or not, he positively smiled at me when he handed me my coffee. Served it in one of Stephen's special Crown Derby cups, too.'

'He certainly makes excellent coffee,' Brenda put in appreciatively. 'And in his odd fashion waits quite competently. It's no wonder Stephen and Pete won't hear of pensioning him off.'

'I don't think much of his coffee.' Gloria was a little supercilious again. 'But of course over in America we get spoiled. We have the best of everything,' Adding hastily: 'Though, of course, Brenda, your coffee is first-rate.'

'Pearl makes it as a rule,' was Brenda's cool reply. 'And now let's get back to our seats before the row gets too full.'

'Okay! But I'm going to have a word with Stephen first. After all, I'm the only member of his family who's here.'

'Second cousin at that,' Penny thought, with irritation, as she followed her mother and stepfather, and then thought suddenly, with pain blotting out vexation: 'But there's been a far closer relationship, if Eric's guess has any truth. Even now, perhaps, it's reviving again—or how could she be so confident? Yet she's gate-crashing this evening, I'm sure of that. And he positively snubbed her over that question she asked him.' She suppressed a deep sigh. God knew what it was all about. She certainly didn't. And if she had a grain of sense she wouldn't be bothering her head about it.

Pete's pleasant voice came now, asking everyone to return to their seats, and as the lights went down, Gloria returned to her place beside Penny.

'Just another short film to show you something you've probably heard about but may not have seen—our famous blue butterflies which can only breed at a very high altitude. After that, Stephen will be delighted to answer all the questions you like to put.'

And now came a series of stills. First, shots of a

gigantic tree, festooned with creepers and vines, in which reddish-coloured monkeys leapt and swung. Then, as they fled, leaping through other great trees, Stephen was shown starting to climb up the first tall trunk, carrying his movie-camera.

' Pete took these,' Stephen explained. ' At that time we had only one movie-camera between us, so he had to use an ordinary one. But to get this last picture he had to do some climbing too, in a nearby giant.'

Now came a shot which made the audience gasp.

There was Stephen perched precariously at the very top of his chosen tree, looking horribly unsafe, but holding his camera steadily at the ready.

' To get the butterflies one has to soar oneself,' he remarked, ' even using a telescopic lens. They spend most of their short, adult lives high up in the ether. Just a minute, and you'll be seeing them.'

And there they were, as large as small birds, and as blue as the sky above them, moving gracefully as ballerinas in intricate dance.

The clapping was thunderous, not only for the beauty of the scene, but for the arduous work which had gone to capturing it.

Thanking them, he observed modestly that though it took only moments to show them the film, it had taken days to make it, searching the forest, and then waiting and waiting for a chance to begin.

Gloria, Penny noticed with surprise, had not joined in the applause. Surely she could not pretend, in bored fashion, that they had bigger and better butterflies in California.

' She'll liven up when questions begin,' she thought impatiently. But not a word did Gloria utter. She just sat back in the uncomfortable chair, staring at Stephen in silence—until suddenly she bent double, uttered a cry and collapsed on to the wooden floor.

There was a stir in the rows nearest the Dale party, and in a moment Robert had pushed past his wife and stepdaughter, and was trying to raise Gloria in his arms.

' I must get her out into the air,' he exclaimed. ' Open the doors, someone!'

' A lady's fainted,' came Stephen's quiet authoritative voice. ' Please, don't panic.' And he called out to

Pete: 'Get the brandy as quick as you can.'

Brenda and Penny, following Robert out into the yard to where the family car was parked, heard Gloria moaning.

'It's colic,' they heard her telling her father in a feverish mutter. 'I'm in terrible pain.'

'All right, child,' came his soothing answer. 'We're taking you home, and soon the doctor will be coming. Meanwhile Pete's bringing some brandy.'

It was Stephen who brought the flask along. He was looking pale, and profoundly disturbed.

'I'll fetch Dr Henderson, if you'd like me to,' he told Robert.

'I would indeed,' came the crisp reply. He put the flask to Gloria's lips, but she jerked her head away. 'I'm sick, deadly sick,' she groaned. 'And the pain—I can't bear it. Morphia, that's what I want.'

'Bring the doctor to our bungalow,' Robert told Stephen. 'And for God's sake go quickly. Sorry to spoil your party, but this is serious.'

'I'll take Penny with me. Gloria will need the back of the car to herself,' Stephen said quickly, with a glance at Penny's white face.

'No; I want her in the back with me,' came Gloria's whining voice. 'She must hold me. I'm scared to be alone.'

Before Brenda could make a move, Penny was in the car.

Cradling the sufferer in her arms, she thought she would never forget that drive home in the starlight. Gloria, so adept at play-acting, was not fooling now. She tried to pillow her head on her stepsister's shoulder, then restlessly moved away, writhing with pain, shifted her position this way and that, now flinging out an arm, now bending double, with no respite from agony and distress.

At last they were home, and Brenda and Penny, without even a word of discussion, got Robert to carry her into the room she had occupied during her stay at the bungalow, and deposit her carefully on Penny's bed.

Time dragged until the doctor arrived.

But at last he was there, following Brenda into the room where Gloria lay writhing on the bed, sweat pouring from her agonised, distorted face.

In the sitting-room Stephen, white with shock and distress, was talking quietly to Robert and Penny.

'I'm so afraid there was something wrong with the food. Stale fish in the sandwiches, or something like that. The best of servants can be careless and unobservant in that sort of way. And Isaac had those youngsters helping him.'

A horrifying thought shot through Penny's mind, but she held her tongue. And Stephen went on desperately: 'If that's so, there will be others suffering in the same way. It will be a minor epidemic—or something very like it.'

'Don't get worked up, son.' Penny had never heard her stepfather speak so kindly to Stephen. 'It may not be food-poisoning at all. May be a sudden violent chill.'

Brenda came out of the bedroom then, running towards the kitchen.

'Please God, it's going to be all right,' she called out to them. 'I'm preparing an emetic.'

Robert went out after her, and Penny, looking haggardly at Stephen said quietly: 'Isaac served her with coffee in a special cup from your best set. We all enjoyed ours. She didn't—and said so.'

Stephen jumped up.

'Penny, you're not implying—'

She shivered.

'I'm remembering what Isaac said to me, the last time I brought up a parcel for you. He spoke of Gloria and quoted from the Bible. "Thou shalt not suffer a witch to live."'

'Crackpot as he is, I can't believe he'd do such a thing,' Stephen exclaimed. 'He's always hated her, but—' And then his face lightened. 'He could hardly have planned anything. She wasn't invited, and he knew it.'

She shrugged her shoulders, thinking: 'If he really went in for voodoo, he might have some very odd things in his possession—herbal poisons included.'

As though by telepathy, he suddenly—taut again— put that very same thought of hers into words, adding vehemently: 'Why did she have to come when I purposely left her off the list? She knew I couldn't refuse her a place on any pretext, when she came with your mother and stepfather.'

Robert came back just then.

'Steve, I can't thank you enough for getting Mr Henderson along so quickly,' he said hurriedly. 'He has just told me how you had to go hunting for him up hill and down dale. It's severe food-poisoning, he says. But the strong emetic worked, before the poison could spread through other parts of her body. He's putting her under sedation very shortly, says she's going to be all right.'

Relief swept over Penny. Gone was any thought of Gloria's maddening behaviour—gone any desire to be free of her disturbing presence. Only thankfulness remained, not only for Gloria herself, or even for her father, but for Stephen, on whose life tragedy might well have cast a lasting shadow.

Soon the doctor was out, too—brisk and ginger-headed.

'She'll do,' was his curt comment. 'She's a fine, healthy lass. Needs cosseting for a few days. Then she'll be as good as new.' He looked at Stephen. 'Shall we be on our way now?'

'Of course. I'm very much at your service.'

'That's fine.' He glanced round the room. 'No symptoms from the rest of you? Mrs Dale says she feels fine, so here's hoping there are no similar cases. If there are, a strong emetic administered at once is the safe thing. But I should be sent for, all the same.'

Tempted as Robert and Brenda were to sit up and discuss how the near-disaster could have occurred, they persuaded Penny to go to bed quickly in that tiny bedroom she had occupied as a child and young schoolgirl. And soon, discovering themselves to be equally exhausted, they turned in themselves.

The effects of Gloria's sedative would last, Dr Henderson had said, at least until early morning. They could hope to sleep in peace.

Gloria was still asleep when, urged by Brenda, Penny drove off to the pharmacy next morning.

It was useless their hanging around, Brenda maintained, racking their brains about last night's happenings, worrying themselves to bits over it. All Gloria needed now was complete rest and quiet, with the lightest possible diet. Far better for them to get down to work, and leave herself and Pearl to cope.

They found, on reaching the shop, that the news of Gloria's sudden and violent attack of colic had trickled to both staff and customers, causing sympathy, but no great excitement. In the tropics digestive upsets were, after all, fairly common. She was recovering, nursed by her kind and competent stepmother, and that was all that needed to be said about it.

Mrs O'Brien had been one of the first to learn of Gloria's collapse. Sybil who, sitting with Joe last night in a corner of the room, had seen the sick girl being carried out to Robert Dale's car, had popped in on her way home to tell her what had happened.

Now, sending Sybil to the shop as her messenger, she expressed warm sympathy, with the promise to call on the patient soon.

But Stephen, dashing in around ten o'clock, was the only person, Penny felt, to show keen concern. He relaxed slightly when Penny assured him that she had left Gloria fast asleep, but still looked so haggard and exhausted that Penny, lowering her voice, said accusingly that she didn't believe he had slept a wink all night.

'No. And neither has Pete,' he admitted. 'But I can't talk about it here. It's too public. Could I have a word with you and Robert in his office?'

Robert was even more startled by Stephen's obvious distress and fatigue.

'Don't take it so hard,' he said gruffly. 'That double journey last night, driving Henderson, must have been grim. But you certainly needn't worry yourself to shreds over Gloria. She'll be as right as rain in a few days.' He went to a wall cupboard and brought out a couple of bottles and a glass.

'Chemists aren't too ignorant to prescribe for simple ailments,' he remarked drily. 'A rum and ginger ale is fine as a pick-me-up, as well you know. Sit down, relax and drink it up.'

Penny, always conscious of the age gap between herself

and Stephen, saw him momentarily in a very different light. Maybe it was the way her father was speaking to him—treating him almost as a youngster—as indeed he was, compared with Robert—or maybe because of that great tiredness, which gave him such a vulnerable look.

He took the drink without arguing, and colour came back to his face.

'Pete and I were up late, clearing the place, and washing up.' He paused. 'Washing up all the cups—except one. That was back, clean as a new pin, among the rest of my Crown Derby set.'

'But what happened to Isaac and his nephews?' Robert demanded. 'How could they leave you and Pete in the lurch like that?'

'Vanished, all three of them,' was Stephen's curt answer. 'Making their way through the hills and woods to the far end of the island, that's my guess.' He paused a moment before asking the older man: 'Do you want me to get the police in? To institute a search for Isaac—to prosecute him for attempted murder?'

Robert stared back at him for a moment in stunned silence.

Then he said heavily: 'No, Stephen, I don't. I shall have to consult Gloria, I suppose, but I'm pretty sure she'll agree. Isaac's a crackpot, and he'll never appear in these parts again, I'm certain. Far better to hush things up.' He glanced at Penny. 'You'll think that's a strange decision, but Stephen will understand.'

'I do,' Stephen said evenly. 'Of course, if Gloria had—had died—'

He broke off, and Robert nodded. 'That would have been different—perhaps. But as things are—well, you can congratulate yourself that she didn't. Fetching Dr Henderson with such miraculous speed probably saved her life. Henderson thought so himself, I know. Another hour and it might have been too late.'

'Thank God for a good car, and some years of experience on these mountain roads,' was Stephen's comment. 'But it's time we had a doctor again in Val Fleury. I know Dr Henderson has a very busy practice in that complex of villages where he works. But Val Fleury's grown in recent years, deserves a resident doctor and a surgery.'

Robert smiled faintly.

'When all this longed-for prosperity comes to the island no doubt our requirements will be met,' he said. 'You're not the only sufferer I've ventured to prescribe for, Stephen, by a long chalk. Though it's not normally such a pleasant-tasting dose as rum and ginger ale.'

'For which I'm much obliged, Robert!'

Stephen left them then, looking in far better shape than when he had first come in, and Penny glanced at her stepfather.

'Dad, I'm a bit bewildered,' she told him. 'But if you don't want to explain—!'

'My darling, some troubles are like wounds which should be allowed to heal and then forgotten.' He spoke with a nervousness foreign to him. 'But as you may or may not be aware, there was a scandal centring round Stephen and Gloria a few years ago. This is an old-fashioned island where the word " permissive " chiefly applies to the poor and uneducated. So when a rumour started there was soon a lot of talk. I was hurt and angry at the time, and though I've got over it now, of course, I should hate a revival of gossip.' He hesitated. 'By accident, Isaac learned more than he should about things. But he's so loyal to Stephen that once Gloria left Santa Rita, he never betrayed any knowledge he had come by—not by the blink of an eyelid.' And then he added: 'Mind you, I'm not saying there was anything seriously wrong. But there was certainly grave indis-cretion.'

She went over to him and kissed him.

'Thank you, Dad,' she said quietly, and went back to her counter.

But at lunch-time something happened to turn her mind away from all this. Eric telephoned, just before she was leaving for home, so anxious for a private conversation with her that she let her stepfather drive off without her. She was going for a very short run with Eric, she explained: he would drop her at the bungalow in ten minutes or so.

'Well, if he wants to come to lunch bring him along, my dear—and let's hope he's more cheerful than he's been lately.' Robert started up the engine. 'I'll tell your mother, and she'll lay another place in case.'

But the moment Eric came into the shop to fetch her, she knew that there was something very wrong.

His buoyant spirits had evaporated. His good-looking face wore a stricken expression, and when he spoke to her the old stammer, which she had slowly and perseveringly helped him to conquer from the very beginnings of her friendship with him was again apparent.

'I can't take this, after all that trouble over Stephen,' she thought desperately. 'It's too much. He's going to tell me that Lopez has let him down—as I've known subconsciously he would—and I don't want to hear anything about it.'

But to imagine she could reject his confidences was wishful thinking. She would have to listen and sympathise: treat him with tact and kindness.

No question of making it plain to him at present that she was in earnest over breaking her half-promise to marry him. That revelation would have to wait. But if only he hadn't come to her with his woes to-day, when she was feeling so played out and depressed.

If she couldn't look as serene as usual, she just couldn't help it, she told herself, as she got into his car. But indeed he was in no state to notice her expression, being utterly absorbed in his own gloomy reflections.

He drove a little way up the road to the mountains, and quickly found a parking space, a small green glade where a few goats were browsing in charge of a tiny boy. One of Pearl's numerous grandsons, she guessed, as he grinned and waved, for the track that led to her cottage was only a few yards away.

The moment Eric stopped the engine, he pulled a folded newspaper out of his pocket.

'Tom Perez gave this to me last night,' he said, adding as he handed it to her: 'He marked the paragraph in blue.'

It took Penny only a second or two to take in the news which had shattered Eric so badly: that 'the famous guitarist', Manoel Lopez, was leaving immediately for a tour of Europe.

'Leaving without a syllable of explanation or advice to me, after all his promises—all the hopes he held out to me,' Eric exclaimed in a stricken voice. 'Oh, *Penny*!'

'I'm terribly sorry, dear.' She slipped a comforting arm through his. 'But it's probably only a case of postponement. The tour may not take very long, and even if it does, he'll be coming back to Rio eventually. You'll be able to contact him there—it's not all that far away—and maybe he'll still want to help you.'

He shook his head.

'Perez says these tours of his last months and months. Admits, too, that Manoel is a creature of impulse. When he came to the Palace Hotel for a rest, Perez expected him to stay for at least ten days. But he didn't. Off he flew again.'

Penny hesitated.

'He said you needed to go to a first-class teacher in Rio—to develop your very evident talent. Though maybe those weren't his exact words. I suppose if you wrote and told your father that, he wouldn't help you out with a worthwhile loan. You could pay it back by instalments when you started to earn.'

Eric gave a hard little laugh.

'You don't know my father. If I'd won a scholarship to a university he'd have backed me to the hilt. But his idea of a guitarist is someone who thrums rubbishy tunes, and puts down an old hat to collect coins from passers-by. My mother's not quite so crassly ignorant, but she thinks I'm the fool of the family, too.'

His tone was terribly bitter, and Penny longed to console and encourage him. But all she could find to say was: 'Don't give up so easily, Eric. Lots of people have a very hard struggle before they reach success.'

He shrugged his shoulders.

'I can't see any hope for me at all. Thank goodness I've not chucked up my job. And Penny, if there's one gleam of light in the darkness, it's having you at my side—helping and encouraging me, as you've done ever since we first came to know each other. How I wished you had been with me last night, instead of that giggling girl from the groceries.'

And then suddenly, deaf to the sound of occasional traffic on the road to and from the mountains, he swept her into his arms, and kissed her—holding her as though he would never let her go.

She broke away from him, ruffled in spite of herself.

'Eric, it's not all that private here!'

'What does it matter?' His voice was jealously possessive now. 'Everyone knows you're my girl!'

If only she could have told him shortly: 'Well, I'm not. I don't belong to anybody but myself!'

Instead she said quietly: 'Time I was home for lunch. Are you coming to join us?' adding: 'Incidentally, you haven't made a single inquiry after Gloria.'

'Good lord! How awful of me—after all her kindness. I won't come to a meal, but maybe I could just pop in and see her for a moment. If she's up to visitors, that is.'

'Mum will know. But let's get going anyway.'

'As you say.' He backed the car very carefully into the road, the small boy with the goats waved cheerily, and in a matter of minutes they were at the Dale bungalow.

Gloria was not, however, visible. She had been awake part of the morning, and taken some milk and cereal, but was now deeply asleep again, and no one was particularly sorry when Eric took himself off.

They were tired, all three of them, longed to be on their own.

By evening, however, Gloria had revived considerably. Enough, anyway, to demand her make-up box and hairbrush.

And Robert, though dreading the inevitable discussion with her over Isaac—whether she wished to prosecute him or not, if he could indeed be traced, or whether she wished to forget the incident—nerved himself to go to her room.

The talk, whether acrimonious or not, was certainly short.

'She's not in the least surprised that suspicion has fallen on Isaac,' he told his wife and daughter, when he came back into the sitting-room. 'And she'd dearly like to have him arrested and punished. But like myself she doesn't want a fuss or scandal, with people singing calypsos about the incident. So I can tell Stephen not to inform the police. Which will be a relief to him, too. It's bad enough for him and Pete that their party was ruined.'

'Not really, dear.' In spite of her fatigue, Brenda

Dale still maintained her habitual air of gentle calm. 'We had all those glorious films. I've not enjoyed anything so much for a long time, and when I next see Stephen I shall tell him so. I couldn't think of anything last night but Gloria, I'm afraid.'

'Mind you, she wants to have a word with Stephen about it herself.' Robert was frowning a little now. 'I told her it wasn't necessary, that it would only tire her, when she badly needed to rest and relax.' He shrugged his broad shoulders. 'But you know what she is. Insists on my asking him to come as soon as possible.'

He went off to telephone, and came back to say that Stephen would call to see Gloria for a few minutes to-morrow afternoon, between three and half-past.

'No doubt he's relieved that she's behaving reasonably,' Brenda remarked. 'As far as trying to have Isaac caught and prosecuted, that is.'

Penny said nothing. She thought, eyeing her mother: 'And she'll expect you to wait on her hand and foot, making her look as attractive as possible for Stephen's visit. If you were a different sort of person, Mum, you'd refuse to take an ounce more trouble—unless, of course, it's dread of a scene. Hysterics, and all that!'

She wasn't, herself, at home next day when Stephen was due to arrive at the bungalow. As usual, she was at work all afternoon, dividing her time between normal duties at the shop and picking up odd scraps of pharmaceutical knowledge behind the scenes to supplement her regular studies.

She was at her counter when he dropped in about four o'clock, and wondered if he was going to say anything to her of his call on Gloria. But to her surprise and hurt he gave her a brief nod, went over to the door of her father's office, and disappeared from view—without one word to her. He emerged in a matter of seconds, went to the cosmetics counter to buy some shaving cream, and went off, again with that curt nod.

More deeply wounded than she cared to admit, even to herself, she fell to wondering whether Gloria, with her genius for trouble-making, had said something to prejudice him against her. But she quickly dismissed the notion. Stephen's fundamental good sense put it out of court. Even if he didn't know his attractive cousin's propensity for lying, and he certainly did, he was the last person to be moved by gossip and scandal. Far more likely that he was in a generally irascible mood, angry with himself for not having suspected what might be the results of Isaac's unconcealed hatred of Gloria, for believing that the old man, daft in some ways, was capable of serious crime.

Why, she herself, though half afraid of Isaac, hadn't for a moment taken seriously his grim quotation from the Old Testament. Surely Stephen, too, would have brushed it aside, had she repeated it to him—even striving, absurdly, to imitate the old man's sinister accents and expression.

At home, asked by her mother to take some tea to Gloria, she found her step-sister looking weary, indeed, but faintly elated. She was in a delightful cotton wrapper, white, splashed with bronze and yellow chrysanthemums, and at her throat she wore the gleaming topaz necklace.

The colour of the flowers and the necklace might have been an unwise choice for an invalid, but she had evidently taken immense trouble with her make-up. Her skin was pale but clear, and her cheeks the tint of roses, and her hair was so simply arranged as to suggest the artlessness of youth.

It was a splendid achievement which Penny was forced, however grudgingly, to admire. Whatever qualities Gloria lacked, determination, and the gift of making the most of her appearance, were hers in full measure. They betokened, she had to admit, a kind of courage, which could battle successfully against illness and fatigue.

'Stephen was sweet to me,' Gloria told Penny softly, smiling to herself at the memory. 'Thinks I'm marvellous to take this barefaced attempt to murder me with so little fuss. But then, as I reminded him, we come of a tough family, he and I—tracing our ancestry on one side back to the fabulously brave Spanish *conquistadores*.' Then a spark of resentment sprang into her glorious dark eyes. 'He ought to have adopted a more worth-while career than that of forestry officer in an obscure little island—just because he happened to be born here, and liked a country life. But it's useless to argue with him. I know that now. Though I wouldn't believe it five years ago.'

'*When you were lovers?*' Dared Penny ask that
question which suddenly sprang into her mind?

But while the words trembled on her lips, Gloria gave
a great sigh and sank against the pillow supporting
her head, the clever make-up powerless to disguise the
unhealthy pallor which spread over her face.

'I'm all in, Penny,' she murmured. 'Utterly exhausted all at once. Take the tea away and ask your
mother to come in and help me undress. That's all I
want—to rest and sleep—and be alone.'

'I hope she isn't going to have a relapse,' Penny told
her mother fearfully, when she flew to summon her.
'She looks pretty ghastly.'

But Brenda shook her head.

'All that fuss about dressing up for Stephen—that's
what's made her so tired. She's not fit for visitors yet,
especially one who excites her the way Stephen does.
Mind, it's not his fault. He would have far preferred not
to come. But with his servant trying to murder her, he
could hardly refuse.'

And she went off to do what she could for her wilful
and difficult stepdaughter.

Mrs O'Brien was Gloria's next visitor. She arrived
fashionably dressed and made-up the following day, but
with an air of uneasiness which Penny, who went to the
front door to greet her, found a little surprising. Surely
Maudie realised by now that the invalid was well on the
road to complete recovery.

'Don't worry about Gloria, Mrs O'Brien,' she said
reassuringly. 'She'll be up and about in a day or two.
In fact, the doctor says that by the end of the week she'll
be as good as new.'

Mrs O'Brien looked relieved.

'I'm glad to hear that. I hope she'll be back at work
well before the Christmas rush—and staying with me
again, if you and your parents can spare her. I miss her.
It's lonesome living alone.'

'We can spare her very well indeed,' was Penny's
coolly amused reflection. But all she said was: 'She'll
be very pleased to see you, I'm sure. I'll just tell her
you're here.'

Gloria, though forewarned of Mrs O'Brien's intention

of visiting her, had made no effort to dress up for her. All her clothes were expensive and most were beautiful, too. But the wrapper she chose to wear on this occasion, though flatteringly rose-coloured, had clearly seen its best days. It needed mending here and there and could even have done with a clean.

Without any intention of doing so Penny showed momentary surprise that she should be receiving a visitor in such a shabby garment, and at once Gloria's lip curled.

'What I'm wearing is quite good enough for Maude O'Brien,' she snapped. 'You should see her in the privacy of her own home, once she's peeled off her foundation and kicked her high-heeled shoes across the room.' She paused. 'Besides, I don't want her to get the idea that I'm rolling in money.'

Remembering what Sybil had hinted over Gloria's generosity to her employer, and the reason for it, Penny asked very casually: 'What on earth is it to do with Mrs O'Brien whether you're in funds or not?'

Just for a moment Gloria looked confused. But recovering quickly she observed in bored tones: 'She thinks that she can under-pay people if they happen to have private means. Not that I bear her any ill-will for her attitude. She's a bit of a muddler over money.'

Later that day, long after Mrs O'Brien had departed, Sybil, dropping in to supper, shed further light on the matter.

Sitting with Penny, after the meal, in her cramped little room, she told her: 'Settling Maudie's overdraft isn't the end of Gloria's munificence. You know we had some new equipment last year at the Salon. Well, I'm pretty sure that Gloria has taken over the monthly payments—possibly because Maudie was getting behind with them. The man from the electricity show-room in Port Leon, who comes to collect the money, dropped a brick by mentioning Gloria's name in my hearing. It was in connection with a cheque—nothing to worry about, it was quite in order. But it made me think, especially as Maudie went pink with embarrassment.'

'Did she say anything to you? Mrs O'Brien, I mean!'

'No. I think she just hoped I hadn't heard. Told

me rather sharply that Mrs Smith had been quite long enough under the dryer—which wasn't actually the case.'

'Well, Gloria can do what she wants with her own money.' Penny tried to speak in an off-hand way. 'All I wish is that she wouldn't pretend to Dad that she's still on the rocks—more or less.'

'You know what I think, Penny. That Gloria's determined to stay on in Val Fleury because of Stephen.'

'So you said before.' Penny's long-lashed hazel eyes were bright with unshed tears. 'But I don't want to talk about Steve. Except that for some reason he seems to have turned against me. Not that it matters. It's Eric I've got to worry about.'

'But, Penny dear, compared with Stephen Eric is—'

'He's my boy-friend,' Penny exclaimed, cutting her short, 'and he's been badly let down by that wretched Lopez. I've got to stick to him, for the present, anyway. He's—broken!'

Sybil looked at her friend in distress tinged with impatience.

'Oh, *dear*!' was all she said. But there was a wealth of meaning in that brief, commonplace exclamation.

CHAPTER VIII

Whatever schemes might be maturing in Gloria's head, she was clearly content for the moment to stay where she was, with nothing to do but sit back and enjoy Brenda's cosseting.

Robert, who felt that his wife was pampering his tiresome daughter far too much, uttered a protest. And when it was disregarded—Brenda secretly feeling that the sooner Gloria recovered her full strength, the sooner she would leave—he went a step farther.

Finding Gloria alone on the back verandah one early evening, he asked her, tactfully he hoped, if she intended to resume work at the Hibiscus Salon in due course.

'Not for a while anyway,' she told him languidly. 'I might go in at odd times during the Christmas rush. Otherwise—well, I heard from my lawyer in America recently, enclosing a small draft. Nothing substantial, but it'll keep me going for a bit—until he sends me something worth-while.' And she added pathetically: 'I'll be able to buy you all some little Christmas gifts, if I can manage to get a lift to Port Leon. Mrs O'Brien would lend me her car, but I'm not up to driving at present. I'm nearly well physically. But the nervous reaction—that hasn't gone yet.'

He repeated the conversation that night to his wife and stepdaughter. Brenda thought, nodding her head in satisfaction: 'If she's in funds, she won't stay here much longer, appropriating poor old Penny's room all over again.' And though Penny's reflections differed in some respects from her mother's—for Gloria had undoubtedly given her father no more than half-truths—she was glad that he would have a respite from worrying about her immediate financial needs, from attempts on her part to sponge on him.

Much of her own spare time now was taken up with Eric. Sybil didn't approve, she knew: thought she was behaving far too chivalrously. And sometimes the strain of his continual laments made her feel frantic. To feel, indeed, that she would after all have to break definitely with him, and quickly.

Once she had been able to help him—pouring self-confidence into him, buttressing his self-esteem. Now the spell was broken. Nothing she could do or say, she found, could break that dark wall of depression or inspire him with even a flicker of hope and courage. It was utterly wearing.

And there was no turning to Stephen now for sympathy and advice. He filled her thoughts, but all to no purpose.

The snub he had given her was nothing. It could well be due to natural preoccupation and anxiety over the attempt on Gloria's life.

What tormented her—tell herself as she might that it was no concern of hers—was the growing belief that at one time he and Gloria had been lovers, and would be again. It hung, this belief, in a corner of her mind like a grey, dusty cobweb. And like all cobwebs, one brushed it away one day, only to see it in the same place on the next.

Oh, she didn't sit in judgment. And to be jealous was sheer lunacy. Stephen, at least, would be horrified if he guessed the feeling he had stirred in her: could well claim that in all these years he had never shown her anything but brotherly affection.

But even brotherliness was gone now. He had changed altogether: was a different man, she sometimes felt, since Gloria's return to Val Fleury.

If only she could forget him, and concentrate more charitably on poor Eric. Find some way of bolstering up his deflated ego.

And then, within days, the totally unexpected thing happened.

Eric burst into the pharmacy at midday, and in a couple of strides with his long legs reached Penny's counter—shifting with visible impatience from one foot to another while she attended to a customer who had brought in a film for processing.

Once the woman, admittedly a ditherer, had concluded a final piece of bright conversation with Penny, and gone, Eric, his face glowing, leant over the counter, and exclaimed under his breath: ' My dear, we've misjudged Manoel badly. I've had a letter from him this morning, written before he left Rio, but posted in London. I'll take you to the cinema-café tonight for supper, and show it to you. Can't stop now.'

And he was away as quickly as he had come—handsome, gay, alert, a different person altogether from the dispirited, pallid young man who had haunted her lately.

Hoping earnestly that his new-found optimism was this time securely based, her own drooping spirits rose a little.

If his news meant that success lay ahead, she would be able at last to make a clean break with him. He would feel, no doubt, that she was treating him badly, but his unhappiness wouldn't last. Other girls would fall for his good looks and the charm which prosperity would keep alive in him. He would soon forget her, or at least come to agree that she was not the right wife for him in the new world he was entering.

Even the shedding of this one load gave her a happier expression, and though her mother was too tactful to comment openly, Penny knew that she had noticed and was pleased.

She could hardly have heard Eric's news. But all the same, when Penny told her that she was going out to supper with him that night, she observed : ' I hope you'll enjoy yourselves, dear,' in a tone which for once indicated cheerful optimism, rather than a pious wish.

The café attached to the local cinema was a humble affair compared with any similar establishment in Port Leon, but the food was reasonably good, the place clean, and a corner table had been kept for them by the stout, smiling proprietor.

While they were still eating their first course, Eric gave her the contents of Manoel Lopez' letter in words that showed he had read it over and over, and knew it almost by heart.

Manoel had been extremely busy ever since leaving Santa Rita, arranging with his agent a long-mooted tour of the main European countries. But he had found time to contact a group of wealthy men in Rio, with far-reaching interests in the field of popular entertainment. They had already financed other beginners on his recommendation, and would do the same for Eric—on the undertaking, put of course in legal form, that when fully trained and launched he would for a term of years be working under their auspices, giving them an agreed percentage of his earnings.

'You see, it's not charity,' Eric pointed out eagerly. 'Manoel has convinced them that I've a future—that to support and help me now will pay them dividends later on. Oh, Penny, his faith in me makes me feel that I don't care how hard I work, or how many sacrifices lie ahead. I'll make good, cost what it may.'

And then he went on to tell her of his more immediate plans.

His manager, George Farrow, knowing that he had been feeling thoroughly unsettled of late, already had his successor in mind—a bright young chap who had worked his way up from messenger boy to junior accountant, and was eager for greater scope and responsibility.

'Farrow says he will release me as soon as I wish,' he ended robustly. 'And that to me means at the end of the week. I shall have time to clear up my rooms, settle one or two small bills, arrange my flight to Rio, and say good-bye to all my special friends.'

Startled at these precipitate plans, she was tempted to ask him, as tactfully as she could, if he had enough money for the fairly heavy fare to Brazil; for clearly he was far from being, as yet, the sophisticated person he hoped one day to become.

But he forestalled her.

'I've been saving every cent I decently could,' he told her eagerly. 'And if I was short by a few dollars, I'm pretty sure I could borrow it. In fact, I've nothing to worry about at all, except—' and he reached for her hand across the table—'except leaving you. For it's impossible, Penny dear, for us to get married until I'm well and truly launched. And unless you could one of these days fix up a job somewhere near me—'

And then at last she told him, gently but decisively, the plain truth. That she could never marry him, because, quite simply, she no longer loved him. She refrained from adding that she knew now that she had never really done so.

'You mean that, Penny?' His astonishment was genuine. 'You've spoken that way before, but I've never taken you seriously. I just thought you were afraid of a different way of life in a strange country.'

'I have felt a bit scared,' she said haltingly. 'And

I still think I wouldn't fit into the entertainment world. All the same, I know that if I really loved you, I'd have a damned good try.' She gave a sigh. 'But you see, Eric, I don't. It's been a boy and girl affair, and there's nothing left in it now for either of us. You'll see it yourself before very long—and be grateful for your freedom.'

'You're saying all this to excuse your own fickleness,' he retorted, speaking under his breath. 'You don't care a damn that you're breaking my heart.'

She wasn't moved. She knew him too well to be deceived. That attempt to sound stricken just wasn't genuine. He was angry and resentful, because his pride was wounded. His heart was not seriously hurt—if at all.

And then he said something to reinforce that belief.

'The truth is that you're throwing me over because you've fallen for another man,' he muttered indignantly. 'But you're a fool. Stephen Vaughan might, I daresay, have come to see you as a desirable woman, if Gloria hadn't turned up again. But once she did, you hadn't a hope in hell.'

She looked at him contemptuously.

'And to think I ever cared for you!' she said, and gathering up her handbag, made her way to the exit, leaving him to settle the bill.

She had not gone far along the road when a car slowed down beside her. She thought it would certainly be Eric catching her up, and she turned her head away.

But it was Joe's cheery tones that met her.

'Hi, whatever are you doing walking the roads alone at this hour?' he demanded. 'Jump in, Penny, and I'll run you home.'

She was beside him in a flash, speechless because she was struggling with her tears. And in a few moments they were at the gate of the Dale bungalow.

He jumped out and opened it for her, observing with unexpected tact: 'I could say a lot, Penny, but I won't. Except that no one so blindly selfish as poor old Eric is worth a tear. None of us tiresome males are, perhaps.'

She gave him a watery smile.

'Joe, you're a dear. No wonder Sybil's devoted to you!'

And, determined to hide her jangled feelings as best

she could, she went into the house.

She had forgotten that her parents would be out at this time, playing Bridge with some neighbours, until she found Gloria alone in the sitting-room, looking even more glamorous than usual in her white and yellow wrapper, the topaz necklace round her slim and graceful neck.

She was mending the exquisite lace on one of her fragile, transparent nightdresses, and looked up from her work with a mixture of surprise and annoyance.

'You're back very early,' she exclaimed, with a glance at a clock on the wall. 'Look as though you'd been howling, too. Had a row with Eric, I suppose. But you'll make it up to-morrow, no doubt—if you've a grain of sense. By what I hear, he'll be a much better match for you than seemed likely at first—if you don't get sick and tired of waiting for him.'

'Can't you ever mind your own business?' Penny exclaimed, stung to anger.

Gloria gave her a fleeting glance, then resumed her stitching.

'A bit touchy this evening, aren't you! But I was only going to say that if you find yourself flung on your own resources, you needn't behave like a nun. Time will go far more quickly if you aren't too prudish. Eric will be amusing himself, no doubt, with the *senhoritas*. And —well, there are plenty of attractive men in Port Leon.'

'Thanks for nothing!' Penny snapped. 'I'm off now, so good-night!'

Gloria raised her eyebrows.

'Going to bed already?'

'No. It's a chance to catch up on my pharmacy lessons.'

'How sensible! Well, you won't be leaving me on my lonesome. I'm expecting a visitor. Stephen wants to see me. He rang up soon after Dad and Brenda left for their Bridge evening. Wanted to see Dad, too, as a matter of fact.'

'Did you say he wouldn't be in?' Penny tried to sound elaborately casual.

Gloria shot her an odd look.

'Steve was in such a hurry, he didn't give me time to say anything. But it doesn't matter. I can always tell Dad whatever it is Stephen wants him to know.'

There was the sound of a car drawing up outside, and without a word Penny, to Gloria's evident satisfaction, went off to her little bedroom. She had no hope now of concentrating on her pharmacy books—nor even on one of the detective novels she had collected, and stowed here, out of the way. She would occupy herself with something mechanical—sort out a drawer, stuffed with old letters and snapshots and greeting cards, discarded painting boxes and crayons, and tubes of dried-up glue, a job she had postponed for far too long.

But one of the first things she picked out was a battered picture postcard of a scene in Barbados, addressed to her at her convent school in Trinidad in Stephen's hand-writing, at the beginning of her first term there.

In kind, big-brotherly tones, he assured his 'dear little Penny' that she would soon get over her home-sickness and enjoy life at school. And that he would be over shortly and would get the nuns to let him take her out on the spree, before he settled down to the new term courses at the agricultural college.

She tore it up and threw it into the waste-paper basket.

Soppy nonsense to hang on to mementoes of one's childhood—precious though they had once been. But what a tiring job such sorting was, especially at the end of a trying day.

She persevered all the same for a while, filling the waste-paper basket with outworn treasures.

And then, dusty and dishevelled, her curls falling into her eyes like a Yorkshire terrier's, she heard Stephen's voice calling her.

'Penny! Will you please come here for a minute?'

She hesitated, then called back: 'If you really need me. But I'm in the middle of sorting—in no end of a mess.'

'It's only for a minute,' he persisted. 'And I bet I'm untidier still.'

She closed the drawer, nearly empty now, and went unwillingly into the sitting-room—horribly aware of the contrast her untidiness made with Gloria's elegance.

'Come along, dear!' Whatever Gloria was thinking of this interruption to her tête-à-tête with her cousin, her manner left nothing to be desired. Indeed her tones were so honeyed that Penny believed for a moment that she and Stephen were about to announce their engagement.

But Stephen said at once, walking restlessly about the room: 'I've been telling Gloria, and I want to warn your father, too, that Isaac is back in the district, if indeed he ever went, as reported, to the other end of the island. So it may be necessary to prosecute him after all.'

'And I've been telling Steve to go ahead—and engage the sympathy of the police and magistrates, so that he won't be allowed to talk a lot of hot air about his motives for giving me a passage to—' she shrugged her shoulders —'to heaven or hell.'

'While I'm trying to explain to Gloria that her suggestion smacks of bribery. However, as I don't want to burden Gloria with messages to her father—seeing that she's in no state to be bothered a fraction more than necessary—I'd like you to tell him that any decision must rest with him.'

An odd little speech, Penny thought. Not in Stephen's usual vein at all. But she said, with a pretence of indifference, aware of Gloria's eyes on her, 'As you please. And then of course he'll get in touch with you.'

'O.K. But listen, you two. I've got my dog in the car, and I want to leave him with you. Any suspicious sound, and he'll give the alarm at once.'

'But he'll recognise Isaac's footsteps—greet him as a friend,' Penny objected.

'The main thing is that he'll make a noise,' Stephen declared. 'It's all I can think of, unless I get police protection for you. And that will definitely lead to a prosecution.'

He went out and returned a moment later with the Airedale, who ignored Gloria, but gave Penny a flattering display of affection.

'Stay here, Larry, and look after the ladies,' he admonished him, and the dog, albeit a little disconsolately, sat down by Penny.

She stroked his rough head, and told Stephen: 'I'll explain things to Dad, of course, the moment he gets in.'

He nodded.

'I'll be in at the shop tomorrow morning to discuss what should be done. Meanwhile, good-night to both of you.'

Gloria made a move to follow him, with a murmured: 'Just a minute, Steve!'

Whether he heard her or not, Penny could not tell, but he certainly did not wait.

He was out of the house before Gloria, impeded by her flowing housecoat, could get up from her low chair, and within a matter of seconds had started up his car and driven away.

Disappointment at her failure to have a private good-bye with him showed clearly on Gloria's face as she returned to her seat.

'The whole thing is a blasted nuisance!' she exploded. 'And it's all due to Stephen's cussed obstinacy. I told him years ago that Isaac was a dangerous fanatic, and that he ought to get rid of him. But no! He was a good and loyal servant. He could stay on until he was pensioned off.'

'I found him a little alarming myself,' Penny admitted.

'Oh, these people who practise voodoo on the quiet—throwing the bones one day, and quoting from the Bible the next—they're always a bit sinister.' She shrugged her shoulders. 'I was never scared of him, though—used to laugh at him. He didn't like that, but his scowls never frightened me, even after he discovered something that he shouldn't have done.'

Penny continued to fondle the Airedale.

'You'll have Larry in your room to-night, I suppose?' she asked, when she could find her voice.

'Not right inside. I couldn't stand that. He can sleep on the mat in my doorway. Then, if there's an intruder, he'll wake us all up.' And she added: 'Make some coffee, Pen. If we're going to stay up for Dad and Brenda we may as well be comfortable.'

Penny, badly shaken, felt very much like suggesting that if Gloria wanted coffee, she could jolly well make it herself. But quarrelling would only increase her exhaustion. She went out to the kitchen, made sure the window, with its wide grating, was securely bolted, switched on the kettle, and got out a home-made cake of her mother's baking.

She was longing now for her parents' return, and she had hardly carried the tray into the sitting-room, before she heard the car being put into the garage, and footsteps coming briskly up the path: sounds greeted by loud barking from Larry, swiftly in position at the front door.

Their astonishment at seeing Stephen's dog, now jumping round them joyfully, would, at any other time, have made Penny burst out laughing.

'Steve here at *this* hour?' Brenda exclaimed, and followed by Robert, observing dourly: 'A bit late for an evening visit, surely,' came into the sitting-room.

Before Penny could embark on explanations, Gloria was well away with her own summary of the situation. In spite of herself, Penny found her eloquence impressive: she never hesitated, was never at a loss for a word. But her father wanted a terse outline of the circumstance, no embroideries, and more than once cut her short, saying only, at the end of her recital: 'I'll discuss it with Stephen to-morrow. Meanwhile I suggest we all go to sleep—including Larry, who can have a mat in the hall.'

There were, as it turned out, no alarms or excursions. When the cocks crowed at midnight, and again at sunrise, Larry gave a protesting yap, then sank down again into slumber, and the humans all slept deeply, confident of their guardian's sharp ears.

Pearl, after her first fright at being met at the back door by noisy barking, quickly accepted the presence of that 'darned dawg' from the Forestry Office. Indeed she seemed almost relieved to have him there.

All efforts at concealing the connection between Gloria's sudden illness, and Isaac's equally swift disappearance, she hinted, had failed. There was no open discussion of the matter, particularly among people of the Dales' standing. But the poorer and less educated folk—the kind to whom Isaac belonged—had much to say among themselves. She had been hard put to it, she suggested to combine loyalty to the Dales with frankness to her friends and acquaintance. They believed she was in the know, and had no scruple about putting sly questions to her—questions which sometimes found an answer in her very silences.

As soon as Robert and Penny had gone off to work, she decided to speak out more plainly, to Brenda, and beckoned her into the kitchen, well out of Gloria's hearing.

'Spec's yo' hear, Mis' Dale, dat Isaac in dese parts again. Dat why Mister Stephen's dawg here, o' course. Well, it true 'nough! Mah nephew Sam, who livin' in one o' dem cottages up in de woods, seen him lurkin' in de trees las' night, lookin' wild like jumbie.'

Brenda nodded.

'It's worrying, Pearl, but my husband and Mr Vaughan are dealing with it. Isaac's mad, poor old man. He'll end by being locked up, I'm afraid.'

But Pearl did not agree.

'No one gwine catch dat one,' she said darkly. 'He got power. If Mis' Gloria have a bit o' sense she pack up an' go away. No dawg ain't gwine save her. Isaac only to put a spell on it—an' it turn on her.'

Brenda looked at her severely now.

'Pearl, you know very well you shouldn't talk such superstitious nonsense. What would Father Alphonse say if he heard you?'

She shrugged her plump shoulders.

'He angry. Or mebbe he jus' laugh, scornful like. But Ah tellin' yo' dere t'ings even Fader, for all his book-learnin', couldn't 'splain.'

'Auntie Brenda!'

For once in a way Brenda was relieved to hear Gloria calling her. Pearl was a dear, but with her rolling eyes and guttural voice, she had given her the creeps this morning.

Gloria, who had overslept, merely wanted breakfast. She didn't—for which Brenda was grateful—wish to discuss the latest developments over Isaac.

All she said, in unconscious agreement with Brenda's recently expressed view, was that lunatics should be put under lock and key, and kept that way.

Meantime Stephen had reached the pharmacy and was in close consultation with Robert.

As before, he didn't stop to speak to Penny on his arrival, and she tried not to care. At least he had given her a vague smile.

But as on a previous occasion, Robert opened the door of his office and beckoned to her; and eager to hear the latest developments, she hurried to answer his summons.

When she went in, she saw at once that both Robert and Stephen looked less worried than she had anticipated.

'Sit down, Penny,' her stepfather said curtly. Then turning to Stephen he went on: 'You'd better tell her yourself, and see what she thinks.'

Stephen hesitated.

'Need we bother her?'

'My dear chap, she's not a child any longer, she's a sensible young woman.'

'I know. I'm very conscious of it! But I think this is a man's business!'

Robert gave a short laugh.

'You can't know much about women if you think Penny will be content to concentrate on her work all day, without wondering what we two have been discussing.'

For the first time Stephen looked directly at Penny, smiling faintly.

'I suppose you're right. Anyway, Penny, here's the way it is. Isaac turned up at the Forestry Office last night, his clothes more or less in rags, and looking wilder than ever.'

A startled expression leapt into Penny's eyes.

'Oh, Steve! Did he attack you?'

Her voice was more frightened and concerned than she realised, and for a moment both men, to her embarrassment, looked at her in surprise.

'Heavens, no! He came to tell me that he was going to live alone in the mountains for the rest of his life, that he would never come to Val Fleury again. The only reason he had come now, he declared, was to give me a warning from the old gods of the forest. They were angry that the witch had not perished, but held him guiltless. He need do no more. Retribution was in their hands, and the people of Val Fleury must expect disaster.'

She could only stare at him incredulously, astonished that he should now be smiling broadly.

'Don't look so worried,' he said. 'It's only a lot of crazy nonsense. The main thing is that he'll be keeping out of the district permanently. He's not mad on every point, either. He knows that if he stays around the police will pick him up. And if there's one thing a chap like Isaac dreads, it's to be put under lock and key. He'd far rather be dead.'

For a moment Penny did not speak. Then she asked haltingly: 'Is there any evidence beyond his own word that he's going to stay up in the forest? How can he possibly survive?'

'He's been spotted up there by some of the workmen, making a little hut for himself near the old shrine. He'll have water at hand, and grow a few vegetables. And from time to time one or other of his many relatives will make their way up there and ensure he doesn't starve.'

'I see.' Penny was relieved. She had hated to think of the crazed old man dying in isolation of hunger and exposure.

A silence fell now on the little room, until Robert asked her with an effort: 'What do you think we should do, Penny? Let's have the woman's point of view. Stephen is sure there'll be no danger from him now. But I'd rather he was safely locked up.'

Penny did not hesitate. She looked at her stepfather with those clear hazel eyes of hers and said steadily: 'If he's arrested and put in jail, with a charge of attempted murder, he'll never get out. He'll be pining away there years after Gloria has gone back to America —unless, of course, he dies of misery, or commits suicide. I believe with Stephen that he'll do no more harm— that he should go free.'

'I'm glad you agree with me, Penny,' was Stephen's quick response. 'And there's something else I must tell you both that I was nearly forgetting. Isaac asked me to fetch a Bible, and when I did, he swore on it to leave the district for all time. And after that he took another oath, which entailed his making a little cut in his wrist and drawing blood—a voodoo oath. It rather gave me the creeps, that business. His eyes were rolling, and he was foaming a little at the mouth. However, he'll never dare break that oath, I'm certain. We'll have no more trouble from him.'

Robert pushed back his chair, and stood up.

'I'm glad to have your views, but the final decision must, of course, rest with Gloria. I'm pretty certain she'll take the same line as you two, though possibly for different reasons.' And then he squared his shoulders. 'She has many faults, my daughter, but cowardice isn't one of them. I can take pride in her for that. And now let's all get back to work.'

Stephen and Penny left him, but once back in the shop Stephen did not, as Penny had expected, leave at once. He asked her quietly if he could speak to her for a moment outside.

Absurdly, her heart beat a little faster. But his manner, as they went together into the yard where his car was parked under the great saman tree, was stiff and awkward.

' Sorry to bother you, Penny,' he said at once, ' but I don't feel like chewing this Isaac business over any more with Gloria.'

' So what?' she enquired with a lift of her eyebrows. ' How does it concern me?'

He reddened.

' I want Larry back as soon as convenient, and if I fetch him I may get involved with her. He's a big dog for you to feed, and quite expensive. Besides, it will add to the gossip if he stays with you.'

' Then I suppose you'll send a servant for him!'

' Unfortunately the new man, Laluji, is a bit scared of dogs as big and lively as Larry. I wonder if it's too much to ask you to run him back yourself when you can spare the time. I may very likely be out, but Laluji will be around, and he's a very pleasant chap. And if he saw you weren't afraid of Larry, he'd take heart.' He gave a wry little smile. ' A perfectly sane fellow, this time—although he can't cook like Isaac.'

' But more reliable at brewing coffee, I hope!' She couldn't help grinning slightly now.

' Oh, Penny, what laughs we've had together!' For a moment his tone, and more, his expression, gave her the wildest notion : that he was going to bend down and pull her into his arms.

But so quickly was he his cool, collected self again, she felt sure that sudden change in him had been a mere illusion, born of her own great longing.

And that sombre thought was immediately confirmed when he said in a pleasant, matter-of-fact voice : ' By the way, I'm delighted to hear that your Eric is set on a bright future after all. I hope it won't be too long before you're able to join him in Rio—or wherever it is you'll be making your home together.' And then he added cheerfully: 'I'm sure you'll be very happy.'

It was a formal little speech, and she should at least have thanked him politely. But instead, she heard herself asking him curtly: 'Do you think we shall be happy, Steve?'

'Riotously so, I should think, from the fervency of your embraces the other day. I have every sympathy with you, of course. But it would have been more discreet of Eric if he had parked his car just a little farther away from the public high road. But there you are,'—and now his tone was mocking—'young love—and all that!'

She turned on him then, scarlet-faced, and words like 'insufferable' and 'insulting' trembled on her lips.

But all she could get out—fiercely—was: 'Get someone else to do your rotten errands. I won't!'

And with that she literally ran back into the shop.

CHAPTER IX

Discussing the matter with the family over lunch, Gloria, to their relief, declared firmly that she had no fear whatever now of Isaac making a further attempt on her life.

Fanatics of his sort, she asserted, would be far too scared to break a voodoo oath of any kind.

'They're not only superstitious, but terribly ignorant,' she went on contemptuously. 'Voodoo only came from Africa with the slaves, within the last three or four centuries. But they've got it all mixed up with the old Arawak gods, who were worshipped here in far earlier times.' And then she added: 'I learnt a lot of their nonsense from that nurse I had for a while. You remember, Dad! You had to sack her because she was giving me nightmares.'

'I do indeed, remember, but let's get back to the point,' Robert returned, a little impatiently. 'I gather, Gloria, that I can let Stephen know you wish to let the matter of Isaac rest. That being so, I shall take his dog back to him this afternoon, and tell him so.'

Penny, at least, was glad to hear that last brusque remark. Angry and sore as she felt with Stephen, she didn't at all want him coming up to the bungalow to claim Larry—and being entertained by Gloria, whether or not she was all dressed up for the occasion—adorned in his favourite yellow!

That petulant retort she had flung at him—she hadn't meant it at all.

But Gloria, leisurely folding up her napkin, intervened, as Penny might have known she would.

'Why on earth should you trouble, Dad? And come to that, why didn't Stephen approach me direct, instead of bothering you with messages? Tell him, with my compliments, not to be so darned lazy—expecting a man of your age to run errands for him!'

'And I'll tell you something!' Robert's temper was beginning to flare. 'Not so much as I could, because we've an audience. Just this—don't try bossing your father. I shall do exactly as I think fit.'

With that, he lit a cheroot and stumped off into the garden; and ten minutes later, whistling to Larry to accompany him, was driving off in the direction of the hills.

'Increasing years haven't improved Dad's temper,' Gloria remarked, sitting back in a comfortable chair while Brenda and Penny cleared the table for Pearl. 'If he was like this in his youth, when he was married to mother, I don't wonder she left him!'

The bitterness in her voice shocked both Brenda and Penny. But neither of them spoke, and Gloria went on frigidly: 'It's decided me to go away again.'

'You mean to California?' Try as she might, Brenda could not achieve even the semblance of regret.

'Not at present—you'll be sorry to hear! Only as far as Mrs O'Brien's. She misses me; wants me back. In fact, I shall soon be working again at the Salon. It won't be long now before people start sprucing themselves up for Christmas.'

'Well, don't hurry away!' Brenda tried hard to fight against her longing to be rid of her troublesome stepdaughter. 'At least wait until you've had a quiet talk with your father.'

But Gloria shook her head.

'We should only quarrel again. I shall pack up and be off before he gets back this evening. Maudie can fetch me in her preposterous old car. I'll be happier in that than in Dad's saloon, or in Penny's Mini.'

'If you feel like that about us, why not ask Eric to give you a lift?' Brenda suggested, struggling not to speak too stiffly. 'He'd be quite willing, wouldn't he, Penny?'

'I'm sure he would,' Penny stammered. 'I haven't seen him the last few days, because he's been so busy, but—'

Gloria opened her eyes very wide at this.

'My dear Penny,' she drawled, 'Eric will be in Rio by now. He flew there last night. Left his car at the airport to be collected or sold. Don't tell me you didn't know!'

It was Brenda who paled with dismay—as Gloria did not fail to observe.

Penny, squaring her shoulders, said steadily: 'Don't

look so distressed, Mum. Gloria may have surprised me a little, but she hasn't hurt me. I knew Eric would be going soon, and it's a relief to know that he's actually gone.'

Brenda, no longer inhibited over showing her true feelings for Gloria, gave her a curt nod, in the direction of the doorway, and with a shrug of her shoulders, the girl left the room.

Alone with Penny, she caught her in her arms.

'My darling! We've realised that things weren't altogether happy between you and Eric, but we certainly didn't expect this. I hope you're not too badly hurt. You don't deserve it.'

Penny shook her head.

'Mum, I'm telling the truth when I say that I'm relieved. It's he who was upset by my ending our friendship. Though I'm certain it's only his pride that is seriously wounded.'

'But why didn't you tell us before? We've been so worried—so puzzled.'

'He didn't want anything definite said until he had left Val Fleury. Now I can be frank—breathe again.'

'We felt, your father and I, that you might have found it difficult to settle to a strange life in a foreign country,' her mother told her a little sadly. 'And then the apparent necessity for a long, indeterminate engagement—'

Penny looked away, unable to meet her mother's eyes.

'I'd have faced all that willingly,' she told her. 'None of it would have daunted me. But I had come to realise that I didn't love Eric, and never would. So can we leave it at that, darling!' And then she hesitated. 'Except that I can't help wondering how Gloria heard.'

'Over the telephone, I expect. In fact, Penny, I wouldn't be too sure that Eric didn't leave a message for you before he went. She's always had the annoying habit of flying to answer the telephone if it rang—even when I was at home.'

'Oh, well, Mum—as I said just now, let's leave it at that. I'm sick to death of the whole thing.'

So once again Gloria was packing up in a temper; though this time it was a swifter operation, since she had only one large suitcase with her.

Unfortunately Mrs O'Brien could not come immediately to fetch her, and her annoyance over this went to swell the already surging flood of anger which she felt for Penny.

Characteristically, she called her young stepsister into her room in so gentle a voice that Penny, suddenly sorry for her, obeyed the summons. But then, still speaking very quietly, but with deadly bitterness, she set about her.

Penny needn't think that now she'd jilted Eric that she could expect Stephen to fall for her. Because he never would.

'I'm going to tell you something,' she went on, sitting on the edge of the bed and staring up at her. 'Unless you've tumbled to it already! Stephen and I were lovers once. He was crazy about me, wild to marry me—but only on his own terms.'

Penny, who had been on the verge of escaping from her, now had the even stronger urge to stay—and listen. For instinct told her that for once in a way, Gloria was speaking the truth.

'He was a junior in the Forestry Department then, but mad keen to stay—to stay here in this potty little island and raise a family—if you can believe it! When I found he wouldn't budge an inch, I broke it up, got Dad to send me to New York to train as a hairdresser. Now, five years later, things are very different.'

'You mean—?'

'That I'm no longer a poverty-stricken youngster. I'm wealthy, or shall be when Greg's estate is finally settled. If Stephen makes it a condition of marrying me that he continues to work in forestry, I've too much sense to stand in his way. Only I shall help him fix up a far better paid job in California. We'll have a lovely home there.'

Penny found words now.

'You really think you can get him back—after all these years?'

Gloria's dark eyes flickered, but her voice was steady enough.

'I'm sure of it,' she said. 'You see, there are things he's never forgotten. Taking me to choose that topaz necklace. He recognised it at once, after all this time, was touched, in spite of himself, that I'd kept it.'

'But you said he'd given it to you quite recently—to wear at the Independence Ball!'

'I daresay I did.' Gloria dismissed the accusation with a shrug, and went on quickly: 'The old song I sang with Eric and Joe on that great occasion—"Remember the Night". We used to dance to it—and it held a clear message for him, which I'm certain he got.'

She hummed the sensual little song to herself, and Penny, sick at heart, turned and left her.

'Let Gloria win him back, if she wants to,' she told herself bleakly. 'For myself, I couldn't care less.'

Answering the door-bell, she found Mrs O'Brien there —a shade flushed and breathless perhaps, but looking like a cat that had swallowed the cream.

She told her politely: 'You'll find my stepsister in her room—practically ready, I think.'

'Thank you, dear, I'll go to her at once.' And along Mrs O'Brien went, her high heels tapping.

'My dear child, I'm delighted to have you back with me,' she heard her exclaim. 'It must be insufferable to be bossed around—not to feel free to have what friends you please to the house, or to visit them without comment.'

Penny did not hear Gloria's reply. Utterly disgusted, she had one cause for gratitude. That her mother, eager to avoid Gloria and her tantrums, was at the bottom of the garden, picking salad, out of earshot of Mrs O'Brien's infuriating remarks—her misplaced expressions of sympathy.

She went out to join her, but said nothing of what she had overheard. Nor, indeed, did she even mention Mrs O'Brien's arrival.

And when they went back together, they found to their relief that the battered old car had disappeared, taking the pair away. No need for insincere farewells, nor, indeed, any possibility of making them. Even Robert, they thought, would prefer it this way. Time later on for a reconciliation. After all, Christmas would soon be here, to bring them together again.

Things began to hum at the shop now, with people coming in to make last-minute purchases of cards and calendars and wrapping paper, of expensive toiletries only stocked at this season, to say nothing of special bargains.

Penny combined the selling of cameras with help at the other counters, trying to subdue her restlessness with sheer hard work. And at home she found plenty of jobs to do, in the way of preparations; for her mother, doubly occupied with other local ladies in organising a party for the poorer children of the neighbourhood, and contriving gifts for them, was glad of her assistance.

Stephen and Pete, she gathered from Sybil, were up in the forest apart from the odd day; and she mentioned hesitantly one afternoon when they met by chance in the street that she had seen Stephen leaving Mrs O'Brien's house late the previous evening.

'That stepsister of yours is a real menace,' she told Penny wrathfully. 'Trying by every trick to get hold of Stephen again. And then all this talk about helping out at the Salon over the pre-Christmas rush! She's not doing a thing now, though she's as fit as a fiddle. Just acting the grand lady. And Maudie O'Brien doesn't raise an eyebrow.'

Penny looked her squarely in the eyes.

'Listen here, Sybil,' she said steadily. 'I don't want to hear another syllable about either of them—nor about Eric. Once this rush is over I'm going to get time from Dad to work hard for my first pharmacy examinations. And the minute I'm qualified I shall apply for a post in one of the bigger islands—if not in England. So that's that.'

'O.K. We'll close the subject—but only after I've given you a word of advice. You love Stephen. Maybe I'm the only person who knows it. But someone else ought to—Steve himself! The dunderheaded fool has, I'm certain, no idea. Probably thinks you're pining for Eric. If you could only make him understand—'

Penny gave a contemptuous little laugh which Sybil, knowing her so well, and loving her so much, found unconvincing.

'I'd rather be dead!' she said, and turned abruptly away.

And then, less than a fortnight before Christmas, the rain began.

Not much the first day, only the kind of light shower that often came just before the start of the dry season. But after that it fell in torrents.

Even then it did not cause any real alarm. A bout of tropical rain, out of the normal season, was not unknown.

But it persisted, and news drifted through of intensive efforts by the Forestry Department to reinforce the work of damming the river near its source, high up by the old shrine. Of an urgent call to the Port Leon authorities to send up to Val Fleury the only bulldozers the island boasted, to deepen the river bed at points nearest the village.

Down and down the rain came, as though a great hole had been torn in the sky—day after day, night after night.

Volunteers were called for to give what help they could to the hard-pressed workmen manning the bulldozers, and the men of the village, Robert included, obeyed the summons. Then Dr Henderson, taking the initiative in relief operations—for Port Leon was facing its own difficulties—organised the more capable women to carry out the work of moving children from scattered homes near the river into the few two-storey buildings in Val Fleury.

Room was made for them—and how many of them there seemed—on the top floor and roof garden of the school, the teachers superintending them. The gallery of the near-by church was cleared to make room for others, and accommodation was arranged with some difficulty at the only other sizeable building, the cinema.

Penny and her mother, and Pearl too, were quickly occupied with feeding arrangements for one particular area, almost working the clock round and snatching what rest they could in an improvised dormitory in the loft.

Tales came through from the men working by the river bed of the swirling muddy torrent bringing down with it torn-up trees, the corpses of animals, including great dead or dying snakes. Yet so far the banks held while the water rushed down to the coast. So far! If once they broke, would even those few higher buildings stand, as the river, widening, found a fresh course and swept through the main street down the road to the coast?

As for the dangers facing that heroic little band up in the high forests, the prayers, spoken and unspoken, that went up for their safety, were never-ending.

More news drifted in. A helicopter was flying in from Jamaica with food and medical supplies, and another might soon be available. Two Red Cross planes had arrived at the airport ready to take off possible casualties.

At last, when it seemed that the heavy rain would never cease, it lessened perceptibly. And before long a report came from the people working at the river bank that the water was beginning to go down, very slowly, but steadily. Everyone breathed again. But that night a helicopter which had been circling the mountain tops brought a fresh warning.

The floods had been diverted into an old water course at the far side of the forest. That was why the river had gone down a little. But there was still a danger—and a very serious one—for anyone who took the round-about minor road from Val Fleury towards the airport.

This road, at one point at least, was threatened, if not by the new sheets of water, by landslides. No one must use it until further notice.

The slightly better news did not make the volunteers relax very much. And the Dale household were up early next morning, swallowing their coffee and sandwich when Pete arrived at their front gate, grey with exhaustion.

Penny's first thought was for Stephen. She was certain, by Pete's expression, that something terrible had happened to him, and she jumped up, knocking over her coffee, and flew down the path.

He caught her in his arms.

' Penny!' he exclaimed. ' You're *here*!'

' What do you mean, Pete?' she demanded sharply. ' Of course I'm here. What about Stephen? Has he—has he been badly hurt—or—or—' She couldn't finish the sentence.

' He's in danger—terrible danger. But I had to leave him—had to come and tell your mother—'

So clearly was he at the end of his tether that Penny, her heart like a great lump in her breast, led him into the bungalow, where he flopped down into the nearest chair.

After one glance at him, Robert went to the sideboard and brought out brandy. And Brenda put his feet, in their broken boots, on to a footstool.

No one questioned him, but after a minute or two, the brandy bringing a little colour to his stricken face, he began his story.

'Yesterday afternoon, just as Steve and I and our men were congratulating ourselves that the worst trouble might well be over, one of the gang came along with a horrifying report. He said that Penny—whose bright blue car they all know, of course—had been killed by a landslide on that side road leading to the airport. Steve—! I thought he was going mad! He leapt up, called out in a tone I've never heard him use in my life: "Penny! *No!* My God, I can't bear it!" Then, suddenly cold as ice again, he called for ropes and something to serve as a stretcher, and went rushing off. I wanted to go with him, but he wouldn't have it. I must go down and break the news to her parents that she was, at least, badly hurt. So I've been travelling through the night, moving as fast as I could in pretty awful conditions, and here I am—to find, thank God, it's all a mistake.'

'But why on earth—?' Robert began, then exclaimed desperately: 'Penny. Your car! The only blue Mini in the island. If it's not in the garage—'

Quickly as he moved, Penny was before him, throwing open the garage door.

'It's gone,' she told him. 'Maybe someone's stolen it! We've left everything unlocked lately. Don't look like that, Dad!'

'I'll ring the O'Brien woman up,' he muttered. 'If Gloria's not there, it's plain what's happened. They'd see the car on the hillside wrecked—!' He broke off. 'Thank God you're safe, child—but oh, my poor Gloria!'

He strode to the telephone and lifting the receiver heard immediately Mrs O'Brien's voice, asking him in a worried, slightly aggrieved tone, if Gloria was with him.

'I didn't fuss at first at her not being around,' she told him. 'She likes to go her own way without being questioned, as you know. In fact I turned in very early, hoping for a good night's sleep at last. But I've just been to her room, and all her things have gone. Do you suppose—?'

But Robert did not wait to hear more. Leaving her still talking, he hurried back into the sitting-room.

'It *was* Gloria in the car,' he said numbly. 'I must go and see what I can do.'

'Mr Dale, you can do nothing!' Pete struggled out of his chair. 'The odds are against Stephen getting down to the car in safety, let alone climbing up again— even with men using ropes. The hillside just there is a sloping sheet of mud. And—don't take offence, I beg you—he's a young man, and a hundred per cent fit.'

And then came the sound of screeching brakes, and Dr Henderson walked quickly up the path.

He glanced from one to the other.

'I gather you've heard of the accident. Well, your daughter is alive, Mr Dale. She's been taken to the First Aid station at the airport—somehow. No details yet. But the minute I have any, I'll let you know.'

He turned to Pete.

'Anything I can do for you, young fellow? You look done in.'

'Just give me a lift to the Forestry Office, please,' came Pete's swift reply. 'I want to collect one or two things there, and get back to my job. I'll snatch up some food and go.'

Dr Henderson nodded briefly, and turning to the Dales said with bluff kindliness: 'Good-bye for the moment. And please, no foolish efforts to get up into the hills, Robert. You might endanger other lives besides your own.'

Robert said nothing, knowing that what the doctor said was true—besides, there must not yet be any relaxation of effort, here in Val Fleury. Work by the river must continue, with constant vigilance on the part of those detailed to watch for any change in the rise or fall of the muddy water, or for blocks caused by uprooted trees or falls of earth. And food for everyone must still be prepared and served in the hastily erected marquee, normally used for charity fêtes.

By tacit agreement no one in the Dale household spoke of Gloria—though she was in the forefront of their thoughts, together with Stephen, who had clearly risked his life for her under the impression that it was Penny whom he was trying to save.

To talk would lead inevitably to discussion and agonising surmise, ending nowhere.

During the day, the rain stopped entirely. With the speed of a curtain rising on a change of scene, the sun came out in glory, shining from a deep blue sky. And when in the evening it sank, it was in a calm splendour of rose-and-gold. People in the streets hugged and kissed each other, many streaming into the church to give thanks. Rightly or wrongly they were confident that the peril was over, that in a few days Val Fleury would be resuming by degrees its normal life.

Early next morning came the news that the river level had gone down by several inches and there was more rejoicing.

But there was still no information from the distant airport, nor from any source that could provide tidings of Stephen.

And then, just as Pete had appeared the morning before, Stephen suddenly arrived, hardly recognisable with a beard of several days' growth, his eyes red-rimmed, his arm in a dirty, blood-soaked sling.

He pushed his way in, and told Robert huskily: 'Gloria's going to be O.K.—badly bruised and shaken, a broken rib. Ought to be brought down to hospital in Port Leon, but flatly refuses.'

'I'll surely be able to get up to the airport by the main road from Port Leon,' Robert exclaimed. 'It'll take hours that way, but—'

'She's already on a Red Cross plane—one that's going to America—in charge of competent personnel. Insisted on it. They'll put her in hospital at the other end.'

'No message, even?' Robert spoke in a stricken whisper.

'I asked her that, and she said to tell you all one word—" Sorry ".' And murmured something about compensation for the smashed-up Mini.'

Robert looked deeply sad.

'She gave no reason for dashing off the way she did?' Stephen hesitated.

'She did. But I'm—I'm sure she'll write to you later

on. Meanwhile there's nothing any of us can do.'

Then, all at once, his face ashen, he swayed and but for Robert's quick action would have crashed to the ground, unconscious, blood seeping now from his clumsily bandaged arm.

CHAPTER X

Helped by the stalwart Pearl, Robert lost no time in getting Stephen, still unconscious, on to the bed in the tiny room which not long ago Penny had been occupying. And while Brenda heated water, and collected antiseptic ointment and clean bandages, Penny flew to the telephone to summon Dr Henderson. But the number was engaged, and after two fruitless attempts at contacting him, she ran to the garage, got out her step-father's big saloon, and drove to the temporary surgery as fast as she safely could.

He was out, but there were two uniformed nurses—strangers to her—hard at work there, and when she stammered out her errand, mentioning Stephen's name, one of them, after a brief hesitation, offered to come with her.

'I ought not to leave the post until Dr Henderson's return,' she told Penny. 'But it sounds as though urgent treatment were required, so I'll see what I can do. My first-aid case is ready—and good for most emergencies.'

By the time they reached the bungalow, Stephen was beginning to regain consciousness, but after one glance at him, the nurse, her face very serious, got down to work.

Brenda would have stayed to help her, but a piteous, pleading look from Penny stopped her short. She told the nurse: 'My daughter is a sensible girl. She'll stay around to fetch and carry for you.'

'Fine. I shan't require anyone else.' And turning to Penny she made a curt request for things she needed.

Penny had to steel herself to great courage and composure when the removal of those grubby bandages, soaked in blood, revealed the state of Stephen's arm. Bruised, badly lacerated and dirty, it looked as though someone had taken a hammer and tried to smash it up. And she was far from surprised when the nurse herself looked taken aback for a second.

But a careful scrutiny, conducted with delicacy and speed, proved reassuring.

'It's only a flesh wound,' she told Penny quietly.
'It's the loss of blood that caused his collapse. That,
and his evident exhaustion.'

Sister Lloyd's examination, gentle as it was, brought
back a degree of consciousness to the injured man.

His face contorted, and he muttered : 'Pete, Penny's
been killed. No, don't hold me back. Oh—*Penny*!'

'But you're Penny, aren't you? Surely I heard your
mother call you that?' the nurse murmured, raising her
eyebrows.

Penny nodded.

'No one has been killed. But someone else, using
my car, was in a serious accident, and Stephen, here,
went to the rescue, thinking it was I.'

'He'll remember all that eventually. But listen, child.
I must get hold of Dr Henderson to authorise a blood
transfusion. Stay here while I go to the telephone.'

She went off, and Penny slipped her hand into
Stephen's. It was an instinctive gesture, and she was
startled when his fingers closed on hers.

And then his eyes opened languidly.

'Penny! What are you doing, sitting here?'

'Looking after you a little—and loving you a lot!'

'Gloria said that you loved me,' he murmured dis-
jointedly. 'It was the very last thing she did say, before
the plane went off. I didn't believe her. She's such a
liar, poor Gloria!'

Penny bent over him and dropped the lightest of light
kisses on his damp forehead.

'She told the truth this time, Steve darling. And not
just as a big brother.'

He closed his eyes again, still holding her hand, and
Sister Lloyd, coming back from the telephone, gave them
both a sharp look.

'He shouldn't be talking,' she said reproachfully.

'Not even to my girl-friend?' Stephen spoke in the
same difficult whisper.

'Now listen, Mr Vaughan,' Sister Lloyd told him
quietly. 'Dr Henderson says I'm to get you down
to the hospital in Port Leon for an immediate blood
transfusion.'

Stephen came to full consciousness then with a
vengeance.

'Take me to hospital?' he exclaimed. 'Not on your life! I ought not to be lying here at all, in fact. I've got to get back to the forest—join my assistant there. As if I'd let him and the other chaps cope on their own just because I was fool enough to trust in a rock that didn't hold.'

'Mr Vaughan, please be reasonable,' the nurse exhorted him. 'The danger is over!'

'How do you know?' he stormed. 'Even if it is, what about our workmen up there—badly hurt, or maybe killed?' He turned to Penny. 'I can't argue with the woman, darling. Tell her to bandage me up, give me a painkiller—and *go*!'

To her relief Penny saw that Sister Lloyd was not in the least offended by this outburst. She stooped over him, wiped the sweat from his forehead, and said mildly: 'What about your poor little fiancée, if you throw your life away?'

'She'd understand, Penny would. She's half a forester herself!' His voice had sunk to a mutter again. 'She knows I couldn't leave Pete to cope on his own. It would be mon—monstrously unfair.'

Suddenly Penny heard her father's voice, calling to her from the doorway in a low whisper. Quickly she went to him, following him into the sitting-room.

'A message has got through,' he told her. 'Colonel Hayward, Stephen's predecessor—the chap who trained him—has been sent up to the Forestry Office to take over from Steve for the present. Pete sent an urgent call, asking his help, explained that Stephen had been badly hurt.'

'Dad! How wonderful!'

She gave him a quick hug, blew a kiss to her mother and Pearl, and slipped back into the sickroom.

'I've good news,' she murmured to the nurse.

'What news?' Stephen demanded hoarsely.

'Colonel Hayward's come to the rescue,' she told him softly. 'He's with Pete now, holding the fort until you're on your feet again.'

To her joy relief spread over Stephen's face.

'Good old Heck Hayward,' he muttered. And looking through half-closed eyes at Sister Lloyd, he went on huskily: 'O.K. If Penny comes with me, I'll go.

Selfish bloke, aren't I? But she'll understand.'

The nurse smiled across at Penny.

'I'll stay until the Red Cross ambulance comes. It had just arrived at our First Aid station when I telephoned. The people manning it will let you go down with Mr Vaughan to the hospital, I'm sure, but you probably won't be able to stay there, as you're only his fiancée.'

'If I only am!' Penny thought, but kept the words back. To say as much might alter Sister Lloyd's ideas.

And she said instead: 'I'll maybe arrange to get hospitality from friends in the Town.'

Her parents were less shaken by her decision than she had feared. They had been through so much of late that they were prepared to take it—and all that it implied—in their stride.

A hurried telephone call made by her mother to old family friends brought her a warm invitation to stay with them at Port Leon as long as she pleased. As for her step-father, he thrust a bundle of notes into her hands, and told her that if she needed more, she could have it. In any case, he and Brenda would come down soon to see how she was managing, and how Stephen was progressing.

Then, hardly giving her time to throw a few clothes into a suitcase, the ambulance was at the gate, farewells were being said, and, seated beside Stephen, her hand once again in his, Penny was travelling down to Port Leon in the smoothest vehicle she had so far encountered.

It was the strangest Christmas she had ever spent. Her host and hostess were kindness itself, and as the hospital was only a stone's throw from their house, she had no difficulty in spending a great deal of her time there, sitting at Stephen's bedside, or helping in the children's ward by playing with the little ones, and putting up Christmas decorations.

For a while Stephen was well content not to talk. All he wished, apparently, was to have her close to him—putting his hand out sometimes to ensure, it seemed, that she was really there.

But there came a day in early January when she noticed a heartening change in him. He was a better colour, and his voice was a little stronger. She could almost believe his eyes held something of their old sparkle; that he might even begin to tease her again.

He was already spending much of his time on the verandah, shaded from the strong Caribbean sunshine, but to-day, when the doctor in charge of him arrived on his rounds, he declared that he could now be wheeled into the grounds, when the first heat of the day was over.

She took him out herself in the wheelchair, and a smiling orderly brought her a wicker chair so that she could sit near him. And when they were settled in the shade of a tall immortelle tree, its coral flowers forming a canopy over them, he told her that he had so much to say to her, he didn't know where to begin.

'I suppose I must talk a little about Gloria first,' he said.

'Not if it distresses and worries you,' she told him quickly.

'My dear, there are things I must get off my mind. Even if you didn't realise I was growing to love you, Gloria did—in her heart. She tried to light old fires—and indeed, I was crazy about her once, as you doubtless know. There was even a scandal about us at one time! But though you were supposed to belong to Eric, and I didn't dream of competing, the ashes remained ashes—so far as I was concerned.'

A silence fell between them, until she asked quietly: 'Steve, why did she come to that sudden decision to leave—to return to America?'

'She asked me to come and have a talk with her. She was at Mrs O'Brien's again by then. I went, but convinced her at last that five years had changed me completely, that I could never love her again. I suppose people thought it was fear of flood disaster overtaking the village that made her rush away. She hadn't rid herself entirely of childish superstitions caused by that disastrous " Nanny ". But it wasn't that at all. She has realised at last—and God knows I've been pretty slow at recognising it myself—that I really and truly love you. Though she could never understand in a hundred years that though passion is involved—and how!—there is also a feeling different from anything I ever knew for her.'

'I've been blind, too,' Penny admitted—adding, crying and smiling at the same time, in the most ridiculous fashion: 'You've been very unkind to me sometimes, Steve.'

'I suppose I was so jealous of young Eric, I just had to take it out on you! When I saw you together in his car—and you enjoying letting him hug you like that—well, I can't tell you how I felt.'

'I was sorry for him, over his plans all going wrong. But I was far from enjoying myself. You see, I'd made up my mind not to marry him, even if the man I really loved didn't want me. And I dreaded telling him'

He took her hand and raised it to his lips.

'I'll be hugging you soon myself, darling. Kissing you properly, too. Meanwhile I'd like to send out for some engagement rings for you to look at. A chap from that shop in the Palace Arcade can easily bring a few on approval.'

Memory stabbed. A picture flashed into her mind, of Gloria choosing the topaz necklace: A gift from her lover. She thrust it resolutely away, and with it threw out, like a pile of rubbish, every thought of the events of five years ago. She and Steve belonged to each other, and always would.

Stephen was talking again.

'Good lord, I've just remembered we haven't actually told your parents that we want to get married as soon as possible.'

'I don't think it has been necessary. They know all right. But we'd better do the right thing and—'

'And ask their blessing! I only hope they'll give it! They never greatly approved of me, after what happened five years ago—and I don't blame them.'

'They'd disapprove a lot more if you jilted me now,' she said sedately, a dimple flickering in and out of her smooth cheek.

And then suddenly she found herself caught and held in his uninjured arm.

'Steve, you're crazy,' she exclaimed breathlessly. 'You may do yourself untold harm!'

'Untold good, you mean,' he returned quickly. 'Even one small kiss will help! So long as I don't upset this damned wheelchair!'

And pulled her closer still.

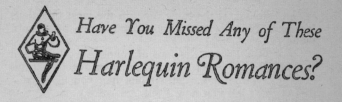

Have You Missed Any of These Harlequin Romances?

HRS. 121